CRIMINAL PROSECUTOR
Killing Yakima

Inspired by True Events

By V. Kusske

Copyright © 2024 by Vic Kusske

All rights reserved. This book or any portion thereof may not be reproduced or used in any manner whatsoever without the express written permission of the publisher except for the use of brief quotations in a book review.

Dedicated to

*the Riegel Family,
the Bustos Family,
the Moore Family,
and to little Sharon Burch,
whose stories needed to be told.*

Even though some true events may have been inspirational to the author, they vary from the fictional events, persons, places, and things written in this work of fiction. The actual county prosecutor during the 1970s and 80s was an honest, churchgoing, family-man who in no way resembles the villain in this work and, all the names, characters, businesses, places, dates, events, and incidents in this book are either the product of the author's imagination or used in a fictitious manner. Opinions expressed are those of the characters and should not be confused with the author's.

Honoring Yakima County Sheriff Detective Lieutenants, Raymond L. Ochs Sr. and Gerald A. Hafsos as fictional characters in this novel.

Contents

Prologue	ix
Chapter 1 Unfinished Business	1
Chapter 2 Raymond "Ray" L. Ochs, Sr.	9
Chapter 3 Gerald Alan "Jerry" Hafsos	11
Chapter 4 Sharon Louise Burch	13
Chapter 5 Lawrence Jay Riegel	19
Chapter 6 Ryan Glenn Moore	22
Chapter 7 Sara Luz Bustos	24
Chapter 8 Public Disclosure Reports & Inquiries	43
Chapter 9 La Fantasma	49
Chapter 10 PDR Responses	52

Chapter 11
Sharon Burch Investigation & Audit   56

Chapter 12
Susan Riegel's Notes   61

Chapter 13
Analysis of Susan Riegel's Notes   68

Chapter 14
Investigator Rod Shaw's Inquiry   76

Chapter 15
Ryan Moore Death Investigation   80

Chapter 16
Sara Luz Bustos Homicide Investigation   85

Chapter 17
Tracy Omar Huitt, Homicide   95

Chapter 18
Bustos Homicide Investigation   98

Chapter 19
Further Analysis of Susan Riegel's Notes   107

Chapter 20
Ryan Moore Death Analysis   142

Chapter 21
Creed's Quandary   158

Chapter 22
Planned Engagement   167

Chapter 23
Bustos Diary   172

Chapter 24
The Rendition   186

Chapter 25
Civil Actions   191

Chapter 26
Special Inquiry Judge — 196

Chapter 27
Grand Jury Investigation — 201

Chapter 28
Unmarked grave location, LiDAR — 204

Chapter 29
No-Body Homicide Prosecutions — 208

Chapter 30
Joe Returns to Yakima — 216

Chapter 31
Conclusion – Sharon Louise Burch — 221

Chapter 32
Conclusion – Lawrence Jay Riegel — 225

Chapter 33
Conclusion – Ryan Glenn Moore — 228

Chapter 34
Conclusion – Sara Luz Bustos — 230

Chapter 35
A Dios — 242

Epilogue — 245

Acknowledgements — 249

Prologue

She was just a child and couldn't understand what was happening to her; she could only react. Her legs and bottom itched and burned from the scalding baths given to her days earlier. She was only half awake, trying to ignore her burning wounds. Pain had been a constant companion for as long as she could remember, and today was no different. She was taken from her cot on the back porch and was tied up again, but this time in an alcove next to the kitchen's wood stove. She was covered with a blanket and gasoline was poured all over her. She tried to move as the liquid covered her body and stung the open wounds on her legs and backside. Frantically, she tried to get loose after being left alone for a few minutes, but she was weak and confused. Suddenly there was an explosion of FIRE covering her, all around her, burning her, causing the worst pain she had ever experienced in her short life. The shock of pain caused her to inhale sharply, drawing 1000-degree heat into her lungs. She tried to scream as the pain in her throat, lungs, and skin was unbearable. She wiggled and struggled against the restraints to no avail as the blaze completely enveloped her. Her frantic movements soon slowed to an occasional jerk and her lips parted slowly, allowing her swelling tongue to protrude between her teeth. After several moments, overwhelmed with torment, her movements became shaky and spasmodic as she slumped forward, her nose dripping. The fire and heat caused her skin to turn black, shrink and split, exposing muscle and tissue. The unrelenting heat turned her face and innocent 5-year-old body into a woeful mass of burned flesh.

1.
UNFINISHED BUSINESS

"Good morning, Mary, I have Yakima Attorney, Ross Manzola, holding on line one. Can you take it now?"

"Yes, thanks, Margaret. Did he say what it was about?"

"He wants Joe Creed's phone number and would like to chat with you."

"Ok thanks, I have it," Mary said as she punched the flashing light on line one.

"Good morning Mr. Manzola, how've you been?"

"Just fine, Mary, please call me Ross. How are you and State Farm Insurance doing this morning?"

"All's well here. I'm looking forward to retirement in a few years. How about you?"

"I keep trying to retire, but I also want to remain available, especially for old friends. I'm trying to contact Joe Creed to discuss some issues, but I don't have his new phone number."

"He's been enjoying his retirement in La Paz, Mexico, for a few months now, Ross, but we expect him back in a couple weeks. I don't have a number for him in Mexico, however his wife, Lydia, would know."

"Thanks, Mary, I have her number. I haven't spoken to Lydia in a while, either. Have you heard how she's doing?"

"I understand she's spending time volunteering at Rick Haze's K-9 training center and enjoying her new home. She's been reluctant to discuss the dreadful events that destroyed their former home and killed Buster, the dog, but she appears to be doing well otherwise."

"Thanks for that info, Mary. I would like to speak with Joe in-person. I wonder why he's spending so much time in Mexico?"

"That worries me too, Ross. I hope he's not planning something serious."

"What do you mean?"

"There's a rumor former Yakima County Prosecutor Karter Truman is alive and living in Colombia and that he instigated the attacks against Joe and Lydia. Just between us, we worry Joe may be planning on going to Colombia to put a stop to Karter Truman."

"Mary, I doubt that, because that's not the way Joe operates. If you hear from him, would you let him know I'd like to talk to him?"

"Sure Ross, if you talk to him first, please tell him to come home soon. We miss him."

"I will, Mary. Thank you and take care of yourself."

Ten days later, Joe Creed, former Yakima City police officer and retired State Farm Insurance investigator, walked into the law offices on North 2nd Street asking to speak with Attorney Ross Manzola.

"Well, this is a surprise. Good to see you, Joe!" Ross declared as he approached.

The two men smiled, shook hands, and walked together into the attorney's office.

"I got the message you were looking for me, Ross. I hope it's not too serious."

"I'm afraid I have a couple serious items which I'd like to share with you, Joe, but first tell me about how you and Lydia are doing and your visits to Mexico."

"Life slowly began to return to normal after our home was destroyed and we survived the attack against us. We occupied ourselves using some of the lawsuit and insurance proceeds to build another home. We wanted a place where we could feel more secure. Getting that accomplished took our minds off of the attempts to eliminate us and helped us begin to heal. The multi-million-dollar lawsuit settlement has also been helpful. We spent time with Rick Haze developing his K-9 Training Center and we volunteer in training new dogs for service in law enforcement. Our lives were completely changed by the assaults against us, however, and we continue to be troubled about the future."

"It's easy to understand how you both feel, Joe, after all that has happened. What about Mexico? Are you doing some sailing again?"

"Yes, I bought my friend Kirk's 63-foot aluminum sailboat after he returned from the South Seas and I'm having her upgraded and refitted for long distance cruising at Bercovich Boatyard in La Paz. It's taking longer than I expected, but she should be ready in a month or so to relaunch. She has 3 staterooms, Ross; you and your family are welcome to join us for some sailing when you have the time."

"I may very well take you up on that offer, Joe, since I'm planning on retiring in about a year, depending on… Which reminds me of why I needed to talk to you."

"I'm listening."

"When I took the oath of attorney, I promised not only to protect and serve our community but also to protect my clients. I want to leave my vocation with the knowledge I accomplished those tasks to the best of my ability. There's some unfinished business that greatly constrains me in that regard, Joe, and I hope you may be able to clear the way for me."

"Of course, Ross, I'll do what I can. What is it?"

"As it turns out there are several client cases that have gone unresolved during my tenure. I need someone with the intelligence and skills to reexamine them by leading a team to investigate carefully and suggest appropriate actions, if possible."

"How many cases are you talking about?"

"Four, the first case is about a 5-year-old adopted child that was killed in a house fire in Wiley City. It happened in 1953, but it wasn't learned it was a homicide until the 1960s. By then, there was very little evidence left which was helpful. Retired sheriff's detective, Rod Shaw, asked me to do an in-depth investigation to the best of our ability. The child's name is Sharon Louise Burch, and she was buried in Yakima's Tahoma Cemetery on September 10th, 1953.

"There are three other cases which need attention; a missing person case where the victim could have been killed by his girlfriend, a suspicious-looking suicide that was investigated by Union Gap Police, and an old Yakima City police homicide case in which a police officer was a person of interest."

"Why me, Ross? I'm sure there are several highly qualified investigators that can work those cases."

"I've recruited two retired Yakima Sheriff's Deputies to look into the cases, but I need someone like you to help develop an investigative plan for each case and then manage the progress. I can provide you with legal support and give you two talented investigators, Joe, with 100 percent of their time dedicated to the tasks."

"Ross, if you knew what I've been dealing with, you wouldn't be asking."

There was a short pause.

"If you tell me about it, maybe between the two of us, we can solve both problems."

"I'll tell you Ross, but you'll have to promise me you'll keep what I tell you in confidence."

"That serious, huh? How about if I consider you to be a client which protects you and the information you provide to be legally privileged?"

"I can accept that," Joe responded with a grin.

"So, what are you up to, Joe?"

"I'm preparing to locate former Yakima County Prosecutor

Karter Truman, wherever he may be, and take him out."

"What do you mean?"

"He will no longer be a threat to us. Whatever it takes."

"Oh, my… I would not have believed it without you saying so, Joe!"

"I have no choice, Ross. I'm convinced as long as Truman is alive, he will continue to launch attacks against me and my family until he succeeds. I consider what I'm preparing to be an act of self-defense."

"Joe, there's no court of law that would consider that to be self-defense. It would be outright murder."

"I know, but that'll not stop me. You know the old law enforcement adage that *it's better to be judged by twelve than carried by six?*"

"Joe, before you act on it, would you do one thing I ask of you?"

"What's that?"

"I know you to be a man with a strong Christian faith and I ask that you discuss the moral implications of what you're planning with a priest before you act."

"Ok, I can do that," Joe responded after a pause.

"I was planning on taking Padre Papa to lunch when I returned to the Baja. It should be interesting to see what he has to say. I have great respect for him as a man of honor and courage, but I can't promise you I'll take his advice."

"Fair enough, Joe. When are you leaving?"

"Soon, I'm waiting on a shipment of Kevlar to arrive so I can take it to the boat."

"Kevlar, for your boat?"

"Yes, I'm having it installed to make SV Hannah as bulletproof as possible."

"While your sailboat is being outfitted, would it be possible for you to return to Yakima to take a look at the four cases I have and put together an investigative plan?"

"Yes, but I want to move against Truman as soon as possible.

I expect it will take some time, however, to get Hannah outfitted. I'll be in Mexico for about two weeks, and I'll get back to you as soon as I return."

"Thanks, Joe. I knew I could count on you. I'll be asking retired Sheriff's Detectives Ray Ochs and Jerry Hafsos to investigate the cases and to make themselves familiar with the details so you three can hit the ground running when you're available."

"Excellent gentlemen and investigators, both of them. I'll see you when I get back," Joe said as he shook hands before leaving the office.

Later that same day, the telephone rang at the Hafsos residence in Yakima and young Michelle Hafsos picked up the receiver.

"Hello?" Jerry's 7-year-old daughter answered.

"Is that you Andy?" caller, Ray Ochs asked.

"Andy's my sister. My name is Michelle. Who's this?"

"This is your dad's friend Ray, Michelle. Is your father available?"

"Hi Ray. You can call me Mo. Here's my dad," she responded, handing the phone to her father.

"Thank you, Mo," Jerry said, smiling as he took the receiver from his daughter.

"Jerry, did you get a request from Attorney Ross Manzola to meet at his office tomorrow at 8 AM?" Ray Ochs asked.

"Yes, and I'm trying to figure out if we're in trouble somehow," Jerry responded.

"It must be you, because I haven't done anything wrong," Ray remarked with a grin.

"Maybe he wants to commend us for the fine work we've done over the years," Jerry suggested with a twinkle in his eye.

Ray looked over the top of his reading glasses at the telephone, saying, "I guess we'll find out tomorrow morning, won't we?"

"Yes Jerry, and you can tell me how much you've enjoyed

your family at the cabin on Chinook Pass, all the fish you've caught from Rimrock Lake since you retired, and that there," Ray quipped.

"Will do, Ray, see you tomorrow morning," Jerry responded, smiling.

The next morning, both veteran detectives walked into the Manzola Law Office and saw four stacks of large ring-bound notebooks heaped on a table.

"Please, come in, gentlemen, and have a seat. Would you like some coffee?" Paralegal, Monique asked as Ross Manzola approached.

The three men had known and worked with each other for many years, and the detectives immediately sensed Ross was relaxed and in a good mood.

"Yes, ma'am. Just black please," Ray responded.

"The same for you, if I remember, right, Jerry?" Ross asked as he closed the door to his office.

"Yes, sir."

"I've asked you here to give you an assignment if you'll accept it."

"A car accident investigation?" Ray asked as Jerry broke out in a smile.

"No such luck. I need you to exercise your skills and knowledge as preeminent investigators to help me with a special assignment. I'd like you to devote your entire efforts to this assignment and you'll have no other responsibilities. You'll receive the standard pay rate," Ross said while placing his hand on the stacks of ring-bound notebooks.

"Preeminent investigators, huh? Are those files on just one case?" Jerry asked, with a perplexed look on his face.

"No, there are four cases here. The first is a horrible murder of a 5-year-old girl; the second a missing gentleman that was possibly murdered, the third a suspicious-looking suicide, and finally a homicide where a police officer is a person of interest. All four cases have been previously investigated and the outcomes are not acceptable to me. I want them each reviewed and re-investigated to the best of your abilities. You can work out of an office here, next to mine. I've asked former Yakima City police officer and insurance investigator, Joe Creed, to return from retirement and work with you. How does that sound?"

There was a long pause as Ray looked at Jerry, who was scratching his head while looking over the stacks of notebooks.

"It'll be good to work with Joe again, but can I ask what's motivating you in these old cases, Ross?" Ray asked.

"Just between us, I'm planning on retiring in a year or so and I want to be able to say I did the best I could during my tenure by not leaving any difficult cases with no resolution."

"You're only going to be around for one more year?" Jerry asked.

"Yes, or until these old cases are cleared."

"I must say I'm honored, Ross. I'll do the best I can," Ray responded.

"Yes, of course, old friend, I understand, and I hope we can live up to your expectations," Jerry agreed.

The two detectives stood up, shook hands again, and took the notebooks to a large office provided for them at the old historic home which had been converted to the Manzola Law Offices.

"The fish in Rimrock Lake should be happy they don't have to worry about you for a while," Ray said as they closed the door.

Ray picked up the file which had formerly been assigned to Detective Rolland (Rod) Shaw of the Yakima County Sheriff's Office and handed it to Jerry Hafsos. Jerry leaned back in his chair, put his feet up on the desk and began reading the old yellowing pages of Yakima Sheriff's case file number 87-0515, a homicide of a 5-year-old child.

2.
RAYMOND "RAY" L. OCHS, SR.

Drawing by Mark Northcott

Occupation	Retired
Employers:	U.S. Navy (hospital ship), U.S. Army (Korea)
	Yakima City Police Department
	Washington State Patrol
	Yakima County Sherrif's Office
Hometown:	Yakima, WA
Married:	LaDena Lou Smith
Children:	Deborah, Raymond Jr, Christina
Memberships:	Yakima County Deputy Sheriff's Association, Elks, Knights of Columbus

Activities: family, wood carving, golf

Ray Ochs (pronounced Oaks) left high school and joined the U.S. Navy, serving on a hospital ship for 2 years. He then returned to Yakima, finished high school, and joined the Army National Guard, serving active duty during the Korean War. Ray and LaDena were married at Saint Paul's Cathedral and Ray started working for the Yakima City Police Department in 1952. He later worked for the Washington State Patrol as a trooper and helped establish the Sunnyside detachment office. He then went to work as a Yakima County sheriff's deputy and was one of the first two deputies to be assigned as a detective, inaugurating the future detective division with the department. Ray enjoys spending time with his family, especially his children, and has played Santa Claus in the community for many years. Daughter, Deborah, described Ray as the best dad any child could have.

3.
GERALD ALAN "JERRY" HAFSOS

Drawing by Mark Northcott

Occupation	Retired
Employers:	U.S. Air Force
	Yakima County Sheriff's Office
Hometown:	Yakima, WA
Married:	Trish Henderson, Linda Sinnes
Children:	Andrea, Michelle
Memberships:	Stone Church, YMCA Youth Programs

After growing up west of Yakima and graduating from Highland High school, Jerry joined the United States Air Force, serving 4 years in Germany. In May of 1971 Jerry began working as a Yakima County Deputy Sheriff. He was later promoted to Sergeant, Lieutenant, and finally Chief Criminal Deputy. On February 2nd, 1980, Jerry and Linda Sinnes were married in Yakima. It was Jerry's second marriage. He enjoys working on his ranch and spending time at his cabin in the mountains with his daughters, family, and friends.

4.
Sharon Louise Burch

Drawing by Mark Northcott

Jerry announced, "I've done some preliminary research on Wiley City, the location where Sharon Burch was murdered in 1953. In 1871, Hugh Wiley settled in the area now known as Wiley City. In 1910, James Wiley, son of Hugh Wiley, received notice that his petition to incorporate Wiley City was approved by the state government. Wiley City is located about seven miles southwest of the Yakima City limits and was connected back in 1910 to Yakima City by an interurban railroad line called the Yakima Valley Transportation Company. The local railroad was used to haul fruit and passengers from the farms and orchards to the large fruit warehouses at Yakima City until 1985, when the railroad company closed down.

"The Yakima Valley Transportation Company is still operating for tourists and is now one of the country's last intact, genuine, electric interurban railroads. The company owns the 75-year-old regularly operating locomotives along with the Class One railroad line. Since the time of the railroad's construction in the early 1900s, it has not undergone any major changes other than a reduction in size. It's an excellent example of classic early twentieth century American interurban railroad construction and service. The railroad and its rolling stock, buildings, and equipment were admitted to the National Register of Historic Places in 1984. The Tampico Saddle club continues to sponsor the popular Wiley City Rodeo on the third weekend in May and has done so since 1949. Wiley City continues to be a quiet little suburban community on the outskirts of Yakima, not a place where what happened to Sharon Burch could be imagined. This case file tells the story, however," Jerry said as he laid the following report on the desk.

Yakima Sheriff's Office Case file report: July 4th, 1988

Sharon Louise Burch was born in Yakima in 1948. Her mother was sixteen years of age, undereducated and not wise to the ways of the world. In 1949, Sharon's parents were divorced, and the father insisted the child be given up for adoption. Sharon was legally adopted in 1949 by Highland and Ella Burch who lived in rural Yakima County. The Burch family were orchard workers who originally came from Arkansas. According to all reports, Ella Burch was the dominant family member, and they all lived in fear of her, including her husband. The other children in the family consisted of Archie (16 yoa) and Sonny (11 yoa). It should be noted that Highland Burch could not read or write and depended solely on Ella Burch for basic things, such as the endorsement required on the back of a payroll check.

In 1953, a house fire took place in Wiley City, a rural area west of the Yakima City Limits. The body of Sharon Burch was found near a wood stove in that house. The fire department which responded to the scene was a private subscription service fire department. Since this was a private service, state mandated rules, regulations, and paperwork requirements were not adhered to. The owner of the service is now deceased, and no files were maintained. The West Valley Fire District was formed in 1960 and no record exists prior to that date. The fire unit from Wiley City, which responded to the 1953 fire, did not file any paperwork or take any photographs. No arson expert was called to the scene.

According to the 1953 Yakima Sheriff's Department report and an article in the local newspaper, the fire was started by Archie Burch, Sharon's brother, who was attempting to start a fire in the wood stove by using gasoline. An explosion took place, which supposedly engulfed Sharon Burch in flames. Archie tried to get Sharon out but was driven back by the heat and flames. Archie was later treated at a local hospital for minor burns and smoke inhalation. The body of Sharon Burch was removed from the damaged house, taken to a local funeral home, then buried at Tahoma Cemetery on 9-10-53.

The responding deputy took four black and white photos of the fire scene, along with several measurements of the area near the wood stove. This information was turned into the department and, on 9-5-53, one day after the fire, the case was cleared: written off as an accidental death.

As of 1953, the sole information pertaining to this case consisted of a one-page deputy's report detailing the facts surrounding the fire and four photographs.

In 1960, Archie Burch was arrested in Decatur, Illinois, on a bad check charge. During the course of that investigation, he informed the authorities he had something he wanted to get off his chest. With that, he told them he was the one who started the fire that killed Sharon Burch. Archie stated his father carried Sharon from the cot and placed her behind the stove, doused her with gasoline, then instructed Archie to wait ten minutes before striking a match. Due to the authoritarian relationship in the Burch household, parental orders were not questioned. Therefore, Archie waited for the allotted time, then struck the match which may have killed Sharon Burch. It is Archie's belief that it was his parents' wish that he would've also died in the fire.

During his conversation with the Decatur authorities, Archie revealed he was the victim of child abuse on numerous occasions, as was Sharon. Facts he mentioned included the following:

1. Being forced to eat excrement as punishment for not eating.
2. Being struck by chains, wood, and electrical cords.
3. Being forced to eat worms, raw onions and a cigar.

Archie said he saw his father place Sharon in a tub of scalding hot water as punishment for not eating all of her dinner. Burch said she was burned badly from the waist down and these wounds never healed. In fact, they resulted in her eventual final illness and/or death. Burch also said Sharon was kept on a cot on the back porch. She was tied by the hands and feet in a spread-eagle fashion in an attempt to prevent her from scratching her wounds. The back porch was not heated but Sharon was always tied there regardless of the weather outside.

Archie further stated that, on the day of the fire, his parents untied Sharon and tried to get her to walk around. Due to the injuries previously received, she was unable to do so. They placed her back on the cot but did not tie her up this time because she was too frail to move about. Sometime on that day, one of the parents noticed the fact that Sharon was not breathing. The father carried the child to the kitchen and placed her behind the wood stove. Archie Burch is under the present-day opinion that Sharon may have been in a coma at that time. He said the body appeared lifeless, but 'she looked like that a lot.' No determination has been made as to whether Sharon died of child abuse/neglect or the fire.

Additionally, Archie said he heard his parents discuss what to do with Sharon's body. Burial was one item he had heard mentioned. The fire was decided upon due to the fact it would wipe any evidence of child abuse or neglect. He also heard his parents say they would need an alibi. For that reason, he was told to wait ten minutes before starting the fire.

The above information was given to the Yakima Sheriff's Department in July 1960 and arrangements were made for Archie Burch to take a polygraph examination in Illinois. This was given on July 28th, 1960, in Springfield, Illinois. The conclusion of the *polygraph examiner is as follows.*

> *After careful analysis of the polygraph of Archie Burch, it is the opinion of the examiner that he is telling the truth concerning the death of his sister, Sharon Louise Burch. However, there is a possibility that this subject could be a non-reactor or pathological liar and, if so, he would show no reaction to relevant questions.*

In July 1960, the Yakima County prosecutor and the deputy assigned to the case proceeded to an address in Portland, Oregon, to interview Sonny Burch, the brother of Archie. A series of questions were asked; however, the quality and value of those questions is subject to interpretation. A polygraph examination was arranged for Sonny Burch, and this was given on 7-29-60 in Portland, Oregon. The results are listed below.

> *As a result of the subject's responses to the relevant questions on the polygraph tests, it is the opinion of this examiner that Sonny Burch answered truthfully to the best of his ability and remembrance.*

A sidebar to the Polygraph examiner's report is listed below.

> *During further interrogation of this subject regarding his brother Archie having given the Illinois authorities the incriminating statement, Sonny Burch stated he believes his brother has fabricated this story to gain sympathy… an attempt to convince the authorities he is mentally ill… or to promote a possible transfer to the State of Washington to gain release from present confinement… Also, that Archie has lied all his life, regardless of whom the lie would injure, in order to gain his own freedom, satisfaction, or escape from punishment.*

On August 2nd, 1960, a neighbor of the Burch family was interviewed by the assigned Yakima Sheriff's Office Deputy. The neighbor stated he believed constant whippings took place in the Burch home; due to the fact he could hear the children screaming from over a block away.

On August 3rd, 1960, the Yakima County Coroner was contacted and asked to review his records concerning the 1953 death of Sharon Burch. This was done, and he informed the department that an autopsy was not performed on Sharon Burch and that the cause of death could not be determined due to the body's extensive damage.

On August 3rd, 1960, the owner of the rental home the Burch family occupied was contacted. He advised the department that the home was remodeled in 1954, one year after the fire. The Burch family had moved out of the house immediately after the initial fire.

As of 1960, the only information pertaining to this case consists of the Decatur PD polygraph results, the Portland polygraph results, and a brief synopsis of the 1953 fire.

End of report.

"Sheriff's Investigator Rod Shaw started working this case after Archie Burch and the child's natural mother visited the Yakima County Sheriff's Office to make a report of homicide," Jerry stated.

"Let me see if I can find Rod's report on the death of this little girl," Ray muttered as he looked through the file.

"We can get back to poor little Sharon Burch later. This missing person case is interesting. You can almost hear the victim crying out from the grave," Jerry responded.

"Who is he?"

"Lawrence Jay Riegel, an airplane pilot. Let's take a quick look at it," Ray replied.

5.
LAWRENCE JAY RIEGEL

Drawing by Mark Northcott

Missing Person, Yakima City Police Department Case # 10-470, National Crime Information Center Case # M868622415

Legal Name:	Lawrence Jay Riegel
Birthdate:	12/15/1952
Place of Birth:	Yakima, WA
Height/Weight:	6' 2" 200 lbs
Eyes:	Hazel
Hair color:	Gray
Scars:	Prominent scar on the right front neck region from a recent cervical surgery, performed in October 2009. One prior full left knee surgery in the 1970s.

Notations by Susan Riegel Vaughn submitted from written documentation.

December 23rd, 2009

I [sister, Susan Riegel Vaughn] last spoke to my brother on December 23rd, 2009, at about 6 PM, as I was driving home from work. Larry had been to Dr. Richard Sloop that day and shared information regarding the nerve damage in his left arm. Larry said they were going to run some additional tests, and they were considering giving him nerve blocker medication. I cautioned him about mixing the medication with alcohol, but he said he was only having a beer once in a while. Larry said he had another appointment after Christmas and they were planning for his next surgery, which was probably going to be on his left knee. We talked briefly about our family dinner, which was planned to be at our mom's house on December 26th at 6 PM. He said he'd be there and asked what he could bring. He sounded upbeat and talkative. I teased him about getting older since his birthday had been on the 15th and told him I was bringing something special. We laughed and chatted for about 20 minutes.

December 26th, 2009

On the afternoon of December 26th, I phoned my brother, as my husband and I were driving to Yakima, but my call was not answered. The family began to arrive at my mom's at about 5:30 PM. By 7 PM. Larry hadn't arrived for dinner. I called his home again and this time (girlfriend) LaDena answered, and said Larry wasn't at home. She said he had left for the coast to visit friends the night before. I asked her why he hadn't called me and she said he just decided to leave suddenly. I asked who he was going to visit, and she said she didn't know, that he had friends over there and was going to stay with them. She also told me Larry was a little blue because he hadn't spoken with his kids on Christmas Day, and that he just decided to go. She also added that the doctors were *treating him for a brain disorder, and that he'd been blue for a while. I asked her, 'A brain disorder? What's that mean?' LaDena said, 'Well, it's not really a disorder, but it's complicated.' I said several times, 'This doesn't make sense. He hates driving to Seattle, and why would he go there?' She said we should probably talk, and I said I'd come over the next day or before I left to return to Snohomish on Monday. I asked LaDena to have Larry call me when he got home.*

"The call never came, and everything gets really complicated from here on out. We can study this later," Ray said, closing the notebook.

"What's the next case about?" Jerry asked.

"It's an unfortunate suicide with a twist."

6.
RYAN GLENN MOORE

Drawing by Mark Northcott

Union Gap, WA Police Department Case Number 10-0669
Domestic Violence — Suicide

Victim:	Ryan Glenn Moore
Date of Birth:	June 17, 1984
Date of Death:	March 20, 2010 (25 years old)
Address:	2209 S. 6th Ave. Union Gap, WA 98903
Witness:	Sue Ann Huntington
	Date of Birth: March 1969 (41 years old)

"I've been reviewing Ross' notes on an interview he did with Ryan Moore's father, Ron Moore. We'll need the investigative case file on the circumstances of Ryan's death from the Union Gap Police Department. I'll send a public disclosure request or PDR to UGPD and see what they have," Jerry said.

"It looks like Ryan's parents have some report copies and I'd expect the Yakima County Coroner's Office will have records of the death as well. I'll send a PDR to the coroner's office, meanwhile here's what we know now," Jerry continued.

> Police Synopsis: *On 3/20/10, 2209 S. 6th Ave, Ryan G. Moore DOB (06/17/84) and his girlfriend, Sue A. Huntington DOB (03/29/69) got into a verbal argument over Moore's drug use. Moore then stabbed himself in the neck and fled on foot down S. 6th Ave. Moore was later pronounced dead at Memorial Hospital...*
>
> *Signed Sgt. C. Kellogg #431 Union Gap Police Department.*

"Attorney Manzola's notes taken during the interview with Ryan's father, Ron, indicate the parents became suspicious that this was determined as a suicide. They state Ryan had been in recovery from a drug addiction for over a month and that domestic violence in his relationship with Sue Huntington was not uncommon, with Sue sometimes being the primary aggressor, according to Ryan. They state there may be records on file. They cannot imagine their son cutting his own throat, and they suspect Huntington could have stabbed him," Jerry remarked.

"Let's wait until we get the public disclosure request back from the Union Gap Police Department and records from the coroner's office," Ray suggested.

"Ok, sounds like a plan."

"This final case is a homicide of a young woman who had a relationship with a Yakima police officer before she was found murdered," Jerry remarked.

"A police officer, suspect?"

"Not a suspect initially, a person of interest."

7.
SARA LUZ BUSTOS

Drawing by Northcott

Incident:	Homicide
Victim:	Sara Luz Bustos
Date of Death:	September 18, 1977 (21 years old)
Height/Weight:	5' 4"/ 115 pounds
Hair:	Brown
Eyes:	Brown
Address:	816 Fair Ave. Yakima, WA 98902
Date of incident:	September 17, 1999
Case number:	YPD 99-16172

Yakima Herald-Republic newspaper article by Jeremy Meyer dated September 18th, 1999, states:

Fisherman Finds Slain Woman's Body in River. A fisherman found a woman's battered, partially clothed body submerged in the Yakima River near Robertson's Landing early Friday evening. Yakima police, who are treating the case as a homicide, worked more than an hour to document the scene and retrieve the body from a back channel upriver from the State Route 24 bridge. Police identified the victim as a Hispanic female, 17—22 years old, between 100 and 115 pounds and between 5 feet and 5 feet 4 with brown eyes and brown shoulder-length hair. Yakima Police Capt. Jeff Schneider said, 'The victim had some obvious trauma to the head. I'm sure she's been hit by something. What it is, I don't know.' Police are unsure how long the woman's body had been in the water. 'Clothing was scattered throughout the bushes,' he said. Schneider mentioned there was evidence where the body had been dragged, but it was unclear if the woman had been killed at the scene. He also wouldn't comment whether there was any sign of sexual abuse. 'We can't identify this person,' he said. 'She doesn't match up with anyone we know as a runaway or missing. Obviously, if anyone knows anything, they should call us at 575-6200.' Schneider said the victim had three distinct tattoos: a cross near her right eye, the letters J M on her right shoulder, and the name Sara on her left wrist. Friday evening, the police had cordoned off a quarter-mile area of the Yakima Greenway and will continue to look for clues today. Schneider said the body was hard to detect because it was about 15 feet from the shore in a back channel, under about 3 feet of water. 'An autopsy was scheduled for today,' Yakima County Coroner Maury Rice said.

"Detective Sergeant Merryman, Detectives J. Martinez, T. Bardwell, M. Tovar, D. Cortez, and R. Hartman were all present at the scene of the body's recovery, and all wrote reports. I must say, Detective Michael Tovar's 11-page report was very complete and thorough. It appears Detective Watts was the lead investigator, with Sergeant Mike Merryman as the field supervisor," Jerry explained.

"Captain Jeff Schneider asked the public for help in getting the victim identified the next day, and this is a copy of one of the first reports written after the body recovery," Jerry remarked as he handed the document to Ray.

YAKIMA POLICE DEPARTMENT
DETECTIVE DIVISION
DETAIL REPORT
DATE: 09-17-99

CASE NUMBER	99-16172
INCIDENT:	HOMICIDE
OFFICER:	J. SALINAS / 3686
DETAILS:	

Officer Posada contacted me in the weight room at 1645 hrs. and told me that Capt. Schneider advised him to instruct me to stand by. A partially clothed woman's body was discovered in the river at Robertson's Landing. The woman had some sort of blunt trauma to her head. At 1705 hrs., I called dispatch and spoke with dispatcher Ybarra. She told me that Capt. Schneider requested my presence at the crime scene at Robertson's Landing.

Detective Hartman and I arrived at the scene at 1740 hrs. When I arrived at the scene, Capt. Schneider pointed out a triangle reflector near the center of the parking lot. He said that the reflector marked a buckle that could be evidence. He instructed me to measure the location of the buckle and collect it. Using the east gate entrance pole as a reference point, I measured the location of the buckle at 187' S and 22' E. I collected the item by placing it in a paper sack. It was a brown strap approximately 6" in length with a buckle attached at one end.

At 1755 hrs., I walked toward the river to the crime scene. Upon inspection of the scene, I found a clump of brown hair near the bank. There was a weed among the clump of hair. Just west of the clump of hair, it appeared as if there were drag marks that led from the west and to the edge of the bank.

A pair of pants was located just south of the ball of hair along the riverbank. There is a small island in the middle of the river. A thin trail of rocks leads from the riverbank to this island. I walked along the rocks to the island and from the edge of the island, I could see the body of the victim floating in knee-high water approximately a foot beneath the surface. The body was that of a young female lying face down, wearing only a bra and a sport top. Along the east end of the small island, there was a pair of pink panties and a small, black shoe.

I returned to the riverbank and began sketching the crime scene. Coroner Maurice Rice was present for the removal of the body. I assisted Rice in the body's removal from the river.

As the body was being removed from the river, I noticed the name 'Sara' tattooed on the victim's left wrist. There was a small cross tattoo on the corner of the victim's right eye. I noticed a wound near the top of the victim's head, wounds on her right temple, and near the corner of the right side of her mouth. The victim had an oblong rock stuck deep into her mouth. Bruising was evident around both eyes, and there was a small trickle of blood trailing from her right nostril. The body was stiff and rigid and the skin around her fingers was very wrinkled as if she had been in the water for quite some time. The victim's hair was similar to the type of hair I saw earlier on the riverbank. There was a similar type of weed mixed in with the victim's hair as the weeds that were mixed in with the clumped hair on the riverbank.

I assisted Rice in the body's removal from the river and helped place her into the coroner's truck for transport.

I left the scene at 1925 hrs. and arrived at the station at 1945 hrs.

At the station, I looked through various high school yearbooks in an attempt to identify the victim. I did not have any success in identifying the victim. In a further attempt to identify the victim, I sent a terminal message to regional agencies and requested that local police agencies check their missing persons and runaway files for any matches with the victim in this case.

Per Sgt. Merryman's request, I left the station at 2145 hrs.

At approximately 0120 hrs., I received a phone call at my residence requesting that I return to the station. I arrived at approximately 0145 hrs. When I arrived, I contacted Sgt. Merryman. Sgt. Merryman told me that the victim had been identified as Sara Bustos.

At 0300 hrs., Detective Tovar and I spoke with Hector Larios Estrada. Mr. Estrada claimed to be Bustos' boyfriend. He has lived in Yakima since 1997. His friends call him 'Fernando' because of his resemblance to a Mexican TV star, Fernando Fiori.

Estrada said that Bustos abused cocaine every day. Estrada said he knew this because he also used cocaine with her often. Bustos, according to Estrada, would steal to support her habit. Estrada spoke of a YPD officer named 'Mike' who was trying to get Bustos into a drug treatment program. Estrada did not know the officer's last name, but said Bustos spoke of him.

Estrada claims he last saw Sara at approximately 1700 hrs., on 09-16-99. He said he remembered well because it was Thursday. Estrada said he took Bustos to her mother's boyfriend's house. Estrada named the boyfriend as Raul. Bustos told Estrada that she had her clothes at the house and wanted to shower and change clothes there. She told Estrada that she would page him later and he could pick her up. Estrada said Bustos never paged him.

On 09-17-99, Estrada said he found out that Bustos was dead. A woman named Maria Elena, who resides in the same apartment building as Estrada, in apartment 12, told him Bustos was found dead.

Estrada said he recalled Sara's sister, Lourdes, telling her that she had better move from Yakima or she would be killed. Lourdes said this because she felt that Sara was a 'snitch'.

Estrada spent approximately a year with Sara. They have no children in common. However, Sara has a child who is currently being raised by her sister who lives in Wenatchee. Estrada said *that Sara's personal items, including her black purse, should be at Raul's house.*

Estrada said Sara had a friend named Jesus who drove a blue BMW. Estrada claimed that he had not seen Jesus in the last four or five days. Estrada did not know Jesus' last name, but described him as a short male of an average build. Jesus speaks in Spanish, and he used to live in a gray apartment building on N. Naches Ave.

Estrada agreed to submit to a polygraph examination regarding the homicide investigation. Detective Tovar and I terminated the interview at 0405 hrs.

On 09-18-99, at approximately 1430 hrs., Detective Watts contacted Detective Hartman and I in the YPD weight room. Detective Watts instructed Detective Hartman that he was to take photographs with the 35 mm camera at the Bustos autopsy. I accompanied Detective Watts and Detective Hartman to the Yakima County Morgue to take photos of the autopsy.

On arrival at the morgue, Coroner Rice, Sgt. R. Light, Officer Henne, and Dr. and Mrs. Sealove were already present. Sgt. Merryman arrived during the autopsy. Also, during the autopsy, Officer Hildebrand arrived, but left shortly thereafter with Officer Henne.

Dr. Sealove conducted a thorough internal and external examination of Bustos. I took 47 Polaroid photos of the victim during the examination process. At the conclusion of the examination, Dr. Sealove determined that his belief was that the cause of death was due to blunt trauma to the head. Detective Hartman, Detective Watts, and I left the morgue at approximately 1800 hrs. I turned over the Polaroid photos to Detective Watts.

Signed
J. Salinas, badge # 3686.

"It looks like Detectives Salinas and Tovar, both Spanish speaking, started following the leads and talking to people. It didn't take them long before they were getting people of interest identified, and were working to come up with a suspect,"

Ray said after reading Detective Salinas' report.

"I did some checking on the officer named 'Mike' who tried to get Sara into a drug treatment program as reported in J. Salinas' report. I believe 'Mike' is Detective Mike Tovar. I think it's possible Detective Tovar witnessed some problems with Sara Bustos. He may have tried to remove her from what was happening but was unsuccessful. I wonder if it's a coincidence that Mike resigned from the Yakima Police Department about six months following the adjudication of this case?" Jerry asked.

"That's possible, but how would we know that, Jerry, since Mike passed away some time ago?"

"His wife would know, I bet."

"But do you want to get her involved in this situation?"

"Probably not, but that should be her decision, Ray."

"It wouldn't hurt to try to locate her, but let's cross that bridge if we come to it later; what do you think?"

"I agree. We may find that our research takes us in a different direction. Sergeant Merryman directed the detectives at the scene to various assignments. Let's take a look at his initial report," Jerry suggested.

YAKIMA POLICE DEPARTMENT
Detail Report
Date: 9-19-99

Case Number:	*99-16172*
Subject:	*Homicide Investigation*
Officer:	*Sgt. Merryman*
Division:	*Investigations*

On Friday, September 17th, 1999, at approximately 1700 hrs., Capt. Schneider advised me to respond to Robertson's Landing, on the Yakima River, to assist with an investigation involving what appeared to be a young female victim. I responded immediately from the station and arrived at approximately 1720 hrs.

Upon my arrival Ofc Dillon advised me that a fisherman had discovered what appeared to be a young female victim in the river who was obviously deceased. Capt. Schneider arrived, and we walked to the crime scene where Ofc Foley and Lt. Finch were surveying the area.

Detectives Watts, Martinez, Guilland, Tovar, Bardwell, Walls, Cortez, Salinas, and Hartman were called to investigate the incident. I made various assignments for the detectives and assisted with searching for evidence and attempting to identify the unknown victim.

The victim was located approximately 15 feet offshore, face down, and partially submerged under the water's surface. It was obvious that she was only wearing a shirt. She did not have any pants, panties, shoes or socks on. She was wearing a light-colored shirt.

As the investigation continued, the victim was identified at approximately 2300 hrs., as Sara Bustos. The identification was made using the photographs we were able to obtain of her and also from the distinctive tattoos that she had on her body.

One possible suspect identified during the investigation was the victim's brother, Salvador Bustos. He was currently awaiting trial from an August 5th arrest, in which Sara had accused him of forcing her to perform certain sexual acts on him. Based on that information, as well as some evidence related to the possible cause of death, we believed that Salvador was a viable suspect.

Patrol was advised of Salvador's description and possible vehicle information. The victim's family was also advised that we wished to talk to Salvador if they came into contact with him.

On Saturday, September 18th, 1999, at approximately 1400 hrs., I was advised by Capt. Schneider that attorney Greg Scott had been in contact with him. Mr. Scott advised that he had been contacted by a client of his, Salvador Bustos, and advised that he thought the police were looking for him regarding the death of his sister. Mr. Scott advised Capt. Schneider that he would bring Salvador to the station between 1700 and 1730 hrs., to talk to us.

Capt. Schneider instructed me to handle the interview of Salvador Bustos if one was allowed.

At approximately 1500 hrs., I attended the autopsy of Sara Bustos. (See Det. Watt's report for details).

At approximately 1745 hrs., I was advised that Mr. Scott and his client were at the station. I went to the station to talk to them. I spoke to Mr. Scott prior to interviewing Mr. Bustos. Mr. Scott advised he would allow an interview with Mr. Bustos with some limitation regarding any question directed at where his client was and who he was with on Thursday night. (9-16-99). Mr. Scott and I went to an interview room where Mr. Bustos had been seated.

Mr. Bustos advised me that Holtzinger Fruit has employed him for the past 1-2 years. He stated that he works with his brother Seferino. Mr. Bustos did not work on Monday or Tuesday of this week, but did work Thursday through Friday. (September 15, 16 & 17) Mr. Bustos reports working at 0700 hrs., each day and gets off work at approximately 1730 hrs. He indicated that 'Grandpa' took him to work all three days.

On Wednesday, he was not sure who gave him a ride home. He got home around 1630-1700 hrs. He stated he was not positive and could have arrived home as late as 1730 hrs.

On Thursday he got a ride home from a subject by the name of 'Nacho'. He stated that 'Nacho' also works at Holtzinger. He said that 'Nacho' stopped and purchased a 6-pack of 'Bud Light' on the way home and they had some beer at his house. Nacho left the house, 816 Fair, at approximately 1730 hrs. Mr. Bustos said that his mother was not home when he arrived home and that was why he had some beer. Mr. Bustos said he would not drink beer if his mother was home because she would get mad at him.

On Friday he got a ride home from Nacho and was home around 1630 hrs.

As mentioned, Mr. Scott did not allow any questions regarding Mr. Bustos' whereabouts on Thursday night after he got home.

Mr. Bustos stated he had last seen Sara approximately three (3) weeks earlier. She was with a subject who was driving a green BMW. He did not know who the driver of the car was, but added that he had observed Sara in his company several times.

I asked Mr. Bustos if he could think of any reason someone would want his sister dead. He said that he had heard that Sara steals from people and the [sic] she might have stolen some cocaine from someone. Mr. Bustos could not provide any specific information regarding whom she may have stolen the cocaine from.

Mr. Bustos stated that his entire family was aware Sara used cocaine. The family tried to get her to stop, but she would not listen.

Ultimately, Mr. Bustos stated he did not know who killed his sister. I asked him if he wanted me to catch the person who did this to his sister. He said that he heard his family talking about how they wanted the person caught. I asked him if he wanted me to catch the person who did this. He said that the person should get [sic] to jail for a long time, but they should not be killed because that would not be right either.

I thanked Mr. Bustos for his time and the interview ended at 1920 hrs.

"What do you think so far, Ray?"

"I've worked homicides by myself, and I know you have too, Jerry. It must be nice to have all the help you need, but I imagine it can get a bit confusing with that many people walking around the crime scene."

"I counted 16 people at the body recovery site, which also turned out to also be the location of the murder," Jerry responded.

"Let's note the names of all the police personnel at the scene," Ray suggested as he took a piece of notepaper and wrote:

Captain Schneider
Lieutenant Finch
Sergeant Merryman
Officer Dillon
Officer Foley

Detective Watts
Detective Martinez
Detective Guilland
Detective Tovar
Detective Bardwell
Detective Walls
Detective Cortez
Detective Salinas
Detective Hartman
Detective Schuknecht
Coroner Mary Rice

"With that many people coming and going, it might have been prudent to assign one detective to list the names, times of arrival and departure of individuals from the scene. They all should have been entering and leaving via one pathway in order to minimize destroying evidence," Ray remarked.

"I'm sure they were careful in their search of the scene. There is one problem, however," Jerry said.

"What's that?"

"There was another person at the crime scene, and I find it alarming that none of the investigators' reports mentioned his name. He was a Yakima police officer assigned to traffic enforcement and on his day-off. Without being asked, he entered the crime scene and assisted the detectives. He was later asked to block the TV camera's view of the victim's body as it was removed from the river. He should not have been allowed to enter the crime scene at all," Jerry revealed.

"How do you know he was there?" Ray asked.

"Because of a report filed by the officer himself on April 12th, 2000, more than six months after the homicide," Jerry responded.

"Who is this officer and why did it take six months to determine he was at the scene?"

"Here are copies of his two reports, written a day apart," Jerry responded as he handed Ray the reports.

YAKIMA POLICE DEPARTMENT
Detail Report
Date: 04/11/00

Case Number: 99-16278
Subject: Bustos Homicide
Officer: K. Twindler # 9999
Division: Traffic

Additional info:

On April 10th, 2000, Sgt. Merryman and I were able to locate my activity log for October 1998, which showed me as being dispatched to 816 Fair Ave, the Bustos residence, in reference to a domestic complaint. The victim had called the police from the Bustos residence and used Sarah Bustos as the interpreter.

Sgt. Merryman and I used my initial report to work up a timeline, and it appears I had contact with Bustos through May 1999.

During my contacts with Bustos, she never mentioned having any problems with anyone other than family problems, nor did I have any contact with anyone Bustos was associated with.

Signed,
K. Twindler #9999

YAKIMA POLICE DEPARTMENT
MEMORANDUM
Date: 04/12/00

To: Capt. Schneider
From: Officer Kensley Twindler #9999
Subject: Sarah Bustos Homicide

My initial contact with Bustos was during a domestic complaint in October 1998. I was dispatched to 816 Fair Ave, the Bustos residence, regarding a domestic complaint where the victim was using Bustos as the interpreter. After taking down the victim's information, I left my business card with the victim and Bustos. It was during this contact that Bustos had mentioned there were subjects living at 735 Fair Ave who were dealing drugs. Bustos had offered to help me arrest these subjects.

A month or so went by and I received a voice message from Bustos stating she was in trouble and she needed my help. I contacted Bustos by telephone, at which time Bustos stated she wasn't getting along with her mother and her mother [was] going to kick her out of the house. Bustos wanted my assistance in finding a job. I contacted Bustos and her brother at their residence and explained to Bustos that I would help her in locating a job as long as she showed up at work on time and did what she was told. I talked to the manager at Taco Bell on 8th St. and Yakima Ave and was told he would hire her if she would come in and talk to him. I passed this message on to Bustos, but she never followed up on the offer.

A couple of weeks had passed when I received another voice message from Bustos stating her mother had kicked her out of the house and she was staying with a friend. Bustos said she was going to church to meet her mother and ask if she could come home. Bustos never left a number, and I was unable to contact her.

Several weeks went by and I received another voice message from Bustos stating she was at home and she and her mother were making fresh tortillas, and I was welcome to stop by and have lunch. I stopped by and met Bustos' mother and had two burritos.

During the next month, I would periodically receive messages from Bustos stating she was OK and she had been going to church with her mother like I had requested.

At one point during the early spring, I had received a page and a voice message from Bustos stating she was at a friend's house and they were doing drugs and she wanted to leave but she was unable to find a ride. I called Bustos back and tried to arrange a ride for her. Bustos did not want to leave the house with any of its occupants, so I told her I would come and get her and take her to a relative's house. I picked up Bustos at an apartment on 20th Ave and Greenway Ave. I pulled up outside the apartment and honked my horn. Bustos came out of the apartment, and I took her to an address near McKinley Ave. Bustos knocked on the door while I stayed in my vehicle. There was no answer at the door, so Bustos asked if she could come to my house and use my phone to contact someone else. Bustos and I arrived at my house and after approx. 15 minutes Bustos was able to contact either a friend or a relative who lived near Garfield Ave. I transported Bustos to this residence and then didn't hear from her for quite a while.

In late spring, I received a phone message from Bustos stating she and her mother weren't getting along and she was, again, staying with friends. I never heard from Bustos again.

On September 17th, 1999, I was riding my motorcycle around town and had decided to stop at the station to pick up paperwork. While at the station, one of our dispatchers, whom I believe was Katie Ybarra, advised me the detectives were out on another homicide at the river near the Greenway. After continuing to ride around for a while, I decided to stop by and see what had happened.

Upon arriving at the scene, I observed several reporters standing near the crime scene tape, which was located on the east side of the parking lot. I walked past the reporters and down the paved path to the river. At the river, I observed several detectives in the river and standing along the riverbank. I also observed Coroner M. Rice and Det. Walls in the water next to the victim. I was standing on the riverbank just to the south of the boat ramp and from where I was standing; I was unable to see the victim in the water. While standing there, Det. Martinez arrived and stood to the right of me. Sgt. Merryman told Det. Martinez and me to stand together and block the view of the TV cameras so as not to let them get a picture of the victim. While standing with Det. Martinez we observed Det. Walls and the coroner bring the body out of the water in a white body bag. Once on shore, one of the detectives asked if he could see the body. Coroner Rice unzipped the body bag, and I observed a white female with brown hair. The female was very white and covered with a green film of algae. The female also had several cuts to her head and face, and she had a large rock sticking out of her mouth. Coroner Rice zipped the bag and place [sic] the victim in the back of his van. I left the crime scene shortly thereafter and continued riding my motorcycle.

On Monday, I returned to work and was told by Det. Cortez that they had another homicide on Sunday. While taking [sic] to Det. Cortez, he advised me that they had identified the female from the river as Sarah [sic] Bustos. I didn't realize until a short time later that it was the Sarah [Sara] Bustos that I had known. I immediately went back to Det. Cortez's desk and told him I knew Bustos. I also told Det. Walls, Salinas and Hartman that I had known Bustos.

Det. Walls showed me the Polaroid pictures of Bustos and it was still very hard to recognize her due to the swelling in her head, her very white skin and the large rock sticking out of her mouth. In the stack of pictures, I noticed a picture of a tattoo of Bustos' first name on her hand.

Later that week, I was told by detectives that they had the subject who had killed Bustos and that was the last I ever heard about the case.

On April 10th, 2000, Sgt. Merryman and I were able to locate my activity log for October 1998, which showed me as being dispatched to 816 Fair Ave, the Bustos residence, in reference to a domestic complaint. Sgt. Merryman and I used my initial report to work up a time using my activity log to show my first contact through my last contact with Bustos.

At no time did Bustos ever stay the night at my residence. She was in my residence once for approx. 15 minutes. I never used Bustos as an informant, nor did I provide her with 'buy money.' During my contacts with Bustos, she never mentioned having any problems with anyone other than family problems. Nor did I ever have any contact with anyone Bustos was associated with. While in contact with Bustos, I was unaware she was a drug user, and

I never offered to send her to treatment in Arizona.

Signed:
Kensley Twindler #9999

"I find it strange that Officer Twindler wrote a very short report about his relationship with the victim prior to her murder, and then the very next day he wrote another report that was three pages long. I can almost imagine Officer Twindler turning in the first report and immediately being told it was not acceptable and ordered to write a more complete report.

"I asked a criminal psychologist to analyze Twindler's reports, and this is the result," Jerry reported.

The first report illustrates that the officer is attempting to distance himself as if he knows very little. In the first paragraph using the words, 'which showed me as being dispatched,' and in the second paragraph 'it appears that' are attempts to distance himself from the content as though it is an afterthought. He does this again by offering up, 'nor did I have any contact with anyone Bustos was associated with.' It appears these are efforts to make this seem routine rather than someone he may have been more familiar with.

In the second report, Sara's full name is used so there is less distance and some familiarity expressed, except he spells Sara's first name wrong several times. Was this done on purpose to make the reader think he is so unfamiliar with her that he doesn't know how to spell her name? It appears so. The thing that stands out to me the most in this report is the officer is functioning as though he is Sara Bustos's social worker more than a police officer. It is difficult to imagine this level of familiarity with a person without the officer receiving some type of gain from the situation. The intimacy of having lunch with Sara Bustos and her mother, being called, and asked to pick her up, and then ending up at the officer's home to use the phone, suggests much more intimacy than is detailed in the reports.

The most obvious attempt at distancing was when her body was found. The statement that the officer didn't realize this was the Sara Bustos he had known was another tactic to distance. The relationship between the officer and the homicide victim appears much more intimate than is stated in the officer's reports.

*L. Cleary,
Criminal Psychologist*

"Also, Ray, did you notice Officer Twindler's report on April 11th, 2000, which was almost 7 months after the murder, listed case number 99-16278. The homicide case number is 99-16172 and this new case number that Officer Twindler listed is chronologically 106 cases after the Bustos homicide case. Why do you think he listed this new case number?"

"That case number might be the investigation into Officer Twindler's relationship with Sara Bustos, so that he could be confirmed or ruled out as a suspect. Why don't you send a PDR to Yakima Police records section for copies of reports under that case number," Ray suggested.

"Good thought, Ray. I'll get that PDR on its way now," Jerry responded as he began typing.

"How many other people are considered persons of interest or suspects in this case, Jerry?"

"There are several men that could have been motivated to kill Sara for various reasons. Her brother, Salvador, was awaiting trial for a sexual assault against his sister and if she was unable to testify, the charges would have been dropped. Sara's sister, Ruby, was also concerned because of several rumors that Sara had been stealing to support her cocaine addiction and that Sara had received death threats."

"Do you remember Officer Kensley Twindler's report dated April 12th, 2000, where he stated in the first paragraph that, 'Bustos had offered to help me arrest these subjects,' at 735 Fair Avenue. Do you think Twindler ignored that offer and did nothing?" Ray asked.

"No, my guess is he accepted her invitation, and he contacted drug detectives either with the Yakima Police Department,

Drug Enforcement Administration detectives, or possibly the City-County Narcotics Unit which consisted of law enforcement officers from the city, county and federal agencies. They could have used her to do a controlled buy from the drug dealers at 735 Fair Avenue or her sworn testimony on an affidavit for a search warrant. The case number for the drug arrest would be close to but numerically less than Sara's homicide case number. I've been unable to locate it for a PDR, however, so I sent in a general request to the Yakima Police Records Bureau. Since Deputy Chief Twindler is in charge of what is provided now, we may not be successful in the search," Jerry responded.

"There's also a rumor that the victim's diary or journal, which is written in Spanish, suffered water damage while in police custody."

"How could that happen when the evidence vault is secured and closely monitored? We need to issue several public disclosure requests. One for the case file, one for a copy of the victim's journal, another for in-person viewing and photographing of the journal for water damage. I'll get those public disclosure requests out the door to see what comes back," Jerry responded.

"We already have a copy of the entire case file from Ross Manzola."

"Come in!" Ray responded to a knock on the office door.

"I hope I'm not interrupting. How's everything going?" Attorney Manzola asked as he opened the office door.

"We've looked each case over and will be sending out PDRs and seeking more information. Poor little Sharon Burch just breaks your heart, doesn't it?" Jerry asked, looking down.

"All four cases are heartbreakers, but the Sharon Burch murder is so cruel it's almost unbelievable," Ross responded.

There was a short silence.

"I have an update on Joe Creed," Ross announced.

"I expected him to be arriving soon to assist in your work on the four cases, but now I'm not sure. Did you notice the young gentleman waiting in the outer office yesterday?"

"Yes, who was that?" Jerry asked.

"He's from the United States Department of Justice, Bureau of Alcohol, Tobacco, and Firearms, or more commonly known as ATF."

"What'd he want?" Ray asked.

"He wanted to contact Joe Creed, but he didn't say why. Joe's wife, Lydia, told him that I may help in contacting him," Ross explained.

"It probably has something to do with either alcohol, tobacco, or firearms," Jerry suggested.

"I like the way Jerry deduces things," Ray quipped, grinning.

"I just hope Joe is not getting in over his head with his nemesis," Ross mumbled.

"What do you mean?" Jerry asked.

"Just between us, I received a receipt in the mail recently made out to Joe Creed for two M 2 Browning .50 caliber machine guns. It came from a Captain Reginald H. Lloyd of the cargo ship, MV Bass Reeves, and said the weapons were delivered at the Bercovich boatyard in La Paz, Mexico two weeks ago," Ross explained.

"Whatever Joe is doing; it has the attention of the ATF. Does he know they're looking for him, Ross?"

"Yes, I left a message and am waiting to hear back from him."

"Meanwhile, there's plenty we can be doing on these four cases," Ray said as he stood up.

"Why don't we get an early start tomorrow morning? I need to pick up a few groceries on the way home to my girls," Jerry responded with a smile.

"Ok, see you at 8 AM. Aren't the Seattle Mariners playing tonight at 6 PM?"

"Yes, they are!" Jerry said, smiling, as he was leaving the office.

8.
Public Disclosure Reports & Inquiries

Retired Yakima Sheriff's Detective Lieutenant Gerald Hafsos opened the door to the Manzola Law Office the next morning, smelling a whiff of freshly brewed coffee.

"Good morning, Monique!" Jerry said with a smile.

"Good morning, Jerry. Help yourself to the coffee and a donut," Monique responded.

"That's nice, Monique. Thank you!"

"Ross has increased the coffee budget to include donuts for you cops," Monique said snickering.

"That was very astute of him."

"He also said that you could order out on the office account if you wanted to work through lunch."

"That's very kind of Ross. It looks like we'll be spending some time here, Monique. Please let us know if we're getting in your way," Ray said as he walked into the office.

"Oh, you're no bother. Let me know if I can help you with anything, please."

After filling their coffee cups and grabbing a donut, the two detectives sat at their desks drinking coffee, slowly eating their donuts, and silently thinking for about 10 minutes.

Jerry looked different since he'd worked on the Nickoloff murders. Not tired, not older, just somehow different. It was obvious the Nickoloff case had taken a lot out of him. He is a decent *gentleman*, Ray thought as he looked at Jerry.

"What are you pondering, Ray? Maybe we should divide the cases between us. Two each, what do you think?"

"Sounds good. Which ones do you want?"

"The little girl, Sharon Burch, has been investigated as thoroughly as possible by Investigator Rod Shaw and I'm familiar with it. There's not much else that can be done on that case, it appears. The Sara Bustos case, on the other hand, could turn into a quagmire of leads going in numerous directions. I can take Burch and Bustos if you think Riegel and Moore would be a fair split?" Jerry asked.

"Yes, that sounds fair. There's not much more that appears could to be done on the Moore case, but the Riegel disappearance could easily turn into a homicide investigation." Ray responded.

"Ok, my friend. Let's see how much our old, retired brains can absorb. Here's a copy of the Sara Bustos case file from Yakima Police. Ross sent in a PDR and received a redacted copy about a year ago," Ray remarked as he handed four full notebooks to Jerry.

"The Riegel file is pretty detailed also," Ray said as he opened that notebook.

"You know, if we still had our badges, we'd just go to the record bureaus and ask for copies of each case file and we'd have it in 20 minutes. Now we have to submit PDRs and wait weeks for redacted copies," Jerry remarked.

"That's because we are no longer deputy sheriffs. We're regular citizens now."

"Yeah, I guess you're right, Ray. We're regular citizens. Do you still pack a gun?"

"Sure, you?"

"Sometimes."

The men spent the rest of the morning reading the investigative files and making notes on the actions they planned to take in each case, with Jerry reading the Sharon Burch and Sara Bustos homicide case files. Ray went through the Ryan Moore domestic violence—suicide and the Lawrence Riegel missing person files.

Later, a knock came at the office door and as it opened Monique said, "Hey you guys, it's 3 PM. Did you go out for lunch and how late do you plan on being here today?"

"I didn't realize the time. No, we've been reading files and kind of lost track, I guess," Ray responded.

"It will only take me another hour or two. How about you, Ray?"

"About the same. Why don't we keep reading and then call it a day? We can put the PDRs together tomorrow morning," Ray suggested.

"Sounds good, Ray. Don't worry, Monique, we'll lock up when we leave," Jerry responded.

"Great, see you guys tomorrow," Monique said as she left the office for the day.

Arriving at 7:30 the next morning, Monique was concerned about finding the front door to the Manzola Law Office building unlocked. The door didn't appear to be damaged; she noted as she approached.

Maybe the retired cops just forgot to lock up when they left last night, she thought to herself as she slowly opened the door to the smell of fresh coffee.

"Good morning, Monique! I hope you don't mind me making coffee," Jerry said with a big smile.

"Absolutely not. Here are some donuts to give you energy."

"I've got a little too much energy this morning, Monique. I woke up at 3 AM. And when I couldn't get back to sleep, I decided I might as well go work on the Burch and Bustos cases."

"You look tired."

"I'll sleep better tonight. You know what the cure for insomnia is?"

"No."

"Lack of sleep," Jerry responded with a grin.

"Good morning, you two. It looks like you've gotten a

head-start on the day," Ray said as he walked into the office.

"Good morning, Ray. Help yourself to the coffee, which was brewed to perfection by your partner, and here are some donuts," Monique announced.

"What time did you get here this morning, Jerry?" Ray asked.

"About 4:00 AM. I couldn't sleep."

"Trying to get the jump on me, huh?"

"That's right, partner. Here's a PDR," Jerry said, handing Ray some paperwork.

Yakima, WA Police Department
Bureau of Records
200 South 3rd St.
Yakima, WA 98901

Public Disclosure Request Sara Luz Bustos homicide YPD case # 99-16172
I would like to look at in-person and take photos of (1)Black Date Book and (1) Purple Spiral Binder (Journal) as noted on the property tag which was signed by R. Watts 3207 on 7/19/00.

After looking the PDRs over closely, Ray said, "I have three as well."

Union Gap, Washington Police Department
102 West Ahtanum Rd
Union Gap, WA 98903

Public Disclosure Request:
Death investigation records of:

Ryan Glenn Moore, born June 1984, death March 20th, 2010, location 2209 S. 6th Ave. Union Gap, WA 98903.
Copy of police investigation records, including initial police

report, detectives' written reports, witness names and statements, death scene photographs, follow-up reports, police supervisor reports, death scene diagrams, names of persons of interest, crime lab reports. Coroner's reports and accompanying documents, photos, emails, texts, video, data and other reports pertaining to the death.

Yakima County Coroner's Office
128 N. 2nd St.
Yakima, WA 98901

Public Records Center:

Yakima County Medical Investigation Records regarding the death investigation of Ryan Glenn Moore, born June 1984, death on or about March 20th, 2010. Address 2209 S. 6th Ave. Union Gap, WA 98903. Please include a copy of the Certificate of Death and accompanying police reports.

Yakima Police Department
Bureau of Records
200 S. 3rd St.
Yakima, WA 98901

A copy of the initial offense report, follow-up reports, investigative reports, lists of evidence, including evidence reports and property tag numbers, copies of photos and outside agency and citizen and witness statements and correspondence and reports, copies of supervisor reports, newspaper clippings, inter-office memos, copies of search warrants and affidavits, return of search warrant document copies, copies of transcribed witness and suspect interviews and declarations. Names and contact information of investigators assigned from the initial report to the current date. A copy of the complete investigative file on the missing and search for:

Lawrence Jay Riegel DOB 12/15/1952, missing since 12/25/2009

"Good, let's get them in the mail. State law says they have 5 days in which to respond," Jerry remarked.

"Why do you want to look at Sara Bustos' diary? Isn't there a copy in the PDR response that Ross received about a year ago?"

"There are places in the copied pages of the diary where her writing is not legible," Jerry responded.

"What do you mean?"

"I've only been able to look at copied pages of the victim's diary, but some pages are not readable even though they're handwritten in Spanish. It appears to me that there's water damage to some pages, but I'd have to see them directly to determine that," Jerry responded.

"Ok, when this information is returned, we'll be able to move ahead with the cases. Where are you at with the Sharon Burch homicide?"

"I worked with Rod Shaw on this case when it was assigned to him at the sheriff's office years ago. I think almost everything I need will be in Rod's file," Jerry responded.

"We can continue reading case files until we receive responses to the PDRs. I suspect how we move forward with the investigations depends largely on the PDR responses," Ray remarked.

Both men went back to reading their case files until there was a knock on the office door.

"I'm sorry to bother you, but there's a woman here looking for Joe Creed and since Ross is away at the moment, I thought you might be able to help her," Monique said, peeking through the doorway.

"Sure, what's her name?" Jerry asked.

"This is Donna Ashford," Monique announced as a woman appeared from behind her.

9.
La Fantasma

Ray and Jerry stood up and greeted the female visitor with handshakes. Jerry noted her hands were dry and rough to the touch and that the little finger on her right hand was missing. She had a breezy scent of the outdoors about her, and her slim, shapely figure was vaguely disguised by her leather pants and jacket. She was wearing a backpack and motorcycle boots and was sporting a short, shaggy hairdo. She appeared to be in her 50's and her bright blue eyes dilated to almost black when she looked directly at you.

"I did some work in Mexico with the DEA and Joe Creed, and I was hoping I could catch up with him if he's around," she announced.

There was a pause while she held up a badge with official credentials.

The gold badge had the wings of an American eagle at the top protecting the scrolled words 'Department of Justice.' Beneath those words was a blue circular emblem with 'U.S.' in the center, 'Drug Enforcement Administration' around the circumference, and the words, 'Special Agent' at the bottom. Opposite the badge in the black wallet were her credentials with a photo in which she appeared much younger and happier. Across the top of the credentials was the name 'Donna Elaine Ashford' and the pronouncement that she was a duly authorized agent of the Department of Justice, Drug Enforcement Administration, etc. At the bottom of the credentials in the area marked 'Assigned' were the words, 'Foreign-Deployed Advisory and Support Team (FAST).'

"I just need to make contact with Joe Creed," she said again as she snapped the badge case closed and stuck it in her pocket.

"He's away at the moment, but we expect him back sometime soon," Monique responded.

"Is he in some sort of trouble?" Ray asked.

"He's in trouble alright, and I'm the solution. There's a message number here he can call, which will get to me. Ask him to contact me as soon as possible," she declared, handing a folded piece of paper to Jerry with a wink and a wry grin.

"Uh, OK," Jerry said, taking the note.

She turned around, walked to the door, and quietly said, "Thanks," before she left.

Ray, Jerry, and Monique all walked to the window and watched her as she approached a black motorcycle parked outside. She adjusted her backpack before mounting the high-powered motorcycle, while eying a police patrol car as it passed slowly by.

"That's a Ducati Monster!" Jerry exclaimed.

The hundred horsepower motorcycle with six gears could easily reach speeds approaching 150 miles per hour, as was evidenced by the sound of its V-twin motor. Putting on her helmet and climbing aboard, she waited for a car as it entered the parking lot and then slowly went southbound on 2nd Street, out of sight.

"Who was that on the motorcycle?" Ross asked as he walked into the office with Ray, Jerry, and Monique still standing at the window.

"That was Donna Ashford of the DEA," Monique responded.

"THAT was La Fantasma? I thought she was dead!" Ross exclaimed.

"What's La Fantasma?" Ray asked.

"La Fantasma in Spanish means the ghost. The last time I heard the cartels sent pieces of her to the DEA office in Washington, DC. It was assumed she had been killed," Ross explained.

"She'd gone rogue and killed over 60 cartel members on her own. She usually takes the little finger of the cartel soldier she has killed and makes the bones into a necklace," Ross continued.

"Oh, my God! Are you serious? She was wearing a necklace that looked like it was made of small bones," Monique exclaimed.

"What did she want?" Ross asked.

"She wanted to contact Joe Creed. She said she was the solution to his problem," Ray responded.

"I wonder what that means?" Ross asked.

"Here's a phone number she asked that Joe call," Jerry said as he handed the note to Ross.

"I'll see if I can reach him in Mexico by telephone and get that message to him if you wish," Monique offered.

"Yes, please, Monique. I want to speak with him if you can find him," Ross said as he handed the note to her.

"Once we get through to Joe and figure out what is going on with this rogue DEA agent, I'll get back to you with an update," Ross announced.

"We need to get our noses back into the case files while we wait for the PDR responses," Jerry said while scratching his head.

10.
PDR Responses

Several days later, Monique entered Jerry and Ray's office while they were reading case files and discussing the information.

"I have some mail for you," she announced while laying a stack of letters on Ray's desk.

"Oh, good! I'll bet those are our PDR responses," Jerry exclaimed.

"I'll let you get back to work," Monique said as she left the office.

"Uh huh," Ray responded while reading a letter.

"Thanks, Monique. We've been waiting for these responses," Jerry declared.

The men spent the next several minutes reading the public disclosure request responses from the law enforcement agencies.

"I sent a PDR to the Union Gap Police Department regarding Ryan Moore's suicide and their response says the records have been destroyed," Ray remarked.

"What does the response say exactly?"

"It says…"

The records you seek are past the retention period with the Union Gap Police Department and can no longer be obtained. The requested records meet the statutory definition of public records, and as such, they are required to be maintained and disposed of in accordance with the provisions of 40.14 RCW. The records were destroyed prior to receipt of your request pursuant to the Secretary of State approved Records Retention Schedule, RCW 40.14.060. Explanation: Agencies may destroy records in compliance with appropriate records retention requirements...

"That's not much help, is it? I wonder why they destroy their records so soon. You'd think they'd hang onto them longer, especially if there was a death involved. If you knew the names of the officers, they may remember details of the incident," Jerry suggested.

"Good idea, Jerry. I'll send another PDR to Union Gap Police asking for the names of the officers that responded to the call. I think maybe a letter to the Union Gap Chief of Police commending his office for their quick response and suggesting they review their records retentions policy, especially when a death is involved, would be in order. A five-year document retention policy seems to be a very short time," Ray responded.

"Here's the response from Yakima County regarding the coroner's reports on the death of Ryan Moore."

Your request will be forwarded to the relevant county departments to locate the information you seek.

"They've sent the Ryan Moore PDR on to the coroner's office, so you should have a response from the coroner soon. Here's the Yakima City police response to your PDR regarding the Larry Riegel missing person case, Ray."

I'm sorry, but we are unable to release the records you requested due to an active investigation. You may request them again at a later date, or please contact Detective Drew Shaw at 509-575-6200.

"I don't understand their refusal to release records about the Larry Riegel investigation. He's been missing for over 10 years, and they say the case is active. I wonder when the last time something was done on the case that makes it active?"

"What about the Sara Bustos homicide case? Did you want to look at Sara's diary because it appears to have been damaged, possibly while in police custody?" Ray asked.

"Yes, here's the response from Yakima City Police on the diary PDR," Jerry responded.

We are speaking with detectives regarding the status of this case and we will provide you with a further status update on your request in about 3 weeks. Recent changes in staffing and technology have created a backlog of requests, resulting in increased response times. Demand is particularly high for email searches, YPD dashcam video and YPD Spillman incident reports. Increased time is required to process these records. Some other record series may also be impacted.

Pursuant to RCW 42.56.520 additional time is necessary to clarify the request and/or gather and review records, to determine whether any of the information requested is exempt from disclosure, and to provide third parties with notice and the opportunity to seek a court order to prevent the release of record(s) in response to your request.'

"A three week wait, is that what they're saying?" Ray asked.

"Yes, I hope they're not going to be stalling us. Three weeks seems excessive just to stop by the police department and look at some documents being held in evidence," Jerry remarked.

"Why would they be reluctant to let us see the evidence?"

"Good question. I hope it's not a case of the fox guarding the henhouse. I guess we'll just have to wait. We'll see what happens in three weeks. Meanwhile, I plan on trying to collect as much information and evidence from the perimeter of this case as possible before speaking with those directly involved," Jerry explained.

"What are your plans exactly, Jerry?"

"I'm going to send out letters to the detectives, officers and others that were not directly involved or assigned to the investigation in an attempt to understand what happened after Sara Bustos' body was discovered. I want to know what the rumors and their source were before I approach the assigned investigators. I want to have a clear picture of the evidence, the actions of those involved, and the suspects first," Jerry explained.

"Good plan, Jerry. Know the answers to your questions before you ask them," Ray remarked.

"It's not necessary to send out PDRs on the Sharon Burch murder investigation because, thanks to retired Deputy Rod Shaw, I have a copy of the entire case file. I'll look closely at the Sharon Burch homicide while waiting for the next response from YPD and the inquiry letters," Jerry explained.

11.
Sharon Burch Investigation & Audit

"Rod Shaw reported that Archie told him he spent a considerable amount of time trying to track down the birth mother so he could explain the true cause of Sharon's death. After finally locating her in Longview, Washington, Archie told her his story, and both decided to come to Yakima and file a report," Jerry disclosed.

The Burch case was assigned to me, and in that time the following has been accomplished:

1. *Taped statement from Archie Burch*
2. *Taped statement from Lorene Dunkle (natural mother)*
3. *Taped statement from Paul Root (natural father)*
4. *Checked with Bureau of Vital Records, Olympia*
5. *Funeral Home was contacted and records obtained*
6. *Library department of local newspaper was contacted and articles were obtained*
7. *Cemetery was contacted and the burial site was confirmed*
8. *Dept. of Social & Health Services was contacted*
9. *Mental Health was contacted*

10. *Superior court was contacted and adoption was confirmed (records are sealed)*

11. *West Valley Fire Dept. was contacted but no records are available*

12. *Coroner's records were checked and confirmed*

13. *The responding deputy in 1953 was contacted but had no recollection of the incident*

14. *The reporting party (1953 fire) was found and contacted*

15. *One 1953 neighbor was located and contacted*

16. *The auto repair shop was found to be out of business; owner is deceased*

17. *The owner of the rental house is now deceased*

18. *The detective in Decatur, Illinois, is now deceased*

19. *Criminal history of Archie Burch obtained from Florida and Illinois*

20. *Contacted Dept. of the Navy for Burch's military records (not available)*

21. *Contacted Burch's former wife and mother-in-law in Minnesota*

22. *Contacted family members throughout Washington*

23. *State arson investigator was contacted and examined photos*

As of this date, the Burch case is active, and the investigation continues.

End of Report,
Rod Shaw, YSO

"I remember Rod Shaw working on this case. We discussed it several times during the investigation. It was horrifying what they did to that innocent child!" Jerry said as he stood up.

Detective Rod Shaw's Report

The 1953 Investigation

Bearing in mind the lack of manpower and training which was present in the Yakima Sherrif's Department as little as ten years ago, it is not surprising that little investigation was done on this case 35 years ago. Another point to keep in mind is that child abuse and/or neglect was not heard of much then as it is today. With those thoughts in mind, coupled with the fact the Sheriff's Department was still considered a 'posse', it does not surprise me that the documentation is nearly nil.

No officer was assigned to the case (detective division was non-existent). The responding deputy failed to question the parents as to their activities prior to the fire. No one contacted or interviewed Archie Burch while he was in the hospital. According to the report, it appears Sonny Burch was briefly questioned while at the fire scene, but this interview did not go into any depth.

It would appear a major blunder took place when the county coroner failed to perform an autopsy on Sharon Burch. He also neglected to have x-rays taken of her body. The coroner's records do not indicate why this was not done other than the statement. 'The body was too badly burned to determine the cause of death.' The coroner who made that statement died twelve years ago.

Critique on the 1960 investigation.

Keeping in mind the fact that conditions in 1960 were not altogether different from that in 1953, the Sheriff's Department failed in the following areas:

> *1. After our department was notified of Archie Burch's statement taken in Decatur, Illinois, no attempt was made to contact him while he was in custody. In fact, he was not*

contacted at all until he arrived at our department in 1987.

1. *Although their exact location was not known, no attempt was made to locate Highland & Ella Burch, the adoptive parents of Sharon. It wasn't known at the time, but they had family members still living in Yakima.*

2. *The reporting party of the fire and other neighbors were not contacted.*

3. *The auto repair shop was not contacted.*

4. *Apparently, a minor review was conducted on the 1953 file report, but the responding deputy was not contacted or interviewed.*

5. *Failure to check with the hospitals for prior child abuse information.*

6. *Failure to contact other family members for info regarding child abuse.*

7. *Poor question selection given to Sonny Burch during Portland interview.*

The questions confronting the present-day Yakima County Prosecutor appear to include the following:

1. *Was the death of Sharon Burch caused by child abuse/neglect? (manslaughter charge)*

2. *Was the death of Sharon Burch caused by fire? (homicide charge) Due to the totality of the circumstances, the cause of death has not and may not be determined.*

3. *Is Archie Burch truthful in his allegations? With his past criminal history, will he be considered a credible witness?*

4. *The adoptive parents of the late Sharon Burch are 65-70 years of age, and both are in ill health... Is there or should there be a viable alternative to prosecution?*

5. Due to poor investigations in 1953 & 1960 and with physical evidence non-existent, is a conviction possible without a confession?

*Rolland (Rod) Shaw,
Detective Yakima Sheriffs Dept.*

12.
SUSAN RIEGEL'S NOTES

"Larry Riegel's sister, Susan, kept very close track of the events surrounding the disappearance of her brother. I'll study her notes and try to pick out any anomalies," Ray announced as he began reading her notebook.

December 28th, 2009

On Monday, December 28th, I arrived at LaDena and Larry's house at 10:30 AM. As I drove up to the house, I noticed I was the only vehicle in the yard since snow had fallen the night before. I noticed fresh footprints going out to the newspaper box, but there was no other activity in the yard. When I walked into the house, the first thing I noticed was the house looked picked up, which was unusual for their home. There were a few Christmas wrappings in a bag which she moved, and she apologized for being in her pajamas. She said she hadn't gotten dressed since Larry left on Christmas night. I placed Larry's birthday presents on the dining room table (a Boeing 787 cockpit poster, a Boeing 787 first flight t-shirt, and a knife and money clip set that had a deer in the woods design on it). I sat in Larry's recliner in the living room, and never left this spot. I didn't go into the kitchen, bathroom or any other area of the house on that day.

1. The first thing I asked her about was the brain disorder comment from Saturday night. She said it wasn't really a disorder, but that he'd been depressed. I asked her if he was taking medication for depression, and she said no. She told me she was with her sister on the afternoon of Christmas Day. When she got home, Larry was depressed that nobody had called him, and that he had to go call lots of people himself. She said he needed money, so he decided he would go to the coast, and he wanted to take his jewelry to pawn at a shop on the other side, because he would get more money over there. She said he was going to take this money and gamble or play poker so he could win more money. She said he was so insistent to go, that she packed a couple of t-shirts for him, gave him clean underwear, packed his toothbrush, put his jewelry in a little Ziploc bag so he wouldn't lose any of it (I distinctly remember her making a little 'closing' gesture when she mentioned the Ziploc bag).

She said he was going to stay with friends on the coast, and that he was going to return to visit his son, Brian, on Monday, December 28th when Brian returned from Portland. I asked her if Brian was aware his dad was in Seattle and she said no. I asked her why he hadn't called me if he was going to be in the Seattle area, because I was home on Christmas Day. I said I thought he would have at least called me to say he was in my area, but she insisted he was going to stay with friends. I asked her repeatedly who these friends were, since I didn't know Larry had any friends that lived in the Seattle area. She kept saying she didn't know who they were. I asked her if he had his cell, and she said he did have it, but that he didn't have his charger, so he wouldn't have any battery life left. She continued to tell me Larry was feeling depressed and stressed out because he needed money to pay taxes and the water on the Harrah farm he was renting from our mom. I kept repeating Larry hated driving to Seattle and didn't understand why he would drive over there on a whim. She firmly stuck to her story.

2. She went on to tell me a long and complicated story about Larry not trusting Brian. Said Brian came over for Larry's surgery back in October; went out and got drunk instead; made a scene when he came home that night; slept on the couch and wouldn't get up at 4:30 AM. when they needed to go to the hospital. She said she dropped Larry off at the hospital, returned to the house and took Brian to the bus station so he could go home since he didn't want to be at the hospital with Larry. She said Brian couldn't be trusted to be alone in the house. Said Larry didn't want him at the house and that Brian would demand that Larry move so Brian could have his own bedroom when he came to visit. She said Brian hated her and tried to turn Larry against her all the time.

3. The next story LaDena told was that our mom borrowed $900 from her. She said Mom called her up one day and told her she had checks bouncing in her checking account, didn't want any of her daughters to know she was having money problems, and needed to borrow some money. She brought $900 to my mom. She said my mom met her at the door, reached out and 'grabbed' the money out of her hands, shut the front door, got into her car and drove away.

She said she repeatedly told my mom that this was her money and not Larry's; that she needed this money to be repaid for bills. She said she 'knew' at the moment my mom grabbed the money from her hands, she would never get repaid. However, she went on to say how she repeatedly asked my mom to pay the money back because she needed to pay bills. She said my brother had also stolen money from her, $2700, on a horse sale. She kept repeating that she couldn't pay her bills because she was missing all this money from my family. It got to the point that I truly felt like she was expecting me to pay her this money on behalf of my mom and brother, and I was actually considering doing just that. I stopped short of doing so because I wanted to discuss the situation with my husband before I gave her any money.

4. The last story I recall her telling was about suggesting to my mom that she sell the farm to one of her neighbors so Larry wouldn't be burdened with trying to care for the house. She felt having the farm sold to her neighbor would keep Larry from having to worry about paying taxes and water, and it would give everyone some money.

I vaguely remember my mom mentioning a similar story to me a year or two beforehand, but I didn't pay too much attention to the details. LaDena had shown up at my mom's house while Larry was out of town on a business trip with CubCrafters. She told my mom she had a buyer for the farm and suggested the house be sold before Larry returned home. I remember my mom was very unhappy with LaDena's interference. LaDena told me my mom had never liked her since this event and that she didn't go over and visit my mom anymore because of this event.

After 1 ½ hours, I got ready to leave the house. I asked her to please have Larry call me when he got home. She said she would. As I was leaving, LaDena repeatedly asked me to hold her confidence in everything we discussed and not to say anything to Larry, Brian, or my mom about any of our conversation, and I agreed.

My impression of the entire visit was that her stories were odd, were not in line with what I knew about Larry's personality and habits, and were random and all over the board. I thought the stories were lies while she was talking to me. There may have been some threads of truth in some of them, but there were details that I felt were untrue. I wondered about the unusual way she gave me details about packing his bag on Christmas night, the jewelry, *and him going to play poker to make some money. My brother enjoyed a good card game, but he wasn't into high stakes poker and certainly didn't have the money to risk losing money.*

I did notice she was laughing and very animated during the entire visit, too much for the stories she was telling me. I was very uncomfortable with the visit and thought something was wrong or she wasn't telling me the whole truth. Up to this event, I had no reason not to like LaDena. We had things in common, i.e. gardening and our love of animals and always had a pleasant visit.

I was mentally and emotionally exhausted by the time I left. An added note here is that Larry's dog, Jesse, sat by me the whole time I was at the house…I sat in the car in the driveway, called my husband and sobbed. I told him something was wrong. I didn't know where my brother was, but something was bad wrong. He told me my brother was a big boy and could take care of himself. He asked me to come home so we could discuss it.

Later that evening, I spoke with my husband concerning the money situation with LaDena. Tim asked me if my mom would get involved between Larry and LaDena if they were having a dispute over money, and I agreed she would. He suggested I call Mom, which I did, and she confirmed that the $900 she took from LaDena was Larry's money. She said she told LaDena the money was for Larry and wasn't for her at all.

My mom continued to tell me a complicated story about LaDena taking money from Larry's wallet and their continuing money disputes. She said Larry had sold two horses for $2700 and that LaDena took this money from his wallet. She also said the $900 was for something else, but that again LaDena had taken the money from Larry's wallet. Because LaDena kept asking my mom to get the $900 back, my mom wrote her a check for this money and gave it to her. LaDena returned the check a couple of days later, saying Larry wouldn't let her keep it. My mom tore the check up and they didn't discuss it again…

Ray leaned back and put his feet up on the desk and said,

"Hey Jerry, I just finished reading some of Susan Riegel's notes about the events following the disappearance of her brother, Larry. What are you working on?"

"I'm still reading the Sharon Burch file and it never ceases to amaze me the horrible things people do to others, especially innocent children."

"Would you be able to take a break from the Sharon Burch investigation and read Susan Riegel's notes about the disappearance of her brother, Larry? I'd like to get your thoughts on a couple of things."

"Sure, Ray. It can't hurt me to take a break from this abomination," Jerry responded as Ray handed him Susan Riegel's notebook.

"I'll look over the Ryan Moore case while you're reading Susan's notes," Ray advised, just as someone knocked on the door.

"How's it going?" Ross asked as he entered the office.

"Good, Ross. Jerry is reading some notes on the Larry Riegel case so we can discuss them. Have you heard anything from Joe Creed?"

"Yes, that's why I stopped by. It looks like Joe is having to deal with a number of problems before he can be helpful to us. He's got the ATF looking at him for possessing illegal firearms and now he's connected with a rogue female DEA agent, known in Mexico as Fantasma, that has Interpol warrants out for her arrest. Monique and I will help you as much as we can, but it looks like Joe Creed will be delayed for an indefinite period of time," Ross explained.

"Interpol has warrants for that DEA woman we met?" Jerry asked.

"Yes, and ATF is aiding Mexico investigating the illegal machine guns Joe had shipped to his boat. Please keep all this to yourselves," Ross explained.

"What did the rogue DEA agent do?" Jerry asked.

"Murder, numerous counts of murder. She could be classified as a serial killer," Ross responded.

"Humm, nicest looking serial killer I've ever met," Ray announced with a grin.

"Who'd she kill?" Jerry asked.

"Some old guy who lived near her cabin in the Finger Lakes Region of New York State, and a whole bunch of Mexican cartel members. She abandoned her DEA assignment in Mexico and went out on her own, killing cartel members in the remote deserts of Mexico. She conducted nighttime surprise attacks on her motorcycle at cartel compounds, killing and taking the little fingers of as many cartel soldiers as possible. She's a nightmare of terror stories among the cartel ranks, and I have no idea why Joe would want anything to do with her," Ross explained.

"Maybe for the same reason he needs the machine guns," Jerry remarked.

"I'll leave you to your work, gentlemen. Let us know if there's anything you need," Ross offered as he left the office.

After about an hour, Jerry said, "Let me grab another cup of coffee and we can start discussing Susan Riegel's notes about the disappearance of her brother, Larry."

13.
ANALYSIS OF SUSAN RIEGEL'S NOTES

"Susan says the last time she spoke with her brother, Larry, was on December 23rd and she notes the time at about 6 PM. I would say she kept a very accurate history of events before and after her brother's disappearance. Her notes can be extremely helpful in understanding Larry's disappearance," Jerry reported.

"He didn't appear to be in the best of health, having recent neck surgery. It would have been prudent for him to allow more healing of his recent surgery before he voluntarily changed living conditions. Also, since domestic violence may have taken place, it should be noted that Christmas can be a very emotional time of year which can sometimes generate domestic violence," Ray remarked.

"Susan and Larry talked about the yearly traditional family dinner on December 26th and not only did Larry say he planned on attending, but he also asked what he could bring. It seems Larry planned on attending the long-established Christmas dinner as he had every past year, and it would have been completely out of character for him to not show up with no notice," Jerry concluded.

"That's what happened. He seems to have disappeared on December 25th and the only person he disclosed his whereabouts to was his live–in girlfriend, LaDena. Even then, he reportedly didn't tell her exactly where he was going, and since his cell phone didn't have a charger, according to LaDena, there was no way anyone could contact him," Ray remarked.

"One day Larry Riegel is alive, happy and doing well and the next he is gone. Just flat gone, nowhere to be found! How does that happen?" Jerry asked.

"There're more notes taken by Susan Riegel. Let's take a look at them," Ray suggested.

December 31st, 2009

My sister's birthday was on December 31st, and I called to wish her a happy birthday, asked about Larry during our conversation and she said she was expecting a call from him because he always called her on her birthday. During the following week, I called and left messages for Larry on his house phone. I asked him to call me when he got back into town, but I never heard from him. As the week wore on, I asked my mom and sisters if they had spoken to Larry, or vice versa, but it was always a 'No.'

January 8th, 2010

On January 8th, 2010, my friends Nan and Wally Lee brought my mom over to see my son perform music at a local venue in Redmond, Washington. I asked my mom if she had heard from Larry yet, and she said no, that she was extremely worried because she kept calling the house and leaving messages, but she wasn't getting any response. She went on to say she couldn't find anybody who had heard from him.

I spoke privately with my friend, Nan, about my brother's disappearance. Nan and I have been friends since 3rd grade, and she is fairly well acquainted with my brother. We both agreed that Larry not returning calls was not like him. He stayed in touch with all of us on a fairly regular basis. Nan used her iPhone to look up numbers in Yakima of Larry's closest friends, and I began making phone calls to people who might have been in touch with

Larry. My calls were made out of my mom's line of sight, and out of earshot, so she would not see my growing concern, and would not become even more worried.

1. I called my nephew, Brian, and discovered that he hadn't been able to reach his dad. Brian was very worried and was angry with LaDena, felt like she was keeping his messages from reaching his dad. (He said he last spoke to his dad on Christmas Day at about 4 PM), tried calling him again on Christmas night several times between 10 PM. and midnight, and couldn't reach him. He said he was calling and leaving messages either with LaDena or on voicemail but wasn't hearing back from him. Brian said a few times when he called, LaDena would say his dad was sleeping and couldn't come to the phone. Brian said his dad and he spoke to one another almost daily and that he hadn't heard from him since Christmas.

2. Next, I called my niece, Bree, and discovered that she hadn't been able to reach her dad either. She'd also been calling and leaving numerous messages but hadn't heard back. She was very worried and didn't know how to reach him. She had discussed filing a missing person's report with her husband.

3. I finally decided to call one of my brother's best friend, Ray Schuel. Ray told me he had made repeated attempts to contact Larry but hadn't heard from him. Ray said he asked his friend, and my uncle, Al Marquis, if he had seen Larry, and if he would ask around, but they couldn't find anyone who had spoken to or seen him. Then Ray told me he was especially worried because LaDena had returned Larry's car.

He said he came home to find Larry's silver VW diesel bug parked in the driveway with the keys in it. He wasn't able to reach Larry, but finally got ahold of LaDena. She told *him Larry wouldn't be able to make any more payments on the car and wanted to return it. Ray wanted to talk to Larry, but she said she didn't know where Larry was.*

"Susan is on the right track. There's a bunch of suspicious circumstances, according to her notes. Let's see if we can list some of them," Ray suggested.

1. "Susan called Larry on December 26th as she and her husband were driving to Yakima and there was no answer. They expected Larry to arrive at their mother's home for dinner at 6 PM. So, when Larry had not arrived at 7 PM, Susan called him again. Larry's girlfriend, LaDena answered. This contact required LaDena to explain where Larry was and why he missed the traditional family Christmas dinner. This would probably be the first time LaDena had to explain Larry's disappearance, I suspect, and she didn't do very well," Ray explained.

"LaDena's story was that Larry left for the coast to visit with friends the night before. The coast probably means a vague area anywhere from Seattle and Tacoma to Everett. LaDena reportedly had no idea which friends Larry left to visit on Christmas night. She also said he had his cell phone but no charger. So according to LaDena, Larry was somewhere in Western Washington State without any way to be contacted," Ray continued.

"It appears that LaDena's goal was to present the scenario that Larry left the area and there was no way anyone could contact him. If the flimsy, out of character story she told about Larry's disappearance is true, it's very illogical, and if it's a lie, it's a bad lie," Jerry remarked.

"Let's look at what else LaDena had to say according to Susan's notes," Ray said.

2. "Larry was a little blue and was being treated by a doctor for a brain disorder, according to LaDena during the December 26th phone call. This appears to shift the focus from LaDena's weak explanation about Larry's disappearance back onto Larry. She must have been feeling some heat for not being able to explain Larry's disappearance more logically, and in mentioning doctors, she must have realized that she was putting herself in a corner if there were no doctors to verify her false statements. When Susan asked LaDena during the call to explain the brain disorder, LaDena avoided the request and ended the conversation, suggesting that they should talk later, possibly so she could come up with a better story. Two days later, when Susan visited LaDena and Larry's home, LaDena completely changed her story and said Larry was just depressed. The fictitious brain disorder explanation disappeared, was never mentioned again, and Larry became even more difficult to locate, in my opinion," Ray remarked.

"So, Ray, are you're saying that LaDena appeared to purposely provide only information about Larry's disappearance that was unverifiable, and that she appeared by her actions to not want Larry found?" Jerry asked.

"That's what it appears to me initially, but let's look closer at this case."

3. "During the visit things purposely get very complicated regarding Larry's disappearance and another important factor is introduced by LaDena—money. In this version of LaDena's explanation about Larry's disappearance, new, unverifiable information is provided again about the disappearance, and then the focus is completely shifted when LaDena brings up money issues. She appears to be much more concerned with financial matters than the strange disappearance of her soul mate

and lover. It even looks as if she's attempting to move the conversation away from Larry's disappearance and possibly blame Larry's family for his disappearance.

"LaDena's money issues made me curious so, at this point I decided to do some background checks on her. She has gone by several different surnames because it appears she has been married several times.

"Her former husbands appear reluctant to get on her bad side, as I suspect she can become aggressive. She spent a couple of years in Las Vegas with one of her husbands and she reveals very little about her activities during that time. She owns several real estate properties, all of which are held in a trust account, and she may have been in collections with the IRS.

4. "LaDena again introduces more money and information about valuable items in her second story about Larry's disappearance on December 25th. She said Larry packed his jewelry with the unlikely story he could pawn it on the coast where he'd get more money; and then, according to her, he planned on playing poker with the funds to increase his bankroll. She talks about $900 that she previously lent to Larry's mother and was never reimbursed; $2700 Larry stole from her horse sale, and how she had tried to help her mom sell the farm in Harrah. LaDena's story was so convincing at the time that Susan considered reimbursing LaDena by writing her a check. Larry's mother later, however, disputed LaDena's stories about the $900 and $2700. Larry's disappearance took a back seat in the money conversation, and it was remarkable to see how LaDena manipulated the inquiry of Larry's disappearance into a discussion about money. She was described as laughing and animated during the conversation. She may have been excited and happy that her stories were being

accepted, but those emotions were very inappropriate during the conversation about Larry's disappearance, especially for someone seriously worried about his welfare, in my opinion," Ray explained.

5. "December 31st is Larry's sister Sandy's birthday. Susan found out there had been no call from Larry to Sandy and that he was still missing. Failing to call his sister on her birthday was very unusual, according to Larry's family," Ray explained.

6. "Larry's son Brian had last spoken with his father on Christmas Day at about 4 PM., tried calling again that night between 10 PM and midnight. He said he left messages with LaDena and voicemails for his father to call him back but heard nothing. I suspect something happened to Larry sometime between 4 PM, when Brian last spoke to his father, and about 10 PM, when Larry was unavailable to come to the phone, according to LaDena," Ray deduced.

7. "On January 8th, while making telephone calls attempting to locate Larry, Susan spoke with Larry's friend Ray Schuel. Larry was buying a Volkswagen car from Ray and making regular payments to him. Ray said LaDena left the Volkswagen car parked in Ray's driveway with the keys in it. Ray said he tried to contact Larry but was unsuccessful. He said he did speak with LaDena, who told him Larry wouldn't be making payments on the car anymore. When asked about Larry, she said she didn't know where he was.

Larry wouldn't be making payments on the car anymore. Fifteen days after Larry disappears, LaDena returns Larry's car saying, basically Larry will no longer be needing a car. How did she know that? What if Larry came home and asked why she returned his car since it was almost paid off? This is the action on LaDena's part, in my opinion, that says Larry is no longer living," Ray concluded.

"I think you're right, Ray; and if she's a suspect, LaDena's focus on jewelry, cash, and the farm property highlights the possible motivation of greed," Jerry surmised.

"There's much more, Jerry, but let's take a break on this case for a while and discuss the Sharon Burch homicide," Ray suggested as he opened the Sharon Burch file.

14.

INVESTIGATOR ROD SHAW'S INQUIRY

Sharon Louise Burch's homicide investigative report by Detective Rod Shaw:

On July 4th, 1988, I was the detective on call for that holiday. The Sheriff's Department called me and said they had a man in their office who wanted to report a homicide. I detailed that location and met with the man who told me 'I killed my sister.' He held out his hands like he wanted me to handcuff him. I told him that was not necessary, and I took him to the Detective Interview Room, where he told me the following story.

He told me his five-year-old sister had been sickly her entire life, but he did not know the cause of her health problems. On this particular day, his parents wrapped the daughter in a blanket and placed her behind the wood stove in the cabin. The father handed the boy a can of gasoline and told him he and his wife had to take their car to a garage in Wiley City for repairs. The father told the boy that after they had been gone for 10-15 minutes, to pour the gasoline from the door of the cabin across the floor to the blanket where the sister was located. They told him, 'This will keep your sister warm'. After the time lapse mentioned, the boy was instructed to light a match, which he did. The cabin burned to the ground, the girl was killed and the boy barely escaped the fire with burns on his face, legs and arms. During the interview, he pulled up his pant legs and showed me the burn scars on his legs and arms.

The next day I reviewed the information with Jerry Hafsos, the Lt. in charge of the detectives. Jerry asked me if I believed the man's story and I said yes, and that he showed me the burn marks on his legs and arms. Jerry said if this is true, we have a case of manslaughter or second-degree homicide. Jerry said he wanted me and another detective to go to Portland and interview the parents.

The parents were interviewed separately and together, but no useful information was arrived at. The parents kept asking, 'Why, after twenty years, are you investigating this?' And my response was that new information had come to light that this may not have been an accident. They kept asking who gave us this information, and they mentioned several names, finally arriving at their son's name. I did not acknowledge that the son had given the information. Whenever a sensitive question was asked, the father would say to the wife, 'You answer that.' And then she would reply, 'No, you answer that.' I observed the man's body language and noticed his leg would start twitching when certain questions were asked. As we left the house, I left my tape recorder in a hidden location, and my partner and I drove around for 15 minutes before returning to the house, telling the parents that I had forgotten my tape recorder. Upon listening to the tape, the average person could only conclude the incident happened as the son described. The very first thing on this tape was the father asking his wife, 'Did you tell them anything?' She replied, 'No did you tell them anything?' The father said, 'We need to notify (an unknown name) and tell them the cops are onto us. We need to tell him to leave town because they are probably coming to see him next.'

Upon returning to Yakima, I reviewed our information with Jerry, and he suggested that I take the information to the Yakima County Prosecutor. I liked the prosecutor. One reason being his door was always open for consultation. I reviewed my information with him, and he said, 'Tell me about the parents.' I told him the parents were in their late 70s and both appeared to be quite sickly. The wife told me her husband had inoperable cancer. He was a very slight man and barely weighed 100 pounds. His wife was a very heavy-set lady who had health problems of her own. The prosecutor asked me about the son, and I told him he was not the sharpest knife in the drawer, and he had a minor arrest record and the son volunteered that he had a dishonorable discharge from the military. I played the tape recording for the prosecutor, and he asked me how I got the tape. When I told him what I had done, he became upset and said that was entrapment. My response was I know what entrapment is and how is that possible when I'm a half mile away? I also asked him if Oregon's entrapment laws were the same as Washington's. He said he did not know.

After additional conversation, the prosecutor looked at me and said he would **not prosecute** this case and here's why. He said with the age of the parents; they did not have much longer to live, especially with their medical conditions. He said if we had Oregon police arrest the parents and they fought extradition to Washington, that would take one month. Yakima County would pay Oregon for the cost of their incarceration and any medical expenses they would incur. Upon returning to Washington, the time frame for the trial would be one to two months and the county would pay for any medications or medical care the parents would receive. When the son was discussed, the prosecutor implied a defense attorney would eat him alive on the stand. Then he mentioned, 'Your damn tape. A defense attorney would try to have that excluded as evidence, and I think a judge would agree with him. So, I am not going to prosecute this case. Then the prosecutor said, 'Let God take care of it.' When I questioned what he said, he repeated, 'Neither have long to live. Let God take care of it.'

This case was never prosecuted. End of report.
Initialed: (RS)

"I remember this case well. What do you do when the prosecutor uses prosecutorial discretion and refuses to prosecute a case?" Jerry asked.

"That's a good question. I've seen that problem occur in the past where a prosecutor refuses to file charges on a case with plenty of evidence. The recourse would be to take the case to another authority with jurisdiction, like the state attorney general or the federal government. Each may have the ability to prosecute, depending on the circumstances," Ray responded.

"It's too late for that now since the parents are deceased and I've been unable to locate the brother," Jerry advised.

"I guess then we will need to *let God take care of it,*" Ray remarked with a discouraged look on his face.

"It took three days, but with the help of cemetery staff we've been able to locate Sharon Burch's grave in Tahoma Cemetery. There's only a small temporary concrete marker with her name on it in the B section of the graveyard, and it was covered by so much old vegetation that no one could have seen the marker for years. There is one thing that can be done, Ray."

"What's that?"

"We could have an invocation at the cemetery and place a proper headstone on this little girl's grave on behalf of the community's remorse and grief for her suffering.

"Good thought, Jerry. Maybe the Wiley Union Church in Wiley City would take this little angel under their wings and remember her somehow."

"I'll contact them and see what they have to say. Meanwhile, what's happening with the Ryan Moore death investigation?" Jerry asked.

15.

Ryan Moore Death Investigation

"The Union Gap Police Department has removed and destroyed their files on the death investigation, but they did report that Officer Kellog collected the knife and Officer Levesque collected the Taser. That evidence was destroyed, however," Ray responded.

"Did the coroner's office have any reports?"

"Yes, we've been fortunate in that the coroner's office provided us with the death certificate and a medical investigation report. Besides that, the parents provided us with a copy of the Union Gap police report," Ray explained.

"Where did they get a copy of the police report?"

"They asked for and received it from Union Gap Police shortly after the investigation had been completed several years ago. We are only missing a copy of witness Sue Huntington's written description of the incident and some photos," Ray explained.

"What does the original Union Gap Police report have to say about the incident?" Jerry asked.

"Here it is. You can take a look at it."

Union Gap Police Department
Officer's Report

Case # 10-0669

Subject: DV-Verbal, Suicide

Synopsis: On 03/20/10, 2209 S. 6th Ave, Ryan G. Moore (06/17/84) and his girlfriend, Sue Ann Huntington (03/28/69) got into a verbal argument over Moore's drug use. Moore then stabbed himself in the neck and fled down S. 6th Ave. Moore was later pronounced dead at Memorial Hospital.

Narrative:

On 9/20/10 at approx. 0950 hrs. I was dispatched to a possible suicide with a gunshot wound at 2209 S. 6th Ave. I am familiar with the residence and have responded there to domestic violences calls in the past between Moore and his girlfriend, Sue A. Huntington (03/29/69). As I was in route, dispatch updated the call stating that it was not a gunshot, the subject had stabbed himself in the neck. As I turned s/b onto S. 6th Ave from Walla Walla, I observed someone standing in the middle of the roadway. As I got closer, I observed Ryan G. Moore (06/17/84) dropping his shirt onto the ground. He was covered in blood from head to toe [sic] and only wearing underwear. I exited my vehicle and asked him to come to me so I could help him. As he turned towards me, I saw what appeared to be a hole in his throat which was bleeding, and he was spitting out blood. I again asked him to stop as I did not want him to run away and lose [sic] more blood and so that I could begin rendering aid. Moore gurgled something and began running s/b on S. 6th Ave towards Valley Mall Blvd. I radioed Officer Santucci and Officer Levesque to get to Valley Mall Blvd in an attempt to stop him from running off or getting struck by a vehicle. Officers Santucci and Levesque sped past me and concentrated their efforts on stopping Moore.

Not knowing everything that was involved, I detailed the residence at 2209 S. 6th Ave. As I approached, I observed Huntington standing in the corner of the living room (the front door was open) shaking. She stated that she was unharmed, and that there was no one else in the residence. There was a blood trail in the kitchen/hall area. Just before the bedroom, I observed a large pool of blood, some of which appeared to have bubbles in it. Just west of the blood pool, I observed a Smith & Wesson Folding pocketknife (approx. 3 ½ inch blade and partially serrated) lying open on the floor. The knife was covered in blood. I had Huntington exit the residence and sit on the front porch.

Officer Santucci advised that he had just had one 'Tased' and on the ground. I detailed his location, Valley Mall Blvd in the median, just south of S. 6th Ave. He was laying [lying] face down in the grass and Officer Levesque had his right hand handcuffed. They informed me that he was combative. I assisted by giving her his left hand. Once handcuffed, he was rolled onto his side. I immediately requested fire to detail our location (they had staged up the block as per their policy).

As fire personnel tended to Moore, paramedics arrived and requested he be un-cuffed. We complied. AMR paramedic Kasey Weigley asked Moore his name, and he answered her. She then asked if his wound was self-inflicted. He nodded yes. A trauma alert was sent and Moore was transported to Memorial Hospital via an AMR ambulance.

I detailed 2209 S. 6th Ave and contacted Huntington. She told me she spent the night last night with Moore at his residence. This morning, they had gotten into a verbal fight over his drug use and some past issues. Moore had gotten upset and began throwing things around and punching things (Huntington stated that no physical assault had occurred). When he again began throwing things, she had turned away and closed her eyes. When she looked back, he had the knife in his throat. She panicked and called 911. The blood trail led from the kitchen/hall out the front door and to a wooden bench in the front yard. From there it led to the end of the driveway where Moore's pants, socks and shoes were piled. It then led down the street where I first observed him dropping his shirt.

Huntington did not have any injuries to her person. I observed a few blood spots on the top of her right hand. I did not observe blood anywhere else on her person or clothing. Digital pictures were taken of the residence and scene. Huntington gave a one page written sworn statement to the facts. The knife was bagged and secured in the trunk of my patrol vehicle.

Peggy A. Moore (06/20/66) arrived on the scene and introduced herself to us and asked how Ryan was. I informed her that he had been transported to Memorial Hospital for a self-inflicted stab wound. She asked if it was serious and if she should call her husband, Ryan's father. I informed her it was very serious.

After processing the scene, Officer Levesque, Santucci, and I detailed our fire station for decon [decontamination] purposes. All of us had blood on our boots. My left leg was sprayed with blood (arterial spray). Officer Santucci stated he had a small drop on the palm of his hand but had no open wounds and sanitized it immediately.

I detailed the office and telephoned Memorial ER. I was informed that Moore had died just after he arrived there. I telephoned Sgt. McNearney and informed him of the situation. I then detailed Memorial Hospital ER. Upon asking, I was informed that Moore was still in one of the ER trauma rooms and that his family had all left. I detailed the room and observed Moore lying on a table, covered with a blanket. With the assistance of Paramedic Weigley, I photographed Moore's body and injury. I was informed Moore was still alive upon arrival at the hospital.

At approx. 1200 hrs. Coroner Hawkins arrived. I briefed him on the incident.

At my office, I removed the knife from the locked trunk. I photographed the knife and placed it into an evidence box marked with BIOHAZARD stickers. The knife was then placed into evidence-see No A13724.

The knife is described as follows:
- metal blade approx. 3.5 inches in length
- blade is half serrated.
- it is a liner-lock folding pocketknife with a metal belt clip
- it has 'Smith & Wesson S.W.A.T.' on the blade
- its blade and handle are black and covered in blood

    I certify (declare) under penalty of perjury under the laws of the State of Washington that the foregoing is true and correct (RCW 9A.72.085) Dated this 20th day of March 2010, at Union Gap, WA.

Signed: Sgt. C Kellogg # 431
Union Gap Police Department

"I located the witness, Sue Huntington, and contacted her twice in an attempt to hear what she has to say about the incident. She refused to respond. There's more information and a horribly unexpected event in this case, Jerry, but for now, let's take another look at the Sara Bustos murder," Ray suggested.

16.

Sara Luz Bustos Homicide Investigation

"Eliberto Diaz Rivera was charged with the murder of Sara Luz Bustos. Her diary was recovered by Yakima Police Detective Mike Tovar and placed in the police evidence vault by Detective Rick Watts 10 months after the murder. It's written in Spanish and mentions Twindler by name and calls him 'my policeman.' It's rumored to have suffered water damage while in police custody, but verifying that with Detective Tovar will not be possible. We won't be able to ask him where the diary was for 10 months and if it had water damage when he found it," Jerry explained.

"Why not?"

"He died recently, leaving a wife and 3 children."

"Oh, that's unfortunate, my condolences to his family. He was a decent, hardworking gentleman. May he rest in peace," Ray responded.

"I wonder how that damage happened. Detective Tovar must have written a report about recovering the diary," Jerry remarked.

"There was no report in the file located from Detective Tovar about finding the diary. The police provided scanned copies of some of the diary's contents but have refused to let us look directly at the evidence," Jerry disclosed.

"What's the reason for not allowing us to look at it?"

"They haven't said. A suspect was arrested, charged with homicide, and was found not guilty at trial, so it's not an open case."

"It looks like this investigation is going to be difficult with the Yakima Police trying to keep secrets about it."

"I hope that's not the situation. They should know better than that, but maybe that's why Ross was suspicious when he looked into it. I suggested filing a superior court claim against the Yakima Police Department for refusing the PDR request to view the diary, but Ross didn't want to litigate the issue. He suggested sending a letter to the county prosecutor, advising him of the circumstances and asking for assistance," Jerry advised.

"Ok, let's send a letter to the Yakima County Prosecutor, explaining the police's refusal to allow us to inspect the victim's diary. He should be able to help," Ray suggested.

"What about the other rumors?" Jerry asked.

"Like what?"

"The rumor that Officer Kensley Twindler was asked to take a polygraph test to eliminate himself as a suspect in the murder and that he refused," Jerry revealed.

"Some people just don't trust the polygraph, Jerry."

"Then why did he hire an attorney who suggested he take a private, confidential polygraph test to see how he'd do?"

"Really? How'd Twindler do on the private test?"

"Rumor was when he didn't pass the secret polygraph test, he then declined the official request," Jerry explained.

"Then there was the DNA test rumor, where Twindler was supposedly given a DNA collection kit, told to take it home, provide a sample and return it later, totally against collection procedure protocols. DNA lab results later determined there were no suspect hits on the DNA evidence collected. Plus, there's another rumor about Sara Bustos' diary. It was reportedly being translated from Spanish to English by a bilingual employee of the police department when she supposedly fell in the police department parking lot and received a head injury. The injury did not allow her to return to work at the police department," Jerry explained.

"Interesting. We should talk to her," Ray suggested.

"I sent her a letter asking for her cooperation but haven't heard back. Then I asked a mutual acquaintance to contact her with no result," Jerry advised.

"What about the rumor that Chief Rizzi hired two Chicago detectives to come to Yakima to investigate and either confirm or eliminate Ken Twindler as a suspect?" Ray asked.

"Chief Rizzi lives in Tennessee, so I sent a letter to him asking for answers to a list of questions," Jerry explained.

"What questions did you ask?"

"Here's a copy of the letter."

Confidential

Dominic Rizzi, Jr.
223 Fourberie Lane
Knoxville, TN 37011

Re: Yakima Police Homicide Case # 99-16172
*   Yakima County Superior Court # 99-1-01628-4*

Greetings Mr. Rizzi:

About a year ago, we requested and received public records regarding the homicide of Sara Luz Bustos, which occurred in September 1999 in Yakima. Sara was found murdered in the Yakima River with a rock in her mouth. There is information in the case file that Yakima Police Officer Kensley Twindler had a relationship with the victim prior to her murder. I've been told that you, as chief of the Yakima city police at the time, were informed of the circumstances and acted in eliminating Officer Twindler as a person of interest or suspect in the homicide. I can find no documentation or investigation, however, that officially eliminates Officer Twindler or other officers as persons of interest in the murder.

Therefore, I have several questions which I hope will satisfy lingering doubts about Officer Twindler's connection to the victim. It would be helpful if you would answer the questions to the best of your recollection. Please keep in mind that repeating rumors can cause harm to the reputation of Officer Twindler and/or others, and that is not my intent. Please do not repeat unsubstantiated rumors in an effort to protect innocent reputations.

1. *Was Officer Twindler considered a person of interest in the case? If so, why? If not, why?*

2. *What action did you or persons under your command take regarding the relationship Officer Twindler or other officers had with the victim to eliminate him (and/or other officers) as persons of interest or suspects in the murder?*

3. *If an investigation was initiated to eliminate Officer Twindler and/or other officers, who conducted the investigation(s)?*

4. *If there was an investigation, where could the written documents of the investigation(s) be found?*

5. *Was the Yakima County Prosecutor's Office made aware of the circumstances mentioned? If not, why not?*

6. *What specific actions were taken to eliminate Officer Twindler as a person of interest? Was Officer Twindler asked to take a polygraph test? What were the results? Was DNA taken from Officer Twindler or other officers and submitted for testing? What were the results? Were recorded statements taken from Officer Twindler or other officers?*

7. *Were interviews and recorded statements conducted regarding Officer Twindler or other officer's relationship with the victim? What are the names of the people interviewed or who provided recorded statements?*

8. *Were you aware of the rumor of the destruction or altering of the victim's diary while it was being held in the police evidence vault? There appears to be water damage to the written Spanish dialogue.*

9. *What information can you provide that eliminates Officer Twindler and/or other officers as persons of interest in the homicide?*

10. *Please respond as soon as possible and feel free to include other pertinent information. Please also feel free to use the back of this letter or add additional pages for your detailed responses. If you choose to ignore this inquiry, please explain why.*

Sincerely,
Gerald Hafsos, Investigator
Manzola Law Offices
Yakima, WA 98908

cc:file

"Former Chief Rizzi's responses should clear things up. What did he have to say?" Ray asked.

"He hasn't responded, except through the grapevine where I heard he was angry about the questions."

"What is it about responding truthfully that makes Chief Rizzi angry?"

"I'm not sure because so far, I haven't heard back from him. He was fired by the city manager for a number of reasons, including lacking information about homicide cases, according to a Yakima Herald newspaper article," Jerry responded.

"Who was the man that was charged with Sara Bustos' murder and why wasn't he found guilty at trial?" Ray asked.

"His name is Eliberto Diaz Rivera, and he was prosecuted by Yakima County Prosecutor Patricia Powers. I sent a letter to Prosecutor Powers, who is retired now, asking to discuss the case with her," Jerry explained.

"What did she have to say?"

"She refused to respond, so I sent this letter to the Yakima County Prosecutor at Ross' suggestion," Jerry explained.

Yakima County Prosecutor's Office
128 N. 2nd St.
Yakima, WA 98901

Re: Yakima Police Homicide Case # 99-16172
      Yakima County Superior Court # 99-1-01628-4

Greetings Yakima County Prosecutor:

There were and continue to be rumors that a Yakima City police officer was identified as a person of interest early in the Bustos homicide investigation. In conducting research about this case, I discovered that the rumors may have some truth to them. The officer in question is now working as a high ranking police administrator.

In attempting to dispel or verify the rumors, we submitted a public disclosure request (PDR) about a year ago for a copy of the Yakima Police case file # 99-16172. We received scanned copies of the large file in installments, including the contents of the victim's diary, concluding in about April 2023. In reading that file, I discovered that a suspect, Mr. Eliberto Diaz Rivera, was charged and prosecuted by Patti Powers for homicide. Mr. Diaz Rivera was defended by attorney Mark Vovos and was subsequently found not guilty at trial in 2001.

Officer Kensley Twindler was identified as a person of interest early in the homicide investigation because it appeared he had a close relationship with the victim immediately prior to her murder. Ken Twindler seems to deny this and says his relationship with Sara Bustos was purely professional in nature. Yet there is information indicating otherwise, including some documentation written by the victim in her diary in Spanish in which she refers to Ken Twindler as her 'policeman' and mentions the name 'Ken' specifically. It has taken some time for me to review the extensive file, including the contents of the diary, which is partially translated into English, and looks to be damaged. Another rumor is that water damage occurred to the diary while in police custody. Because of this rumor, and what looks like water damage to some of the scanned pages of the diary, I submitted another PDR (YPD Request # 23-3155). I asked to be allowed to view and take photos of the diary and an address book directly, in person. Allowing me to view the evidence directly and photograph the pages of both the victim's diary and the address book may answer questions about the rumors. It would be a simple matter for the police to take the diary and address book from the police evidence vault and allow me to inspect and photograph it. Unfortunately, the PDR has been delayed repeatedly. I've also been denied direct viewing of the diary and address book by the Yakima City Attorney. There was no reason given for denying me access to the evidence. The city attorney reported that staff is preparing to scan the document and provide me with scanned copies of the diary within the next 3 months, but they continue to deny me inspection of the evidence. They may not realize I already have a scanned copy of the diary.

 I contacted attorney Ross Manzola for advice on how to proceed. We developed an informal research plan which included contacting you and providing you with a general description of my activities. I attempted contact with defense attorney Mark Vovos and found that he had recently died. I also attempted contact with Patti Powers, but she has yet to respond. Some witnesses have responded and reluctantly discussed their knowledge of the investigation verbally, also expressing great concern about reprisals from Yakima Police Deputy Chief Kensley Twindler. Other officers have just ignored my attempts to discuss the circumstances of the investigation.

 Mr. Prosecutor, at Ross Manzola's suggestion, I ask that you intercede in the PDR denial, which was submitted several months ago to the Yakima Police Department. I ask that you request that the Yakima City Attorney be encouraged to let me view and photograph the evidence directly without interference.

>There are several other rumors which may connect Deputy Chief Twindler and other officers and investigators to the death of Sara Luz Bustos. I plan to continue to look for evidence that verifies or denies these rumors. Besides helping me achieve direct access to the diary and address book, I ask for assistance in the matter from you by encouraging Patti Powers and others to discuss the case with me. If you are interested, sir, I would be willing to share other disturbing details of this case with you in person.
>
> *Sincerely,*
> *Gerald Hafsos, Investigator*
> *Manzola Law Office*
> *Yakima, WA*

"It would be nice to know that the county prosecutor is willing to support our investigation and assist if necessary. What was the prosecutor's response to your letter, Jerry?"

"I haven't heard back from him yet."

"Don't hold your breath. There seems to be an endless list of challenges he has to face on a daily basis. Lately, he's been having to release criminal suspects from jail because there are not enough public defenders available. When he deals with one problem, two more issues surface that need his attention. His job lately has been likened to a game of Whack a Mole," Ray explained.

"If Chief Rizzi did hire Chicago detectives to investigate and eliminate Ken Twindler as a suspect, there should be a copy of a contract for services in the city files, so I sent a PDR in an attempt to get a copy of the contract," Jerry explained.

"Any luck?"

"Here's a copy of the response."

The Finance Department was unable to locate a vendor with the name you provided. They provided the following response: 'The vendor number listing was searched. Out of 6500 +/− vendors searched, the words Chicago, Police, Detective, Detectives,

Sara Bustos and Illinois did not bring back a viable result. I also searched Laserfische with the name Sara Bustos and found an irrigation layout from 2012. The search term Chicago brought up information regarding future Police Officer Rizzi. (former YPD Police Chief Dominic Rizzi). YPD and the City Clerk's office have searched contract files for both City Manager Approved Contracts and Resolutions and have been unable to locate any responsive records. YPD is still searching records in their department to determine if they are able to locate additional records.'

Brandy Bradford.

"Then, a couple of weeks later, we received this response."

No records have been located that are responsive to your request. According to Deputy Chief Twindler, there was no contract or payment to the Chicago Police Department.

Thank you.
Brandy Bradford.

"Notice that it was Ken Twindler who provided the PDR response from the Yakima Police Department," Jerry pointed out.

"It will be difficult, if not impossible, for us to find worthwhile evidence in this case against Deputy Chief Twindler, while the goat is guarding the cabbage patch, as the Germans say," Ray declared.

"Besides that, the PDR requested a copy of an outside contract with Chicago detectives regarding the Sara Bustos homicide investigation. Ken Twindler's response was that there were no contracts or payment to the Chicago Police Department, a slippery, arrogant way of responding, wouldn't you say?" Jerry asked.

"Obviously. What's your next move, Jerry?"

"We need to look at another homicide that occurred 3 days after Sara Bustos was discovered murdered," Ray announced.

"Sara was discovered on Friday and the next Yakima

homicide was reported on Sunday. Both murders had a drug aspect connection to them, and I'm wondering if the Sunday homicide was related to Sara Bustos' murder," Jerry stated.

17.

TRACY OMAR HUITT, HOMICIDE

The Tuesday, September 21st, 1999, Yakima Herald Republic newspaper headline read,

"*Two Held in 'Execution' Shooting.*"
Drug dispute believed to be motive for slaying, by Greg Tuttle, reporter.

A Yakima man was held on a $1 million bail Monday in a case police are describing as the execution of a drug dealer.

Dustin Eric Day, 22, is scheduled to be arraigned Wednesday in Yakima Superior Court on a possible charge of first-degree murder for the slaying of 29-year-old Tracy Omar Huitt, who was shot to death this weekend.

Meanwhile, a second suspect, Daniel Loren Scribner, 23, is scheduled to make a preliminary court appearance today. He also faces a possible charge of first-degree murder in connection with the ninth homicide in Yakima this year. Both men were arrested late Sunday. Huitt's bullet riddled body was found about 11 AM, Sunday in a vacant lot on South 14th Street across from the Washington State Fairgrounds. An autopsy Monday determined Huitt died of multiple gunshots to the neck, Yakima Coroner Maurice Rice said.

"This is an execution," said Capt. Jeff Schneider

A dispute over drugs may have led to the shooting, police said Monday.

According to court records, Huitt was picked up from a home on Swan Avenue at 4 AM, Sunday by Day and Scribner. The trio set out to make a drug deal for 4 ounces of methamphetamine, police said.

But the drug deal was a setup, and a hit man was supposed to be waiting in the bushes next to an abandoned house when Huitt and the suspects arrived, according to court documents.

When the hit man failed to fire, Day allegedly shot Huitt three times with a .357 caliber revolver. Scribner, according to court records, then pumped seven .45 caliber slugs into Huitt after he fell to the ground.

Neighbors reported hearing gunshots, but few telephoned the police. Contrary to an earlier report, someone reported gunshots in the neighborhood at about 5 AM, but officers checked out the area and found nothing.

A man who lives in the neighborhood called police around 11 AM, after finding Huitt's body face-down in the dirt next to a junked car.

Police found several empty .45 caliber bullet casings at the scene. Two spent bullets were also found in the dirt near Huitt's body.

According to court records, one suspect allegedly told police Huitt was ordered killed by a California drug dealer because he had been robbing local drug dealers and 'hurting business.'

Schneider said police have been unable to confirm the hit man allegation and the stated motive for the slaying. All three men have a long history of criminal activity, he said.

"They lured him down there to execute him and that's what they did," Schneider said.

Day's criminal record includes convictions for first-degree escape, possession of a controlled substance, theft and burglary. Scribner has been convicted of charges ranging from second-degree assault and vehicular assault to malicious mischief and harassment. Huitt was sentenced to more than 5 years in prison in 1991 after pleading guilty to first-degree robbery.

No weapons used in the shooting have been recovered. One

of the suspects allegedly told police the guns were given to the would-be assassin and a woman at a Union Gap motel after the shooting, according to court records.

Day and Scribner were arrested after police were tipped to their possible location at the Swan Avenue home on Sunday. The suspects were not at the home when officers arrived at about 8:30 PM but were seen driving past.

Schneider said the suspects tried to flee in the car but smashed into a parked car in the parking lot of a restaurant at the intersection of North First and I streets. "The two men were arrested after a brief foot pursuit," Schneider said.

18.

BUSTOS HOMICIDE INVESTIGATION

"The Yakima Police Department case number for the Huitt homicide is 99-16217, and in looking at the case and the subjects involved I could find no connection to the Bustos murder at this time," Jerry added.

"We need to keep this murder in mind as we research the Bustos case to see if anything connects," Ray suggested.

"So, let's list the suspects or persons of interest and possible motives in the Bustos murder," Jerry suggested.

Hector Larios Estrada aka Fernando	Sara's current boyfriend
Raul Zaragoza	Sara's mother's boyfriend
Jesus R. Diaz	Another boyfriend of Sara, drives blue or green BMW
Salvador Bustos	Sara's brother awaiting trial- indecent liberties
Officer Kensley Twindler	Sara's current lover
Eliberto Diaz Rivera	Sara informed police of his drug dealing
Other Unknown	Unknown motive

"Hector Larios Estrada, also known as Fernando, doesn't seem to be the jealous type. He considered Sara Bustos to be his exclusive girlfriend, but he didn't appear suspicious of the time she spent with other men. He has an alibi and is not considered a viable suspect.

"Raul Zaragoza is a person of interest only because it appears he may have been intimate with Sara. The fact that she left some of her clothing at his apartment indicates a possible relationship. He is also eliminated as a suspect.

"Jesus R. Diaz, another boyfriend who does not appear to be jealous of Sara's friendship with other men. Jesus' alibi checks out.

"Salvador Bustos, Sara's adult brother who she accused of sexual molestation, has a strong reason to not want Sara available to testify. He immediately lawyered up.

"Officer Kensley Twindler's relationship with the victim is officially non-existent until forced to admit it when the victim's diary is found. The county prosecutor declares he wants this relationship investigated thoroughly, but the only investigative report found is written by Officer Twindler, which only explains things from the officer's point of view. There appears to be no follow up unless it's done under a different case number with no reference to the Bustos homicide case.

"It appears investigations into Salvador Bustos and Officer Twindler ended with the discovery of a reported eyewitness to the homicide and the arrest of Eliberto Diaz Rivera," Jerry surmised.

"Kinda makes you wonder what really was going on between the cute little drug addicted gal and the rookie policeman," Ray remarked.

"What would motivate the detectives to want to keep Officer Twindler's relationship with the victim quiet?" Jerry asked.

"Possibly a large embarrassment or challenge to the police department and city. Let's imagine that Officer Twindler takes Sara Bustos up on her offer to help arrest the drug dealers at 735 Fair Avenue like she offered. That's where Eliberto Diaz Rivera lives, right? So, Officer Twindler gives Sara some buy money, and she makes several controlled buys from Eliberto at 735 Fair Avenue. A short while later, an affidavit is typed up explaining Sara's activities in buying drugs from Eliberto at the address, which provides the judge with probable cause to sign a search warrant for Eliberto's apartment. Eliberto is arrested for felony drug possession and is booked at the county jail. Somehow, he is able to come up with the money to bail out and 3 days later, Sara Bustos is murdered.

"Here's the kicker. The prosecution is required by the judge to not mention Eliberto's recent arrest and totally ignore the probable motive that Eliberto killed Sara Bustos to keep her from testifying against him on the drug charge," Ray explained.

"Then the eyewitness tires of sitting in jail on a material witness warrant. She recants her original story and says she didn't see anything, hoping she'll be released," Jerry responded.

"I like where Detective Tovar just overlooked her denials when they took her to the scene from jail. Tovar proceeded ahead, having the witness explain in detail where she was at and what she saw while Tovar made the measurements. Her explanations to Tovar at the scene of where she was and what she saw made her a credible witness, in my opinion, Jerry."

"It wasn't enough for the jury, however. Why was the prosecution required to leave out the information about Eliberto's arrest and his probable motive to kill Sara Bustos?" Jerry asked.

"It was ordered by the judge, because it was viewed as prejudicial."

"That leaves the prosecution with no way to explain the motive for the murder."

"There's another possible scenario. Sara Bustos falls in love with a handsome young police officer who is kind to her. They have an intimate relationship and may have participated in some illegal drug activity together, or he may have given her money when she was dope sick instead of trying to get her into recovery. She wanted to please him, and she needed to feed her addiction, so she agreed to back up her offer to act as a confidential informant. She was instructed and acted on behalf of the police in obtaining enough evidence for a search warrant and the arrest of Eliberto Diaz Rivera. The problem is Rivera was one of Sara's connections for cocaine and he figures out, after he bails out of jail, that it was Sara who got him arrested. Rivera has a supplier who then becomes worried about Rivera giving them up in exchange for a reduced sentence, or even dropping the charges completely. So, they decide together to kill Sara, the witness, and the potential source of some serious jail time. None of this is rocket science, Jerry. Most cops and all narcotics detectives know the serious dangers of being an informant in the violent world of illegal drugs."

"What did they do to protect Sara after she did what they asked?" Jerry asked.

"Absolutely nothing, Jerry, as far as I could find. What do you think?"

"It appears they let her continue to abuse cocaine and probably gave her 'buy money' to score cocaine to be used as evidence in a trial. My guess is not all the cocaine made it to the police evidence vault. They left her in the community, abusing drugs and associating with those who suspected her as a snitch, with little regard for her safety. They could have at least bought her a bus ticket to visit family in California, just to get her out of town for a while," Jerry remarked with a piqued look on his face.

"If that was the case, I suspect it was kept quiet to avoid a lawsuit from the victim's family," Ray added.

"Yeah, a multi-million-dollar lawsuit. Since the 3-year statute of limitations has long passed, I suspect it's too late to file," Jerry responded.

"If Officer Twindler had an intimate relationship with Sara Bustos and if they used cocaine together, she would be a liability to Twindler's law-enforcement career if she talked about it."

"And Officer Twindler might be motivated to make sure Sara Bustos never exposed his indiscretions," Jerry explained.

"So, the next question is, was Officer Twindler, now Deputy Chief Twindler, capable of killing Sara Bustos?" Ray asked.

"He must not be worried about a lawsuit because the statute of limitations has expired, so why is he still attempting to cover up the incident? Is it because there's no statute of limitations on homicide leaving him in jeopardy of an arrest at any time in the future?"

"You know Jerry, I can imagine Eliberto Rivera making bail with the help of his supplier and contacting Officer Twindler and threatening to expose Twindler's relationship and drug use with Sara Bustos unless the charges were dropped," Ray explained.

"Maybe that's why the eyewitness recanted, and Rivera was found not guilty of killing Bustos. Officer Twindler, Eliberto Rivera, Rivera's supplier, and the Yakima Police Department were all in the clear with the death of Sara Bustos and Rivera's not guilty verdict." Ray suggested.

"Who do you think was Eliberto Rivera's cocaine supplier, Ray?"

"I find it interesting that three people at Final Choice Auto Sales all provide an alibi for Rivera, and I wonder if they helped Rivera make bail. Background checks of the owners, Chuck and Debbie Chambers, would be in order along with Debbie's son, Frank Hernandez," Jerry remarked.

"This is a response from Yakima City Police Records regarding case number 99-16278 which we discovered in Officer Twindler's report, which differed from the homicide case number 99-16172. It appears to be an investigation of Officer Twindler, but we're not sure because they won't release it," Jerry explained as he handed a copy to Ray.

Open, active police investigation file is exempt from disclosure.

The following investigative, law enforcement, and crime victim information is exempt from public inspection and copying under this chapter:

(1) Specific intelligence information and specific investigative records compiled by investigative, law enforcement, and penology agencies, and state agencies vested with the responsibility to discipline members of any profession, the nondisclosure of which is essential to effective law enforcement or for the protection of any person's right to privacy;
RCW 42.56.240 Investigative, law enforcement, and crime victims.
We hold RCW 42.17.310(1)(d) provides a broad categorical exemption from disclosure all information contained in an open active police investigation file and reverse the superior court.
Newman v. King County, 133 Wash. 2d 565, 575, 947 P.2d 712, 717 (1997)
Your request no. 23-3155 remains open for the remaining portions of the datebook, which is being reviewed by Spanish-speaking staff.
With production of these records, the city has completed its response to your request. Thank you.

Regards,
City of Yakima Records App

"I'd sure like to take a look at this investigation into Officer Kensley Twindler, but it remains undisclosed and in a classified file at the Yakima Police Department. It also looks like they're still translating the diary and datebook, Jerry. It surprises me the victim's datebook hasn't been translated to English until now because it's critical evidence in the homicide investigation. I doubt we'll ever be able to see the file investigating Officer Twindler as a suspect in this murder, unless..." Ray's voice trailed off.

"Unless what?" Jerry asked.

"Unless the prosecutor applies for and receives approval to empanel a grand jury to investigate this case."

"How would that work, Ray?"

"It's complicated and expensive, but it's becoming the only

way I can see to find out what really happened in this case."

"What about the feds? Do you think they could help?"

"That's possible, Jerry, but I'm not sure. They need to have jurisdiction before they can prosecute for murder. If the homicide happened on federal property, crossed state lines, or was in other categories, the feds could prosecute."

Jerry got up from his desk, walked over to a bookcase that took up the entire wall of the office, pulled out a large volume, opened it and handed it to Ray, saying, "Take a look at 18 U.S. Code § 1512—Tampering with a witness, victim, or an informant."

(1) Whoever kills or attempts to kill another person, with intent to—

(A) prevent the attendance or testimony of any person in an official proceeding;

(B) prevent the production of a record, document, or other object, in an official proceeding; or

(C) prevent the communication by any person to a law enforcement officer or judge of the United States of information relating to the commission or possible commission of a federal offense or a violation of conditions of probation, parole, or release pending judicial proceedings;

shall be punished as provided in paragraph (3).

(2) Whoever uses physical force or the threat of physical force against any person, or attempts to do so, with intent to—

(A) influence, delay, or prevent the testimony of any person in an official proceeding;

(B) cause or induce any person to—

(i) withhold testimony, or withhold a record, document, or other object, from an official proceeding;

(ii) alter, destroy, mutilate, or conceal an object with intent to impair the integrity or availability of the object for use in an official proceeding;

(iii) evade legal process summoning that person to appear as a witness, or to produce a record, document, or other object, in an official proceeding; or

(iv) be absent from an official proceeding to which that person has been summoned by legal process; or

(C) hinder, delay, or prevent the communication to a law enforcement officer or judge of the United States of information relating to the commission or possible commission of a federal offense or a violation of conditions of probation, supervised release, parole, or release pending judicial proceedings;

(3) The punishment for an offense under this subsection is—shall be punished as provided in paragraph (3).

(A) in the case of a killing, the punishment provided in sections 1111 and 1112;

(B) in the case of—

(i) an attempt to murder; or

(ii) the use or attempted use of physical force against any person;

imprisonment for not more than 30 years; and…

"According to this, the feds would have jurisdiction. The trick would be getting the feds to accept this old case," Ray responded as he handed the lawbook back to Jerry.

"Wouldn't the suspect be able to claim he is the victim of double jeopardy since he was tried in state court and found not guilty? Would it be legal to try the suspect again in federal court for a crime that he'd just been acquitted of in state court?"

"I'd say yes, it would be legal and not double jeopardy because each jurisdiction is able to enforce its own laws. If a crime violated both state and federal laws, then each jurisdiction is allowed to charge the suspect with the crime, but that's just my humble opinion. Getting the feds to accept the case would probably be difficult," Ray responded.

19.
FURTHER ANALYSIS OF SUSAN RIEGEL'S NOTES

"Let's see. Where are we in this case? Ray asked.
"Greed could be a motivator, so I did some research on the problem," Jerry responded.

"What about greed?"

"Greed is one of the seven deadly sins. It is called a 'deadly' sin because immersing oneself in greed and the other deadly sins leads to eternal death," Jerry explained.

"What's eternal death and how many deadly sins are there?"

"Eternal death is also called Sheol, Hades, Gehenna or Hell, and there are seven deadly sins. They are, Lust, Gluttony, Sloth, Wrath, Envy, Pride, and Greed."

"What does greed have to do with Larry Riegel's disappearance?"

"Maybe nothing, Ray, but I suggest we keep the motivator greed in mind when we are analyzing Susan's notations about the circumstances of her missing brother," Jerry remarked.

"Ok, sounds reasonable."

"Here are some more of Susan's notes from her journal on January 8th, 13 days after Larry's disappearance."

I hung up and immediately called my sister, Candy. I asked her to call the police and file a missing person's report and she agreed to do this. Later that evening, she called back to say her husband got *a call from a Yakima Police Officer who said there was no missing person's case because there was a report of a domestic violence issue at Larry's house, reported by LaDena on January 4th. The police said they had contact with Larry and that he left the house and was probably just lying low for a few days. I asked Candy if the police had actually seen Larry during this reported event, but she hadn't thought to ask that question.*

I asked my sister, Candy, to call the James Gang Tavern (a known tavern my brother would sometimes frequent). Her husband called the tavern and asked the bartender if anyone had seen Larry. The bartender asked the crowd, and someone came to the phone and said Larry hadn't been in there for at least four months or more. I felt this was inaccurate and said so to my sister.

January 9th, 2010

On Saturday, January 9th, I continued to call my niece and nephew (Larry's children) about the last time they spoke with their dad. I called my sister, Sandy, to see what she knew. She said she stopped at the house a couple times, but either LaDena said Larry was sleeping or wasn't there. I was growing more concerned with every call I made. I called the James Gang Tavern myself and spoke with a bar patron by the name of Nelda. At first, she said Larry hadn't been there for a long time, but I told her that I knew Larry had recently been there with his son. She then said LaDena had called the tavern on January 2nd and said Larry was headed down to the tavern for a beer run, asked Nelda to give him the money that she owed LaDena, also told her she wanted Larry to come right back home because she was holding dinner for him.

(I will say here that she does not cook, my brother does all the cooking and is very good at it. When Nelda said LaDena was holding dinner, I was alerted to this because I knew that wouldn't have been true. Any dinner would have been from my brother, not the other way around).

Domestic Violence Clarification

I had many questions lingering about the domestic violence issue, so I called a friend of mine, who is a probation officer at the Kitsap County Jail. She helped me find weekend phone numbers for the police stations, jails, and hospitals. We thought there was a chance he was in jail, that maybe he was in jail for the domestic violence report. Since it was the weekend, I hadn't gotten very far in trying to confirm this. I called the 911 Dispatch offices in Union Gap to ask about the police report from January 4th. I explained to the dispatch person that my brother was missing, and I gave her his home address. I was told that the domestic event didn't occur at that location, and she suggested I talk to an officer about the report. At 10:30 PM, on January 9th, I got a call from Officer Gordon, who said he stopped at LaDena's house to ask about Larry, and she told him he wasn't there, and hadn't seen him since January 4th. She told him there was activity at the house while she was gone, and she believed that Larry was coming and going. She told him Larry was probably at the Harrah Farm.

I asked about filing a missing person's report, and he said there was no time limit to file; we only needed to feel there was a credible threat to a person's welfare. I asked him if the officer who took the report had spoken with Larry at the time and he said he didn't know. Officer Gordon suggested I speak with Officer Esther Cyr directly. I requested a call back when she got in the next day.

January 10th, 2010

On Sunday, January 10th, at about 10 AM, I called dispatch and left a message for Officer Cyr. She called me back and said LaDena walked into the police station on January 4th and filed a report. She said Larry, and her had fought, he hit her and knocked three teeth loose; she said she was paying all the bills; they were having money disputes and told the police that he walked away from the house after the fight, but that she didn't want him back at the house and couldn't take it anymore. Officer Cyr told me there was no physical evidence on her face of being hit, but she said she was crying really hard and was very upset.

Officer Cyr said the police didn't go to the house and had no contact with Larry. Also, there would be no charges filed against him because it was basically her word against his because of the lack of evidence. I explained to her that we believed Larry was missing and that nobody had seen or spoken to him, except LaDena, since Christmas Day. I told her about the chain of events, the people I had spoken to and that I couldn't find anyone besides LaDena who had any contact with him. She suggested I come to Yakima that day and file a missing person's report. I hung up the phone crying and asked my husband to drive me to Yakima.

Inconsistencies

On the way to Yakima, I continued making numerous phone calls to my sisters, niece, nephew and my friend, Nan. We agreed not to say anything to our mom/grandma until we found out more information on what might have happened to Larry. During these conversations, I found inconsistencies in the stories we were being told.

1. *On the morning of December 28th, my nephew, Brian, called his dad at 8 AM, and LaDena said his dad was sleeping and couldn't come to the phone. This was the same day I was at the house from 10:30 AM, until noon, was told Larry wasn't at home and hadn't returned from the coast yet. Plus, I could obviously see there hadn't been any vehicle activity in the yard due to the fresh snow. I have most recently been told by Detective Blankenbaker of the YPD that Larry was sighted at the Yakima Costco, in the parking lot, on the morning of December 28th. The person who saw him didn't speak to him, but he said he saw him walking with his head down and in a hurry. The detective didn't give me the name of the person who supposedly saw him.*

On February 14th, 2010, my husband and I walked into the Yakima Costco and spoke to one of the managers. We explained about Larry's disappearance and the sighting on December 28th. They looked up Larry's account and said his card was last renewed in 2007, which means it would have expired in 2008. They looked under Larry Riegel, Larry's Construction, and LaDena. LaDena was on Larry's account but had no membership in her own name. They mentioned they could tell what everyone had bought for the last 10 years, and there was no activity with Larry's name on it. This indicated to us that all of these stories were contradicting one another.

2. *On Tuesday, Jan 5th, my sister Sandy passed LaDena at the intersection of 10th and Washington Avenue. LaDena motioned for her to pull into the parking lot of the Airline Market so they could talk. LaDena had a passenger in the car with her, a woman with shoulder-length hair, blunt cut gray hair. Sandy noticed she wouldn't make eye contact with her at all during the conversation, but only sat in the car, staring straight ahead.*

LaDena explained to Sandy that the woman had helped LaDena drive Larry's car to Ray's house, because she and Larry had fought, and she didn't want Larry coming back to the house. She went on to tell Sandy that Larry had knocked three of her teeth loose, but Sandy noticed there was no physical evidence or marks on her face.

Sandy and I both remember LaDena telling us about two teeth she had to super glue back into her dental partial plate. She said she needed some dental work but couldn't afford it. We were told this at a BBQ at our mom's house at least two or three summers ago.

I have suggested that police identify and question the woman who was LaDena's passenger that morning. To my knowledge, this has not happened.

Missing Person's Report

My husband and I arrived at the Yakima Police Station at 200 S. 3rd St at about 3 PM. We went through the jail area and waited for an officer to take our report. Officer Tim Cruz arrived and talked to us while we all stood in the hallway. I explained the circumstances and told him we felt there was foul play, and that the girlfriend was somehow involved. He took some basic information and gave us Case Number# 10-470. I noticed his card said Officer T. Cruz, looked closely at him and recognized him. I had been the maid of honor at his first marriage but hadn't seen him since 1976. We reacquainted ourselves and my husband and I left the station. My husband and I decided we would visit the taverns we knew my brother would sometimes go into, hoping I could get a clear understanding of the real story.

James Gang Tavern

Tim [Susan's husband] and I walked in and ordered a soft drink, then asked for Nelda. She came over and spoke to us; I would describe her as middle-aged, short and petite, with shoulder-length brown/gray hair. She appeared to be intoxicated. She said she was a friend of LaDena's and repeated the story about Larry coming down on a beer run. I asked if she saw him, and Nelda said he never showed up.

I talked to several other bar patrons, including Phil Benseoter. He said he'd known Larry since they were kids, lived in our old neighborhood. Phil said he hadn't seen Larry for a couple of months. Other patrons said the same thing; they hadn't seen him for a while. Someone asked where his car was, and we told them that he was reported to have walked away from the house; that LaDena had returned his car to Ray Schuel. It was suggested we try the Old Town Pump or Boomer's. I left my cell number and asked for a call if anyone thought of anything else.

Old Town Pump in Union Gap

We talked to the bartender first, Kelly Wimberly. She knew Larry, but hadn't seen him since the holidays. We went from table to table and asked people if they had seen him.

Dan Martinez said he saw Larry at Boomer's Tavern the night before Christmas. Again, lots of people knew my brother, but nobody had seen him since Christmas. People again asked about his car. When we repeated the story about Larry walking away and LaDena returning the car to Ray, there was almost an audible gasp in the bar. People repeatedly said he wouldn't walk anywhere, that he always drove, and that he loved his car and would never return it to Ray.

This seemed to be the common theme at every place we had visited so far…

Susan Riegel

"These are some excellent notes. Let's continue looking at the anomalies or apparent suspicious circumstances, based on Susan's entries, besides the seven we've identified so far," Ray suggested.

"Susan and her family were beside themselves, trying to find Larry. It's so heartbreaking, you can almost feel their emotional pain, Ray."

"It's hard not to let emotions overwhelm us, but what we need are the facts. So, in a recap, the anomalies we've identified so far in my opinion are:

1. LaDena's weak and confusing first report to Susan was that Larry was missing, had a brain disorder, and it was impossible to contact Larry.

2. LaDena's story changed about the brain disorder and doctors. This appeared to be an attempt to redirect concern about Larry's disappearance to focusing on Larry's family problems.

3. Another apparent attempt by LaDena to redirect their concern for Larry toward complicated family money issues, revealing her interest in possibly acquiring the Harrah farm and other valuable items like Larry's jewelry and a rare silver chalice from the Middle Ages.

4. LaDena's continued complicated stories about money stolen, borrowed and owed were so impassioned that Susan considered writing LaDena a check for what LaDena claimed was owed to her. It's apparent that Susan's focus on finding her brother was successfully derailed by LaDena's manipulative claims that day.

5. No traditional phone call from Larry to his sister Sandy on her December 31st birthday.

6. Larry's son, Brian, spoke with his father on Christmas Day by telephone at about 4 PM. When Brian called back sometime between 10 PM and midnight, Larry was not available. After speaking with LaDena, Brian suspected she was not being honest as to his father's whereabouts at that time. Brian appears to be the very last family member to speak with Larry. If Larry was murdered, it probably happened on Christmas Day sometime between 4 PM and midnight.

7. On January 8th Susan learned that LaDena had returned Larry's car to the seller, saying Larry wouldn't need it any longer. It's this incident that alerted Larry's family that something terrible might have happened to him.

"There's more information, starting with LaDena's assault complaint that lacked evidence in my opinion," Ray said.

8. Susan and her sister Candy learn that Yakima Police declined to take a missing person report on January 8th because LaDena reported she was assaulted by Larry

in a domestic violence incident on January 4th. LaDena claimed Larry hit her and caused three teeth to be loosened. According to Susan's notes, LaDena reported Larry walked away from their residence on January 4th, and she has not seen him since. Police did not file domestic violence assault charges against Larry, even though LaDena was reported to be very emotional and crying about her injury, because there was no visible evidence to LaDena's claim of assault.

"This incident where LaDena goes to the police department and reports she was assaulted by Larry is very interesting. If it was a false report, could she have been attempting to provide a defense for herself if Larry was discovered dead?" Ray asked.

"You mean like there was a fight, and she supposedly killed him defending herself? That's a possibility. Maybe Larry's body had not yet been disposed of at that point and if it was discovered she could claim her report was evidence she was defending herself from Larry," Jerry speculated.

9. On January 5th, Larry's sister Sandy encountered LaDena and another woman in a car near 10th Avenue and Washington Avenue. They made contact and LaDena told Sandy the passenger in LaDena's car had helped return Larry's car to Ray Schuel, the seller. This woman acted suspiciously and may have more information about the circumstances. She needs to be identified and questioned. Do the police know who she is and have they interrogated her?

10. Larry was last seen at Boomers Tavern on Christmas Eve by several people who know him.

11. While posting fliers in the neighborhood, Susan was told by a neighbor that on January 4th she observed

LaDena moving a number of items from her home. It appeared to the neighbor that LaDena may have been moving.

12. On January 10th, Larry's mother went to LaDena's house and asked her point-blank if she killed Larry. LaDena would not respond with a yes or no, and instead stated to Larry's mother, 'Why would you ask that? I'm a gentle person.' LaDena's obvious failure to deny she killed Larry is very significant, we believe.

13. On January 11th, Susan and her sister Sandy met two police detectives for a walkthrough of Larry and LaDena's home. Larry's expensive hunting rifles, jewelry, and a special silver chalice were missing. LaDena claimed Larry took the jewelry and chalice with him when he left for the first time. Pawn shops checked for Larry's missing property, without success.

14. On January 11th, LaDena claimed Larry's disappearance was not out of the ordinary, that he always went away for weeks at a time and wouldn't call anyone. When pressed about it, LaDena appeared flustered and began saying Larry had been using hard drugs and told a story about a 'drug girl' and a drug house on the reservation. There was no evidence of drug use and, to the contrary, Larry was under the care of a physician at the time. It is suspected LaDena was not being truthful and was trying to provide a reason for Larry's disappearance.

15. On January 11th LaDena said that Larry left in his car to visit friends on Christmas Day, pawn his jewelry, and earn money playing poker over on the coast. She says he returned on December 28th, and they got into an argument on January 4th, after which he walked away, leaving his car, never to be seen again.

16. On January 12th, Susan went to the drug house recently frequented by Larry according to LaDena, and was advised they had not seen Larry in months.

17. Larry's cell phone records were checked by the police and the last recorded phone calls were on January 4th, which were very short calls to family members and a friend, Lisa Hill. Larry reportedly left a message for Lisa, but it was deleted before it was listened to. Was this really Larry? There has been no activity in Larry's bank account.

18. LaDena's cell phone and the landline phone records at the house have never been checked by detectives.

19. Don Martin was renting the Harrah farm at 7811 Lateral C Toppenish, WA. He reported a burglary at the farm where some of Larry's stored property was stolen. Don was a friend of LaDena's, and she had visited the property and was interested in some of the stored items. She was told she was not to be on the property.

20. A neighbor witnessed LaDena loading bags of items into her car on Monday, February 8th, 2010. She said she previously heard LaDena argue and yell at Larry around Christmas time and at other times in the past.

21. Another neighbor also saw LaDena loading a lot of stuff into her car. The neighbor said there had been a blue car in LaDena's driveway recently and she said they noticed LaDena coming out and giving money to a person in a different blue car. They also observed a man wearing a beanie cap and a woman helping LaDena move boxes out of the house.

22. Owner, Mike, at Boomer's Tavern said LaDena had tried to remove Larry's Missing Person posters. He said this was the second time he'd had problems with her,

so he called her at home and told her never to return to Boomer's Tavern again.

23. Tenant and LaDena's friend, Donald Lee Martin, born in September 1948, has criminal records in Oregon for harassment and assault, domestic violence assault, violation of protective order, and theft. He refused to let Riegel family members upstairs at the rental home on Lateral C, looking for Larry's stolen guns and other property.

24. In March 2010, three months after Larry disappeared, Yakima Police Detective Blankenbaker advised a charge of $237.34 had been recently made against Larry's credit card at the Couger Den in White Swan, WA. He suspected it was for cigarettes as LaDena had mentioned she bought cigarettes on March 8th, with Larry's Chase credit card.

25. All of Larry's posters had been taken down from Big Red's Diner in Moxee in March.

26. A memorial of flowers and photos for Larry Riegel was set up by his mother, across from Larry and LaDena's residence in Yakima. It was destroyed and removed several times by unknown persons.

27. What happened to Larry's dog, Jesse?

28. LaDena and her lawyer sued Larry's mother for $2200 in an unpaid loan and request a protection order, saying Larry's mother, Cecilia Downey, had been harassing LaDena.

"The best defense is a good offense, maybe?" Ray asked.

29. LaDena changed her mind on February 10th, to take a polygraph test, and explained it was because Larry still lived with her and was not needed, according to Yakima

Police Detective Blankenbaker.

30. Larry's sister, Susan, reported that about 18 months prior, while she was visiting her brother Larry, she noticed a large bruise on the inside of his leg. She said it went from his groin area all the way down to his calf. When she inquired about it, she said Larry told her that LaDena got mad at him when he was drunk and beat him up when he was unconscious. Susan said she wanted Larry to go to a doctor because he may have a blood clot, but he declined, saying LaDena has a terrible temper and if anything happened to him, it was probably LaDena that did it.

"All these anomalies or suspicious circumstances add up to circumstantial evidence that LaDena was involved in Larry's disappearance, in my opinion. But I don't believe there's quite enough probable cause to arrest her at this point," Jerry remarked.

"Your opinion may change, Jerry, when I tell you LaDena was later arrested – but not for murder. We can go over her arrest and conviction later. Meanwhile, I have to report that the Yakima Police Department has again refused to provide us with a copy of the case file," Ray responded as he handed a copy of the PDR response to Jerry.

Records Withheld. We cannot provide the records you requested. Sgt. Noah Johnson has stated this is an open active investigation and therefore exempt from disclosure pursuant to the following exemption:

The following investigative, law enforcement, and crime victim information is exempt from public inspection and copying under this chapter:

(1) Specific intelligence information and specific investigative records compiled by investigative, law enforcement, and penology agencies, and state agencies vested with the responsibility to

discipline members of any profession, the nondisclosure of which is essential to effective law enforcement or for the protection of any person's right to privacy;

RCW 42.56.240 Investigative, law enforcement, and crime victims.

We hold RCW 42.17.310(1)(d) provides a broad categorical exemption from disclosure all information contained in an open, active police investigation file and reverse the superior court.

Newman v. King County, 133 Wash. 2d 565, 575, 947 P.2d 712, 717 (1997)

Please contact Detective Drew Shaw or Sgt. Noah Johnson at (509) 575-6200, for additional information.

"Hmm, open and active investigation, huh? How many years has it been since Larry was reported missing?"

Jerry asked as he handed the letter back to Ray.

"The Yakima Herald Republic newspaper reported the story after Larry went missing and followed along with the investigation in their news articles over the years. We have a copy of those articles and, in reading them, it appears the reporters found out much more about the investigation than what our fellow detectives are willing to share with us now. Would you like to see what has been publicly reported thus far?" Ray asked.

"Absolutely! Thank God for the Yakima Herald Republic newspaper."

Handing the first copy of the article to Jerry, Ray said, "I've tried to arrange these in chronological order with the first article reported on January 14th, 2010, which was about 20 days after Larry disappeared."

Family, friends search for missing man

Yakima Herald-Republic

Relatives and police are looking for a Yakima man who hasn't contacted family since Christmas.

Further Analysis of Susan Riegel's Notes

Larry Riegel's disappearance is unusual because he normally calls his son and other loved ones almost daily, his family said Wednesday. The 57-year-old lives in the 1500 block of South 12th Avenue. His sister, Susan Riegel Vaughn of Snohomish, Wash., said he missed a family dinner Dec. 26 and hasn't answered phone calls. Yakima police Sgt. Tony Bennett said officers have been checking leads without success. Nothing suspicious has surfaced so far. "We just haven't found a good reason for him to be gone," Bennett said. His girlfriend came to the police station Dec. 5th, to report that they had argued the day before. She said he became upset and walked away from the house, that was the last she saw of him, according to the police report. Riegel is currently unemployed, police said. He has worked as a contract pilot for CubCrafters, but his federal license had been temporarily suspended due to recent surgery, his sister said. She said he was a lifetime Yakima resident who was well known in the area. He frequented several local bars, including Max's, Boomer's, the Old Town Pump and the James Gang Tavern. Friends and relatives are circulating fliers in an attempt to develop information about his whereabouts. He is 6 feet, 2 inches tall, 195 pounds, and has gray hair and hazel eyes. A large vertical scar from the recent surgery can be seen on the right side of his neck. Any tips may be reported to the police department at 509-575-6200.

"There appears to be an error. It says the girlfriend came to the police station on Dec. 5th, to report that they had an argument the day before. I think the correct date should be January 5th," Ray remarked as he handed a copy of the next article to Jerry.

It was a short article, dated January 20th, 2010, stating the family is offering a reward for information leading to Larry's return and cited the assigned detective's phone number 509-576-6573 and a website (www.findlarryriegel.com). He then handed another article copy to Jerry. It was dated January 23rd, 2010, 28 days after Larry disappeared.

Family of missing man is keeping the faith

Larry Riegel has not been seen since Jan. 4th

By Erin Snelgrove
Yakima Herald-Republic

Searching for her brother has become Susan Riegel Vaughn's fulltime job. She's created a Facebook page and posted ads on Craigslist. She's hung hundreds of posters across the Yakima Valley and has sent fliers around the country for people to copy and distribute. She's also given interviews to newspapers and television stations throughout Washington, and is in the process of listing her brother with America's Most Wanted Missing Persons and the National Center for Missing Adults. But nothing has worked. Yet. "We've talked to hundreds of people. A lot of people have been helping," said Riegel Vaughn of Snohomish, Wash. "We're really hopeful that maybe he's having a medical situation or that we're going to find him. It's not easy thinking of the alternative."

Larry Riegel's family, which normally talks to him daily, knew something was wrong when the 57-year-old missed dinner the day after Christmas. According to the police report, his girlfriend hadn't seen him since Jan. 4th, when they had a fight. According to the report, she said he became upset and walked away from their house in the 1500 block of South 12th Avenue. He hasn't answered his cell phone. He is 6 feet, 2 inches tall, 195 pounds and has gray hair and hazel eyes. A large vertical scar from a recent surgery can be seen on the right side of his neck. He has worked as a contract pilot for CubCrafters of Yakima, but his federal license had been temporarily suspended due to his surgery to fix four broken vertebrae in his neck, and he'd been unemployed. He was a lifetime Yakima resident who frequented several local bars, including Max's, Boomer's, the Old Town Pump and the James Gang Tavern. Yakima police Capt. Greg Copeland said foul play is not suspected. The case differs from other missing person cases in that the family has made extensive efforts to find the man, Copeland said. "As we get tips and leads, we follow up on them," he said. *"The bottom line is, we don't know where he is."*

Debbie Beaman-Zorrozua of Yakima said the uncertainty about her distant cousin's whereabouts had been hard on the family—especially Riegel's mother and two adult children. *"Some family members hold out hope Riegel will be found alive. Others believe they're searching for a body,"* Beaman-Zorrozua said. *"It's hit home now,"* she said. *"We're at rock bottom."*

The family is hosting a candlelight vigil for Riegel at 6 PM, Monday at Franklin Park in Yakima. Anyone with information is asked to call the police department at 509-575-6200. Riegel's family is offering a reward for information leading to Riegel's return.

"Some family members think he's deceased, all are extremely worried, and yet the police department thinks foul play is not suspected," Jerry remarked.

"I wonder if the disappearance had been taken more seriously in the beginning by the police, there may have been a different outcome. Here's a copy of the next Yakima Herald-Republic article, dated March 10th, 2010, 74 days after Larry's disappearance," Ray responded, handing the copy to Jerry.

MISSING *(By Phil Ferolito)*

Most days you can find Cecelia Downey out looking for her 58-year-old son, Larry Riegel. She and her daughter, Candy Jarvis, are out every day posting flyers at restaurants and businesses across the Valley seeking information about Riegel's whereabouts. A contract pilot for CubCrafters, he planned to attend a dinner at his mom's house on Pleasant Avenue in Yakima the day after Christmas. But he never showed up. The family, desperate to find him, has been working closely with a Yakima police detective, while also creating a Facebook page and Web site, www.findlarryriegel.com. "We've got posters from Pine Mountain to Moxee to clear to the lower valley and to Roslyn," Downey says. "I try to keep busy. Every once in a while, it hits hard."

Riegel is among the nearly 200 missing persons cases reported in Yakima County every year. Yakima County Sheriff's deputies handled roughly 130 missing persons cases last year. And Yakima police saw about 50, averages that have held steady over the past decade. There are only seven open cases in each department, one of them dating back to 1989. Most of the cases are solved within a few days or weeks, authorities say. Overdue hunters, hikers and snowmobile operators make up the bulk of the cases deputy's handle. Other times people just want to be left alone, and they simply drop out of the lives of their family and friends, says Stew Graham, chief of detectives at the Yakima County Sheriff's Office. "There're a million reasons under the sun why people step out of their lives, and eventually they'll step back. There's a wide variety of resolutions to that."

One case in point is that of Teri Smith, who had family and authorities worried after she went missing in September 2004. Smith, then 40, was last seen leaving Target. Her Chevrolet Trail Blazer was found in the parking lot with her purse, money, keys, shopping bag and cell phone inside. Four days later, she wandered into Yakima Regional Medical and Cardiac Center dazed, dirty, and dehydrated. She apparently suffered a nervous breakdown. "Usually, it will be somebody who just leaves home and doesn't tell anybody," says Yakima Police Sgt. Tony Bennett. "Usually, it may be someone who just wants to get out of a situation."

Rarely do missing cases involve foul play, authorities say. But when they do, the outcome can be devastating for the families they leave behind. Bennett points to the case of 14-year-old Francisca Hernandez-Ramirez of Sunnyside, who was last seen in October 2008, at a party in Outlook. Her body was found in a canal four months later, with her throat cut. "That was terrible," Bennett says. "Also, thank God that it's very rare." Sunnyside police sensed foul play from the start and posted fliers in local schools. After hearing the girl's body had been dumped in a canal, deputies borrowed underwater equipment to look for her.

Bennett says all missing persons cases are handled by the major crimes task force. After someone is missing for a month, local agencies send dental and any other records of the person to the Washington State Patrol's missing and unidentified unit. "We really don't hold back," Bennett says. "We really pour our resources into them."

Eventually the person's information, such as dental records or DNA, is forwarded to the National Crime Information Center's Missing Persons File, which compiles records for the FBI.

According to the federal agency, there are more than 102,000 active missing persons cases in the country. In 2008 alone, there were more than 778,000 such cases reported. Most of them were resolved.

"Oftentimes, cases are left open because authorities aren't alerted when missing people return home, Bennett says. Sometimes people will show up and the family, friends—even the people that report the missing person—don't think to call the police," he says. "We would like to clear them. We'd hope that someone would call so we can close out the case."

When a child goes missing, Yakima police immediately search the home and contact friends and neighbors, comb parks, anywhere the child may frequent. Information about the child's friends, such as addresses and phone numbers, is crucial to a case. "You'd be floored at the number of people that don't have that information," Bennett says.

When an adult goes missing, police make a similar effort to contact friends and family and make routine follow-ups until the person either returns or is found. "We just tell them not to give up, and keep looking," Bennett says. "You can't give up—it's your family."

In Yakima, Riegel's family has continued to actively search for him and has even compiled a 36-page investigation by talking to everyone who has been a part of his life. Relatives remain convinced he wouldn't have dropped out of sight—or moved somewhere else—without telling his family.

His mother drives around in a car plastered with bumper stickers seeking him, and has done radio interviews as well. The family has even put Riegel up on eBay to sell him, in hopes of finding him.

Police say at this time there is no evidence Riegel was a victim of a crime, but the family remains suspicious.

His sister, Susan Riegel Vaughn, of Snohomish, Wash., can't imagine her brother would have intentionally missed dinner. She says she spoke with her brother for about 20 minutes by phone two days before the Dec. 26th dinner, and that he seemed upbeat. "He just had a birthday, and I was kind of joking around and told him he was getting old," she recalls. "We laughed, we joked—it was really a good conversation. He asked me what he should bring (to dinner), and I said, 'Nothing,' I just wanted him to show up."

The Yakima Herald-Republic newspaper also listed,

Open Missing Person Cases:

Yakima County Sheriff's Office

- *Samantha Rios, 20, was reported missing in March 1992. She was last seen boarding a bus in White Salmon bound for Yakima.*

- *John D. Whitner, 48, was reported missing in January 1995 by family members who said they had not seen him in weeks.*

- *Roger M. Seawright, 34, of Toppenish was reported missing in 1998 after he didn't return from a store to get ice.*

- *Reyes S. Macias, 42, of Selah was reported missing in July 1999. Family members said they left the house briefly, and that he was gone when they returned.*

- *David W. Door, 39, of Terrace Heights was reported missing in October 2001 after his empty boat was found floating in Lake Chelan.*

- *Linda M. Adams, 15, a chronic runaway, went missing from Pamona Road in Yakima in 1978, but her* appears the Samantha Rios case has been cleared with the recovery of her body from a shallow grave. The suspect is no longer living and may have committed suicide.

"John Whitner appears to still be missing.

"Joseph E. John was found on April 8th, 2010, in the Marion Drain canal near Highway 22 and Track Road, badly decomposed. He was shot once in the arm and in the heart.

"I was unable to locate any other information on the missing persons listed and assume they are still missing. Here's a copy of a May 2013 Yakima Herald-Republic newspaper article that I think you'll find interesting."

Girlfriend of missing man charged with welfare fraud

Woman accused of using Larry Riegel's EBT card now a person of interest in 2009 disappearance.

By Chris Bristol
Yakima Herald-Republic

The case surrounding a Yakima man who has been missing for nearly three and a half years took an interesting turn Friday. Larry Riegel, a disabled 57-year-old contract pilot, has not been in contact with his family since Christmas Day 2009. His face has periodically been plastered on billboards around town and he was recently listed on the Project Jason missing-persons website. His family has offered $10,000 for clues about his disappearance.

Yakima police consider him a possible, if not probable, victim of foul play. And they consider his girlfriend, who was the last person to see him alive, a person of interest in his disappearance.

Against that backdrop, Riegel's girlfriend, 51-year-old LaDena Mann, appeared by summons Friday in Yakima County Superior Court on felony welfare fraud charges linked to Riegel's disappearance. According to state welfare fraud investigators, Mann used Riegel's electronic benefits transfer (EBT) card several times in the weeks after Riegel's disappearance for $1,503 in financial assistance, including groceries. They said she also filled out an *disappearance wasn't reported until 2004, at the request of the Green River Task Force.*

- *Jesus Gus Rodriguez, 28, was reported missing after his burning car was found on January 23rd, 2005, in an orchard on Summitview Road. His remains were not found in the car.*

Yakima Police Department

- *Kathleen R. Paulson, 52, a transient, was reported missing by family in 2004.*

- *Sally Stromberg, 51, a transient, went missing sometime in 2005.*

- *Gregory L. Holt, 51, who lived in the 3600 block of Fairbanks Avenue, was reported missing in February 2008 by his landlord.*

- *Jose Ortega Jimenez, 26, worked as a laborer in Naches. Fellow workers reported that he ran from the worksite in March 2008, and no one has seen him since.*

- *Juan L. Hernandez, 28, was originally from Yakima but moved to Seattle. He was reported missing in July 2009 by family who said they had not heard from him for two months.*

- *Joseph E. John, 19, was reported missing by family in January 2010.*

Help find Larry Riegel

Anyone with information is asked to contact the Yakima police at 509-575-6200 or Susan Riegel Vaughn at 425-293-5564. More information can be found at www.findlarryriegel.com.

Ray leaned forward, tapping the documents and said, "It

believe Riegel's disappearance was out of character and to confirm Mann was the last person known to have seen him alive.

Asked if that made her a suspect, the veteran detective said, "The last person to see someone alive would certainly be a person of interest."

Told of the charges against Mann, Riegel's sister and family spokeswoman, Susan Riegel of Snohomish, emphasized the family continues to maintain a $10,000 reward in the case. She also said the reward money is for information that leads directly to the recovery of her brother's body.

"Let's just say we've been waiting for justice for a long time," she said. "And were hoping this (the welfare fraud charges) will kick-start something."

"It looks like police detectives went to work on the Riegel case again 12 years later, according to this Yakima Herald-Republic newspaper by Chris Bristol dated July 12th, 2013, Ray," Jerry remarked as he picked up the article.

Still Missing

Yakima police use cadaver dogs to search two properties for missing man but come up empty.

By Chris Bristol
Yakima Herald-Republic

The long running case of Larry Riegel, Yakima's best-known missing person, ramped up Thursday as investigators and cadaver dogs searched locations in Yakima and Moxee. The use of the cadaver dogs to search the properties and homes of Riegel's former girlfriend and her sister left little doubt as to what investigators believe happened to Riegel.

What had been a missing person case is now a death investigation, said Yakima Police Department spokesman Capt. Rod Light.

No remains were found, however, leaving investigators stumped as to their next step in the search for Riegel, a 57-year-old contract

Further Analysis of Susan Riegel's Notes

EBT card eligibility form claiming Riegel still lived with her in the 1500 block of South 12th Avenue, even though by then he had been missing for more than two months.

As a result, prosecutors filed three charges against Mann: first-degree theft (welfare fraud), second degree perjury and false verification for public assistance. All three charges are felonies.

Mann, who is free on her own recognizance, spoke with the *Yakima Herald-Republic* after the arraignment and said she was unaware that investigators consider her a suspect in Riegel's disappearance. According to Mann, Riegel called several people—including his boss, whom she didn't identify—in the first two months after his alleged disappearance.

Describing herself as 'absolutely' certain Riegel is still alive somewhere, possibly in Idaho or Montana, Mann lashed out at his relatives, accusing them of having a vendetta against her. She disputes claims the 6-foot-2 Riegel was physically vulnerable after having had neck surgery, and claimed his mother has suspiciously left town every Mother's Day for the past three years.

"Right off the get-go, they started saying horrible things about me," she said. "They didn't have no reason to say those things... It's just snowballed."

Riegel was an abusive drunk, Mann said, alleging he took off the night of Jan. 4, 2010, and hasn't been seen since because he assaulted her that night and she got a warrant against him for domestic violence the next day.

As to why she used his EBT card, she said she always did the shopping, and that she expected him to return home someday with his tail between his legs—and expecting food in the pantry.

"I'm the only one who ever used it," she said regarding the card, adding, "I didn't know when he was going to come home... I'm so stupid. I took him back every single time."

In a brief interview earlier Friday, Yakima police Lt. Nolan Wentz confirmed he recently took over the missing-persons case following the retirement of the original detective assigned to it. Wentz was hesitant to discuss the case in detail, except to say investigators *pilot who was last heard from by family members on Christmas Day 2009.*

"We'll round table it now and figure out where to go next," Light said.

Riegel's disappearance has been well publicized by his relatives. They put his face on billboards around town, plastered the city with missing person fliers, and have maintained the website findlarryriegel.com, offering a standing reward of $10,000 for the recovery of his body.

Previously, police said they considered him a possible, if not probable, victim of foul play. And they considered LaDena Mann, his girlfriend and last person to see him alive, a person of interest in his disappearance.

Their suspicions became public in May when Mann, 51, was charged with theft for using Riegel's electronic benefits transfer (EBT) card several times in the weeks after his disappearance.

The searches were carried out at Mann's home on South 12th Avenue, where Riegel was living at the time of his disappearance. The other property was a home on Bell Road in Moxee, owned by Mann's sister.

Light said investigators have interviewed countless witnesses and developed probable cause for the search warrants based on conflicting information from some of those witnesses.

Although no remains were found Thursday, he said investigators did collect some items as evidence. Asked to elaborate, he declined.

In a brief interview Thursday afternoon, a tearful Mann said she felt harassed by police and by Riegel's family, but otherwise declined to comment on the advice of her attorney in the theft case.

In May, she told the Yakima Herald-Republic she was certain Riegel was still alive somewhere, possibly in Idaho or Montana, and accused Riegel's family of having a vendetta against her. She called Riegel an abusive drunk who left the night of Jan. 4, 2010, after assaulting her, and also said she got a warrant against him for domestic violence the next day.

Also on Thursday, just blocks away at the home of Candy

Jarvis, one of Riegel's four sisters, family members of the missing man, gathered to discuss the day's events. They refute allegations of any assault and say it would be highly uncharacteristic for Riegel to go any length of time without contacting family members.

Susan Riegel Vaughn, another sister and spokeswoman for the family, praised the efforts of the investigators in recent months and said she hopes the searches yield some useful clues. She said her relatives are convinced Riegel is dead and that the goal now is to bring his killer or killers to justice.

Toward that goal, she emphasized that the $10,000 reward remains in effect, providing it leads to the recovery of his remains.

"Someone saw something," she said. "Somebody saw something unusual in the middle of the night or something strange going on in somebody's backyard. ... They may not even realize it, but they know something."

She noted the family will soon be unveiling a new round of billboards asking, "Who killed Larry Riegel?"

"Idaho or Montana, huh? She gives no reason for saying Larry is in Idaho or Montana. She wasn't trying to misdirect the investigators, was she?" Jerry asked.

"She also said she got a domestic violence warrant of arrest out for Larry Riegel. That's blatantly untrue and an obvious attempt to demonize Riegel and shift the focus away from herself. She's done that sort of thing numerous times during the investigation, in my opinion. The Yakima Herald-Republic newspaper continued to follow-up on the story. Here's another news article dated December 31st, 2013, with information the police department released to the newspaper, but refused to share with us," Ray announced with a frown on his face as he handed the clipping to Jerry.

Still Searching

Larry Riegel went missing four years ago. His case is now a homicide investigation, and his family shows no sign of backing away from its campaign to keep him in the public eye.

By Rafael Guerrero
Yakima Herald-Republic

Susan Riegel Vaughn can so clearly recall her older brother Larry's outgoing personality that she can easily imagine what he'd be doing if he was with her at the moment.

"If Larry was in the room, he'd be front and center right now," Riegel Vaughn said in a recent interview.

But Larry is not in the room. In fact, no one has seen him in years.

Larry Riegel was last heard from on Christmas Day four years ago. Once considered a missing-person case, his disappearance is now considered a homicide investigation. Family members and police continue searching for answers in the case, which has achieved an unusual prominence, thanks to his family's diligence in keeping it before the public, including by paying for large billboards around the community that feature his image.

Vaughn and Yakima police recently sat down to discuss the case with the Yakima Herald-Republic.

"It's down to the point where we're trying to bring this to everybody's forefront again," said Yakima police Lt. Nolan Wentz.

Riegel was a 57-year-old contract pilot with a carpentry business when he was last seen. He was supposed to have a belated Christmas dinner with his sister on Dec. 26, 2009, but he never showed up or called. No one has seen him since. His girlfriend said in May that he was still around on Jan. 4, 2010.

This summer, investigators searched locations in Yakima and Moxee for his body. No remains have been found, and investigators are frustrated that there is still little physical evidence of his whereabouts. However, police have released new details surrounding the events leading up to and just after Riegel's disappearance. Two months before he went missing, Riegel underwent neck surgery. Wentz, who now helms the investigation, spoke with Larry's doctors and surgeon in March and concluded that he would not have been able to travel on his own because he was still recovering from the surgery. "He was a 'mess' physically," Wentz said.

Riegel's oldest son, Brian, tried calling him numerous times from Christmas night, through early January, but did not get a reply, said Vaughn. The sister, who now lives in Issaquah, said his[her] brother and nephew would usually talk to each other about [a] "half dozen times a day."

Wentz said they have also refuted reports from the public that Riegel was seen in some Lower Valley bars and homes, as well as reports he had left for Idaho, Montana or Alaska. There is a lot of speculation as to what really happened, he said. "This is a really big puzzle," said Wentz, who took over the investigation in [the] fall of 2012. "The longer it goes, the more pieces of this puzzle are out there. We're finding the puzzle keeps growing."

Riegel's family, meanwhile, continues to raise public awareness of his disappearance in hopes of finding new clues. They have put his face on billboards around town, plastered the city with missing-person fliers, maintained the website findlarryriegel.com, and are offering a $10,000 reward for the recovery of his body. This week, the family will renew its billboard campaign, asking, "Who killed Larry Riegel?" They say they are convinced foul play is a factor in his disappearance. The billboards will be on the First Street corridor, with plans to add more in the Lower Valley.

Wentz said there are now at least 'two or three' persons of interest in the investigation. He only added that they were 'very close to Larry.'

Police have previously identified LaDena Mann, Riegel's girlfriend, as a person of interest. In May, Mann was charged with welfare fraud, perjury and false verification for using Riegel's electronic benefits transfer (EBT) card several times in the weeks after his disappearance.

Yakima County Prosecuting Attorney Jim Hagarty said Mann was placed into a diversion program, which will see charges dismissed if she reimburses the state and meets other provisions. Court documents show she will finish the program in August. She could not be reached for [a] comment Monday.

Further Analysis of Susan Riegel's Notes

Last July, Mann told the Herald-Republic she has felt harassed by the police and Riegel's family but declined further comment on the advice of her attorney in the theft case. Two months earlier, she told the paper she was certain that Riegel was still alive elsewhere and accused his family of having a vendetta against her.

Discussions with top Yakima police officials last year were encouraging, said Susan's husband, Tim Vaughn. "They said, 'We apologize, we have not done our job better and we are going to,'" he said. "It blew us away, it really did."

Vaughn said she looks forward to the day police call her with the news her family seeks. When she speaks, she often mentions how close she was to her brother.

"I know if the roles were reversed, he'd be out looking for me," she said.

"What do you think about that newspaper article, Jerry?" Ray asked.

"I know Nolan Wentz; he was a Yakima County Deputy Sheriff until he was hired by the Yakima Police Department. He is an excellent investigator. If anybody could have solved this case, it would be Nolan. I think he'd still be actively working this case if he hadn't retired."

"I think it's important that Larry Riegel's doctors declared he could not have been able to travel on his own. That's critical information," Ray declared.

"Do you think it's possible the cadaver dogs missed his grave, Ray?"

"Sure, that's possible. I have some ideas that may help with finding Larry Riegel, but I'd like to share them with the team when the time comes. Here's another article, dated December 26th, 2019, 10 years after Larry disappeared," Ray commented.

Remember him?

Another billboard campaign underway, with a $25,000 reward for information

By: Tammy Ayer
Yakima Herald Republic

Whenever she can, Cecelia Downey leaves her cozy home near Lewis and Clark Middle School for long drives deep into the vast irrigation network of the Lower Yakima Valley.

Downey, who is 90, scans ditches and canals and ponds. She looks past dead animals and gutted appliances, broken glass and graffiti, debris caught up in dark corners under bridges and on rough dirt-banks. None of that grim scenery stops her. This petite great-great-grandmother is on a sorrowful mission that began 10 years ago. Her only son, Lawrence Jay 'Larry' Riegel, was supposed to join his family for a belated Christmas dinner on Dec. 26, 2009, but he never showed up or called. No one has seen or spoken to the 57-year-old contract pilot and carpenter since Christmas Day 2009, when he called several relatives and friends. Downey last saw him that morning and last talked to him the same afternoon, when he called to thank her for the Adidas sweats she gave him.

The family has owned a small farm on Lateral C Road, between Fort and Larue roads, for decades. Downey and her four daughters well know the area's broad grid of blacktop and dirt roads, farms and wide-open spaces. She's not sure what she might find, but continuing to look for any trace of her son, physical or tangential, is important.

They strongly believe Riegel's remains are in the Lower Valley, so Downey keeps driving.

"I go out all the time," she said matter-of-factly.

Riegel's 67th birthday was Dec. 15th. A few days later, a new billboard went up near Eakin Fruit Co. in Union Gap. Alongside a big photo of a smiling Riegel are these words: "Remember Me? 10 years and the search continues."

The billboard includes a new $25,000 reward for tips that lead to the recovery of Riegel's remains and urges those with information to call the Yakima Police Department.

That billboard and two more posted since then are "A little provocative," said Riegel's younger sister, Susan Riegel Vaughn of Ronald. One stands at 10th and Washington avenues, and the other at the intersection of Lincoln Avenue and North First Street. Family have previously bought billboards in those locations, all high-traffic areas.

The missing person case became a homicide investigation years ago, and relatives have heard all kinds of stories. They include rumored sightings in Lower Valley bars and homes, mysterious phone calls, and supposed car rides and reports that Riegel left for another city or state. None have been verified by the police. A father of two—now a grandfather of two—Riegel didn't disappear on purpose, his family said. They suspected foul play early on. But without a body, the case lurched along. Investigators have searched locations in Yakima and Moxee, and relatives have brought a cadaver dog to the farm property, which Riegel was renting out when he went missing. Until Riegel is found, they will keep looking. While his remains are crucial to the investigation, they're even more precious to those who love and miss him.

"I want the body, and for my mom and his kids and my family. That's really important," Vaughn said. "If somebody points out where the body is, I'll cut a $25,000 check for them. We're a big Catholic family and everybody is buried at Calvary Cemetery. We don't have anything there for Larry. I know it would give everybody a sense of peace."

A chatty Cathy

Riegel kept in close contact with his family and friends, noted former Yakima Police Department investigator Nolan Wentz. He got the case in late 2013 and retired in June 2016, but stays in touch with Riegel's family. "There have been a lot of stories about what may have happened, but Riegel's disappearance was out of character," Wentz said. "The circumstances tell us this was not a missing person."

Riegel was gregarious—just ask any of his fellow regulars at the James Gang Tavern and Old Town Pump Saloon in Union Gap.

They may not have known his name, but they would probably say he talked a lot. Vaughn likes to call her brother a 'chatty Cathy,' and Wentz mentioned his social nature, too.

"He can't go a day without talking with somebody," Wentz said.

They know Riegel made Christmas dinner that day at the house he shared with his girlfriend a few blocks from Downey's home. At the time, a tenant lived on the Lower Valley farm and owed a back rent of $3000, Vaughn said.

Riegel called the renter that evening. Scanning Riegel's phone records from Dec. 1st, 2009, to Jan. 1st, 2010, Wentz noted that Riegel's last three calls started at 5:16 PM, on Christmas Day. The final call he made was at 5:23 PM.

In the family since 1962, the 10-acre farm was Downey's home until 2000, Vaughn said. It was rented for about a year and a half until Riegel took it over and later rented it out again.

Riegel's oldest son, Brian, tried calling him numerous times from Christmas night through early January but did not get a reply, Vaughn has said. They talked often, so it was yet another reason for alarm. He had no reason to leave, his family said, and they don't believe the talk that he chose to. Riegel was also recovering from recent neck surgery and likely would not have been able to travel on his own. With no confirmation of Riegel's whereabouts, his family filed a missing person report with the Yakima police on Jan.10, 2010. "By now, everyone's worried," Vaughn said.

Persons of Interest

Wentz previously said there were at least 'two or three' persons of interest in the investigation—people who were 'very close to Larry.' He mentioned it in a 2014 interview with the Yakima Herald-Republic; at that point, investigators had already identified LaDena Mann, Riegel's girlfriend, as a person of interest. She was the last person known to have seen him alive.

Late on the morning of Dec. 28th, 2009, Vaughn went over to the house the couple shared. Mann told her Riegel had gone to Seattle on Christmas Day, Vaughn said. In a May 2013 interview, she said he left again on Jan. 4*th*, 2010, and hadn't been seen since because he assaulted her that night and she got a warrant against him for domestic violence the next day.

Riegel's family confirmed that Mann went to the Yakima Police Department to make a domestic violence report. Vaughn talked to an officer on Jan. 10*th*, she said.

"The officer said it was a 'he-said, she-said' issue," Vaughn said. "Nothing filed, no physical injuries."

In May 2013, Riegel's girlfriend was back in the spotlight when she was charged with welfare fraud, perjury and false verification for using Riegel's electronic benefits transfer (EBT) card several times in the weeks after his disappearance.

Yakima County Prosecuting Attorney Jim Hagarty said Mann was in a diversion program, which would see charges dismissed, if she reimbursed the state and met other provisions. She completed those requirements in February 2014.

Attempts to reach Mann for this story were not successful.

A killing field

In the years since, Riegel's family members have continued to investigate on their own and publicize his case with billboards, flyers, and social media posts. They have also supplemented efforts as much as they can by spending money from fundraisers—and their own pockets—on a private investigator, cadaver dog searches and other efforts.

They have provided DNA, and the vertebrae in Riegel's neck, if found intact, could identify his remains quickly. "If I find a skeleton that has those vertebrae, I'll know that right away," Wentz said.

Every time human remains are found in the Yakima Valley; Vaughn calls the coroner. She and her family are among many with loved ones who have gone missing over decades and plead for more attention to their cases. They see the need for more resources for investigators and more money to fund already-strapped law enforcement agencies struggling with gang and drug violence amid the rugged landscape of one of Washington's largest counties.

"You've got this perfect environment to hide human remains," Vaughn said. "This is a killing field. That's what the Yakima Valley is—a killing field."

At least one person of interest has died since Riegel went missing. But anyone could have heard something crucially important to the case, Wentz said. It could be anything.

"It would probably be something really innocuous in conversation," Wentz said.

Vaughn will continue to lead her family's efforts to find their brother, son, father and grandfather, uncle and friend. She and Riegel were particularly close. He took her to school for show and tell when she was an infant, and he was in first grade. She was his bookkeeper for 20 years.

"He was my friend," Vaughn said. "I know he'd be doing the same thing for me."

Their mother sings to Riegel's picture every night, Vaughn said. "She shouldn't have to be looking for him. She should know what happened to her only son before her time on Earth is done."

"My mom deserves that," she said.

"A very well-written article by Tammy Ayer, that tells us a few things we didn't previously know. First, it's good to know Lt. Nolan Wentz took over the investigation of this case. Nolan was one of Yakima PD's best investigators, and if there was any chance this case could be solved, Nolan could do it," Ray remarked.

"Yes, but unfortunately, after the passage of time and the loss of potential evidence, even Nolan Wentz couldn't produce a miracle. You would think a $25,000 reward would give rise to some results," Jerry responded.

"The family has now raised the reward to $50,000," Ray added.

"Wentz could have received a number of tips, if so he's not sharing them. I would really like to see a copy of the probable cause affidavit that was submitted to the judge for the search warrants. Judges don't sign search warrants unless there is some strong evidence presented in the affidavit, Jerry."

"I think I know another possible person of interest. There are records showing Donald Lee Martin lived on Lateral C Road Toppenish, WA—the Riegel farm. He's the man who refused to let Susan search for Larry's guns at the farmhouse, but I'm not sure he's still living," Ray remarked.

"Where do we go with this case now, Ray? It seems if we wanted to continue investigating, there would be a few more things we could look at, or maybe we should confer with the team and Ross before we dig deeper into this case. What do you think?"

"I think this case is ready for Ross and the team to examine before further actions are taken."

"What about the Ryan Moore death investigation? Are you ready to draw some conclusions?" Jerry asked.

"A shocking event occurred in the examining room as Ryan died that day, but we can go over it later," Ray announced as there was a knock on the door.

Ross Manzola appeared with a smile on his face, saying, "I hope I'm not interrupting."

"Not at all, Ross, come in," Jerry responded.

"I just wanted to say that I will be unavailable for a week or so. Just between us, I'm going to meet with Joe Creed in Mexico. When the ATF came looking for him, it concerned me, but when La Fantasma said she was the answer to his problems, it caused me to become concerned enough to go see him. Please keep this to yourselves. If you need any legal advice while I'm away, do not hesitate to contact my good friend and attorney, Gary Collier," Ross announced.

"Sure, Ross, let us know if we can help you or Joe with whatever is happening. Have a safe trip to Mexico," Ray responded.

"Thanks guys, I shouldn't be long," Ross said as the door closed.

"Let's take a break and then go over the death of Ryan Moore next," Jerry suggested.

"Sounds good to me, let me grab my notes," Ray responded.

20.

RYAN MOORE DEATH ANALYSIS

"So, the call initially came out as a gunshot victim but was later corrected to a man who had a self-inflicted knife wound. How did the dispatcher know it was a self-inflicted wound?" Jerry asked.

"It appears a 911 call was made by Sue Huntington, who must have provided the information," Ray remarked.

"The officers had information it was a self-inflicted injury before they even arrived so, just because Sue Huntington said the wound was self-inflicted doesn't automatically make it so," Jerry observed.

"You're right Jerry, but the more you know about a call before you get there, the better it is, as long as the information is correct and not a diversion or misdirection. Police officers and first responders must have an open mind when they're investigating an incident. Even though a reporting party claims something happened in a certain way, officers must be open to look at every possibility. Do you remember a few years ago a man in Gleed claimed a horse kicked his wife in the head, killing her? He had the detectives convinced it was an accident, but the victim's family didn't believe it. When the Yakima County Prosecutor refused to prosecute the husband, the family appealed to the governor. The governor sent an assistant state attorney general and an investigator to Yakima, and they got the husband convicted of murder. With those thoughts in mind, it could have happened just as Ms. Huntington reported, but since she is the only living witness to the stabbing, we need to compare what she tells us to what the evidence reveals. There is some evidence Ryan's actions were fueled by drugs. The low nighttime temperature on September 20th was 45 degrees and at about 10 AM it was 60 degrees with no wind, according to records. Ryan removed all his clothing except for his shorts and ran down 6th Avenue, away from the responding officers while gushing blood from a neck wound, according to the officer's reports. An overdose of methamphetamine causes the body to overheat and can cause hallucinations, and that may be the reason Ryan removed his clothing," Ray reasoned.

"It would be interesting to read Sue Huntington's written explanation of the incident, but unfortunately, we don't have it. In the report narrative Sue says she looked away when Ryan stabbed himself in the neck and didn't see the actual stabbing, however, observant Sergeant Kellogg reported he looked Sue over closely and saw no blood on her anywhere, except blood spots on the 'top of her right hand'."

"How did those blood spots get on her hand and what did they look like exactly?" Jerry asked.

"I must say the Union Gap Officers were exemplary in their actions regarding this incident. They made quick assessments and even though contact with another person's blood is dangerous, they responded swiftly. Ryan was known to them as a drug user whose blood may have been carrying contagious diseases, yet they contained Ryan and treated his injury, called an ambulance, and soon had him transported to the emergency room before cleaning and decontaminating themselves at the fire department. Amazingly, thanks to the Union Gap police officers, Ryan was still alive when he arrived at the hospital," Ray explained.

"Since Ryan was still alive when he arrived at the emergency room, why weren't they able to save him, Ray?"

"I was able to locate the Advanced Life Systems ambulance paramedic and spoke with her on the phone recently. After a few moments, she said she remembered the call, that she would never forget it because of what happened at the hospital. According to the ambulance paramedic, a doctor walked into the examining room with a nurse, took a quick look at Ryan's wound without touching him and said, 'That's a fatal wound,' and turned to leave. The paramedic said she asked the doctor to try to stop the bleeding, and he replied again that it was a fatal wound as he left, with Ryan struggling for his life on the examining room table.

The nurse then said, 'We need more blood!'

To which the paramedic responded, 'We need a doctor!' as Ryan expired.

"Did she think Ryan could have been saved?"

"Maybe not, but that's not the point."

"Who was this doctor, Ray?"

"The paramedic said she couldn't remember his name. She did say she reported him to his supervising physician who declined to address the issue saying the doctor was about ready to retire, anyway."

Jerry leaned back in his chair and looked at the ceiling while Ray tossed the file he was holding onto his desk.

The office became very quiet.

"Don't doctors take an oath?" Jerry asked after a few moments.

"The Hippocratic Oath. I looked it up."

"What's it say?"

"Here's an oath that is taken at the Penn State College of Medicine."

By all that I hold highest, I promise my patients competence, integrity, candor, personal commitment to their best interest, compassion, and absolute discretion, and confidentiality within the law.

I shall do by my patients as I would be done by; shall obtain consultation whenever I or they desire; shall include them to the extent they wish in all important decisions; and shall minimize suffering whenever a cure cannot be obtained, understanding that a dignified death is an important goal in everyone's life.

I shall try to establish a friendly relationship with my patients and shall accept each one in a nonjudgmental manner, appreciating the validity and worth of different value systems and, according to each person, a full measure of human dignity.

I shall charge only for my professional services and shall not profit financially in any other way as a result of the advice and care I render my patients.

I shall provide advice and encouragement for my patients in their efforts to sustain their own health.

I shall work with my profession to improve the quality of medical care and to improve the public health, but I shall not let any lesser public or professional consideration interfere with my primary commitment to provide the best and most appropriate care available to each of my patients.

To the extent that I live by these precepts, I shall be a worthy physician.

"Well, I'd say Ryan's emergency room doctor failed his oath. Since it's been more than 3 years, I suspect an attorney would tell the parents it's too late to file a lawsuit," Ray added.

"Besides, it wouldn't bring their son back."

"I asked the paramedic if Ryan's blood had been checked for drugs and she said with the transfusions he'd been receiving, his blood had been completely replaced and a drug test would be invalid," Ray explained.

"Here's a copy of the coroner's report," Ray explained as he handed it to Jerry.

Yakima County Coroner
Yakima County Courthouse
Yakima, WA 98901
(509) 574-1610   fax: (509) 574-1613

Yakima County Coroner's Report   Case number: 2010-126

Narrative

March 20th, 2010, at 1121 hrs., I (JB Hawkins) received a call from nursing supervisor Valerie from Yakima Valley Memorial Hospital. Valerie advised me that Ryan G. Moore DOB 6/17/1984, a 25-year-old white male, had been brought to the hospital via ambulance. Ryan had a severe laceration of the neck. He had lost an incredible amount of blood. Ryan did not survive his wound. Valerie advised that she had been told this was a self-inflicted wound.

I detailed Yakima Valley Memorial Hospital. I contacted Kasey Weigley, contact number – of Advanced Life Systems (ambulance service) and Sgt. Chase Kellogg of the Union Gap Police Dept. Kasey Weigley is a paramedic with Advanced Life Systems Ambulance Service. Kasey advised that when she arrived, Ryan was down, and it appeared he had been struggling with the police. She asked him if he was going to fight her, and he advised he was not. She also asked him if he had stabbed or cut himself and he stated he had done this to himself. Sgt. Chase Kellogg advised that he did hear Ryan Moore say he cut himself. Kasey Weigley advised that Ryan had been given 6 liters of blood at the hospital. Sgt. Kellogg advised he received the call at 0950 hrs. The call came out as a shots fired call. When he arrived, he observed Ryan Moore standing in the middle of the road, undressed. He was bleeding very badly from his neck. Ryan took off running when he saw Sgt. Kellogg. Sgt. Kellogg and Officer Curtis Santucci arrived. He also went after Ryan. Ryan turned and came back running toward Officer Santucci and Officer Santucci shot Ryan with a taser gun and he went down. EMS arrived,

Advanced Life Systems and paramedic Kasey Weigley attended to Ryan. This is when Ryan stated that he cut himself. Ryan was transported to Yakima Valley Memorial Hospital. Medical personnel were unable to revive Ryan, and he was pronounced dead at 1044 hrs., 3/20/2010.

    I removed Ryan from the emergency department of Yakima Valley Hospital. I transported him to the County Morgue. I contacted Dr. J. Reynolds and scheduled an autopsy for 1400 hrs., on 3/20/2010.

    March 20th, 2010, Dr. J. Reynolds performed the autopsy on Ryan G. Moore. Dr. Reynolds advised that the cause of death was Cerebral Hypoxia, due to Hypovolemic Shock, Esophageal Intubation, due to Self-Inflicted Knife Wounds to the Neck. Dr. Reynolds advised that Ryan had stabbed himself two or more times in the neck and used a sawing motion during the neck attack on himself. These were self-inflicted wounds. Present during the autopsy was officer Curtice Santucci UGPD and I (JB Hawkins).

    March 20th, 2010, at 1700 hrs., I received a call from Jeremiah Wandell, who was calling to see if we had received any information as to the death of Ryan Moore. Jeremiah advised that Ryan was his roommate and had lived with him on and off during the past few years. He advised that Ryan was a heavy drug (meth) user and had been acting strange the last few weeks. He came and went from Jeremiah's at 611 S. 8th Ave. Yakima and his Union Gap home, which had been foreclosed on. I advised Jeremiah of Ryan's death. He stated he thought it would be drugs or something like this, as Ryan had been having drug problems lately.

    March 20th, 2010, at 1710 hrs., I called Ron Moore Ryan's father. I advised Ron that we did perform the autopsy. I advised him that Ryan had cut himself two or more times in the neck. He had lost a lot of blood and did a considerable amount of damage to himself. Ron advised he was not surprised as Ryan had been having problems with drugs (meth). Ron advised he had talked with his x-wife Ryan's mother. Ryan had visited her in the last month, and Ryan was very angry. They talked and were trying to *think of something they could do to help him. But Ryan did not want help. He continued to use drugs. Ron advised that they were going to have services for Ryan in the Tri-Cities. He would advise when a funeral home had been contacted.*

04/06/2010, I received the Washington State toxicology Report results: Blood Ethanol—negative, Blood Analysis—not performed, Urine Test Results—CNS drugs none detected, Glucose 1000 mg/dL and Vitreous—Ethanol negative

Note: Ryan received 6 to 10 units of blood, his blood was diluted with the blood he received.

The Cause of Death was Cerebral Hypoxia, due to Hypovolemic Shock, Esophageal Intubation, due to Self-Inflicted Knife Wounds to the Neck.

The Manner of Death was Suicide.

Signed: Jack B. Hawkins, Coroner

"Ryan's blood had been replaced by transfusions so a blood test for drugs would not be valid, and a urine test could take 12 to 14 hours before positive results could show up. I see where the report says there were no drugs found in Ryan's urine test. (*Urine Test Results CNS drugs none detected*). CNS drugs mean central nervous system drugs such as methamphetamine, and if Ryan had been recently using meth, the urine test would not be valid since it can take 12 to 14 hours for the drug to be found in the urine," Ray explained.

"So, it's still possible Ryan was under the influence of methamphetamine at the time of his death," Jerry remarked.

"Yes it's possible, and here's a copy of the pathologist's 5-page report," Ray said as he handed Jerry a file folder.

Jeffrey M. Reynolds, MD Forensic Pathologist

4001 Tieton Drive
Yakima, WA 98908
Ph: (509) 965-1770

Autopsy Number:	A10-036
Date of Report:	25 March, 2010
Name of Deceased:	MOORE, Ryan G.
Age:	25
Sex:	Male
Date of Birth:	17 June, 1984
Date and Time of Death:	20 March, 2010; pronounced 1044 hrs.
Date and Time of Autopsy:	20 March, 2010
Place of Autopsy:	Yakima County Morgue Yakima, Washington
Responsible Party:	Jack Hawkins Yakima County Coroner Yakima, Washington
Prosecutor:	Jeffrey M Reynolds, MD, Pathologist

FINAL PATHOLOGIC DIAGNOSIS

I. *Single Edge Knife Wound to Neck.*

    A. *Multi-Angled cuts consistent with three partial entry / exit motions.*
    B. *Transection of trachea, esophagus and right jugular veins.*
    C. *Minor injury to right carotid artery.*
    D. *Acute aspiration of blood and gastric contents*

II. *Multifocal perivascular chronic myocarditis, mild*

    A. *Consistent with chronic toxin use*

III. *Emergency endotracheal tube in esophagus*

IV. *Cause of Death: Knife wound to neck*

V. *Mechanism of Death: Increasing cerebral hypoxia secondary to hypovolemic shock and esophageal intubation.*

Signed:
Jeffrey M. Reynolds, MD
Pathologist

BRIEF HISTORY

Deceased was a known drug user who apparently committed suicide by cutting his throat, and when an officer arrived at the scene, he was standing in the street and fled the officer, bleeding profusely. Multiple units of blood were administered at the hospital, but the patient succumbed.

EXTERNAL EXAMINATION

Body is that of a Caucasian male appearing approximately his stated age, measuring 69 inches in length and weighing an estimated 160 pounds.

JEWELRY – None seen

MEDICAL PARAPHERNALIA – Tracheal tube is inserted in the wound on the lateral side of the right neck and extends to the [sic] trachea, presumably. Intravenous catheter is present in the left antecubital fossa and two are present in the right antecubital fossa. Another intravenous catheter is present in the right inguinal region, and a urinary catheter is in place with the collection system holding a small amount of hazy yellow urine.

HEAD – Hair is brown in color, trimmed neatly to within an inch of the scalp in most areas, with no evidence of trauma to the scalp visible or palpable. Anterior chambers of the eyes are clear, irises hazel in color, and pupils larger than mid position, equal and round bilaterally. Some mild injection of the conjunctivae is present, but no evidence of petechial hemorrhages. Subconjunctival edema is noted, as is lid edema. A small amount of blood is present in the nares and mouth, with no evidence of trauma to the teeth, tongue, or lips noted. Food particles are present in the oral cavity. Onset of rigor mortis in the muscles of the jaw is just beginning, and the jaw is easily mobile. No evidence of direct trauma to the face is seen. Goatee is present and neatly trimmed and brown in color.

NECK – The neck is notable for an incisional wound, and the presence of the incisional wound crosses midline slightly extending approximately 1 cm to the left but begins at the right angle of the jaw and proceeds anteriorly in a sawing motion showing one, two, three, four separate different cutting areas to the edge of the wound. Edge is smooth, with no evidence of serration noted. Total length of the wound is about 10 cm and further description will occur after tracheal tube is removed. The neck is otherwise atraumatic and unremarkable.

THORAX – Aside from assorted smears of blood, the thorax appears atraumatic, symmetric and unremarkable.

ABDOMEN – The abdomen is soft, atraumatic and unremarkable. Two small, superficial, linear scars are present at the right costal margin near the anterior axillary line, but these are old and well healed.

UPPER EXTREMITIES – The right upper extremity shows a superficial scratch just distal to the elbow, measuring some 4 cm in length, but not even penetrating into the dermis. The hands show no evidence of defensive wounds, although multiple areas of blood are present. Nails are trimmed to less ¼ inch overhang, and all are soiled. No evidence of defensive wounds or injuries to the [sic] right upper extremity are noted. No scars, tattoos or other identifying marks are noted. No scars, tattoos or other identifying marks are noted on the left upper extremity, but on the proximal portion of the dorsal left # 2 finger is a taser injury with a small amount of burning at the edge. This is a single penetrating wound. Nails are similar in that they overhang less than ¼ inch and all are soiled. No evidence of recent defensive wounds aside from the taser wound is noted. Older superficial scratches are present on the dorsal aspect of the left # 4 finger over the middle phalangeal area, and these show an eschar and healing changes at least several days old. These are superficial injuries.

PELVIC REGION – Genitalia are circumcised male with both testes present intrascrotally. Some edema of the scrotum is noted. No evidence of mechanical non-medical trauma is noted.

LOWER EXTREMITIES – The left lower extremity is noted for a medial calf bruise measuring some 2 x 4 cm, which appears recent. Taser wound similar to that noted on the left hand is present above the left patella with less thermal injury noted. The left lower extremity is also notable for a pigment nevus measuring 2 x 3 cm present medial to the left patella. The right lower extremity shows no evidence of trauma, and no scars, tattoos or other identifying marks are noted. Some dried blood is present on both feet, consistent with this same prospect.

BACK – The back is notable for an ornate, very well-done tattoo extending from the scapular region to the lumbar region. No evidence of recent trauma to the back is noted. The back is otherwise unremarkable.

INTERNAL EXAMINATION

Body is opened in the usual Y-shaped fashion revealing approximately 1 cm of subcutaneous fat over the anterior thorax abdomen. No evidence of recent trauma to the internal or external aspects of the thoracic or abdominal walls is noted. Subcutaneous emphysema is present, especially prominent substernally. Small amounts of pale, cloudy, almost white fluid are present in the peritoneal cavity, consistent with lymph fluid. Approximately 20 cc of blood-tinged fluid is present in the pericardial sac, and no appreciable amounts of free fluid is present in the pleural spaces.

HEART – Great vessels enter and leave the heart in their usual locations, and the epicardial and pericardial surfaces appear normal. Serial sectioning of the myocardium reveals a left ventricular wall averaging 1 cm thick and a right ventricular wall 3 mm thick. Total weight of the heart is 400 grams. Serial sectioning of the coronary vasculature reveals widely patent coronary arteries with normal anatomic distribution. Valves are all delicate without evidence of atresia, regurgitation or vegetations. There is no evidence of pulmonary embolic phenomena in the pulmonary outflow tract. Coronary ostia are widely patent, and the aorta is unremarkable.

LUNGS – Both lungs are heavy, weighing approximately 500 grams each. There is a mosaic pattern of aspirated blood present both externally and in section. Pulmonary edema is present, but is not severe. Some small amount of gastric contents is present in the main stem bronchi, but there is no evidence of pneumonic consolidation or pulmonary embolic phenomena in any section. All lobes appear approximately equally affected. Endotracheal tube is not present in the trachea but is present in the esophagus.

GASTROINTESTINAL TRACT – Stomach contents show a moderate amount of liquid and particulate food, which matches that seen in the endotracheal tube at the level of the neck wound. Some of the particulate matter is similar to that found within the large airways. The esophagus, duodenum, jejunum, ileum, and colon are all within normal limits, and the appendix is unremarkable.

LIVER – The liver is present in its usual location and appears normal both superficially and in section. Gallbladder is present and contains approximately 30 cc of dark green bile.

SPLEEN – The spleen is present in its usual location and appears normal both superficially and in section. The spleen weighs 180 grams.

PANCREAS – The pancreas is present in its usual location and appears normal both superficially and in section.

ADRENAL GLANDS – Both adrenal glands are present in their usual suprarenal locations and appear normal both superficially and in section.

KIDNEYS – The kidneys appear well perfused and appear normal both superficially and in section. Ureters appear normal, and the bladder is empty. Prominent emphysema is present within all the mesentery of small and large bowel, and the lymphatic vessels are prominently obvious throughout the mesentery. Prominent emphysema is present in the retroperitoneal tissues throughout.

CENTRAL NERVOUS SYSTEM – Scalp is reflected in the usual fashion, showing no evidence of trauma to the subcutaneous tissues or galea.

NECK WOUND – Exploration of the neck wound noted grossly shows complete transection of the right internal and external jugular veins, complete transection of the esophagus where the endotracheal tube enters, complete transection of the trachea, and transection of the thyroid arteries bilaterally. The right carotid artery shows minor damage due to the knife blade, but no substantial blood loss from this artery is seen.

TOXICOLOGY

Two tubes of blood, one tube of crystal clear vitreous, two tubes of urine, and one tube of bile are retained by the coroner for toxicologic analysis, if necessary.

MICROSCOPIC EXAMINATION

Sections of the myocardium are noted for both chronic and acute inflammatory cells present in peri-small vessel locations, but these inflammatory cells are predominately lymphocytes with a few plasma cells. This is consistent with repetitive exposure to some substance toxic to the heart. Diffuse myocarditis is not present within the myocardial parenchyma, and only a few microscopic areas of fibrosis are present. Sections of lung show gastric aspiration with food debris present in many small airways. Inflammatory response to this aspiration is minimal, consistent with its occurrence less than an hour prior to death. Aspiration of blood is also present, again with minimal inflammatory response.

Signed
Jeffrey M Reynolds, MD

JMR: gfb   *Pathologist*

"So, what do you think about the autopsy, Jerry?"

"I had to look up a few words in the dictionary as I read the report to understand it. We are very fortunate to have access to someone like Doctor Reynolds, who did exemplary work. I would like to examine a couple of things in the autopsy report."

"Like what?" Ray asked.

"Well, to start off with, I'm curious if Ryan was right or left-handed?"

"Right-handed, according to his father."

"That makes a difference when we're looking at the description of the neck wound. If Ryan was right-handed, then it's probable that he used his right hand to cause the wound—if it was suicide. If the wound was caused by someone other than Ryan, then the wound may look different if Ryan caused it," Jerry explained.

"I would say your hypothesis is valid in this case, Jerry. So, where does it take us?"

"According to the autopsy, the wound begins at the right angle to the jaw on the right side of Ryan's neck and travels to just left of the midline of the neck. So, if Ryan caused the wound himself, he would have most probably had the knife in his right hand. He would have inserted the blade of the knife into the right side of his neck, below the jawline, and then drew the knife in a sawing motion, to the left—just past the midline of his neck, correct?"

"The autopsy describes what the wound looked like, and your hypothesis of the event could have made that wound, but I wonder, wouldn't it have been easier for Ryan to make the cut from left to right, since he was right-handed?"

"You mean like drawing the knife across his throat instead of pushing it?"

"Exactly, Jerry."

"Good point."

"The autopsy report also shows no sign of defensive wounds on Ryan's hands. I think this is important because if Ryan was attacked it would have been natural for him to try to stop the knife attack by grabbing the weapon and possibly receiving cuts on his hands or arms," Ray explained.

"Yes, it is important. Along with the report that there was no petechial hemorrhaging in the conjunctivae of the eyes," Jerry responded.

"Petechial hemorrhaging of the conjunctivae of the eyes could have been an indication of strangulation. We believe Ryan was not strangled, correct?" Ray asked.

"Right, and I don't have any further questions about the autopsy. How about you, Ray?"

"Not at the moment. I did take a closer look at Sue Huntington. Ryan's father said Sue appeared to take after the Goth lifestyle. Ryan asked his father to help him have Sue legally evicted from his home sometime early in 2009. Prior to that, there were a number of domestic violence calls to Ryan's home. Sue was later evicted, but it appears Ryan invited her back to his home before the incident."

"How would you describe the Goth lifestyle?" Jerry asked.

"Here's a good synopsis from the Wikipedia encyclopedia." Ray responded.

The Goth subculture can be defined as lovers of Goth rock, Gothic literature, Victorian and medieval history, and contemporary horror cinematography. Members of this subculture are often accepting and non-violent intellectuals who are sometimes just cynical of societal evils and have a fascination with death.

"Fascination with death, huh? Ryan's father also said he received information from a Spanish-speaking neighbor about activities at Ryan's home just before the incident."

"What did the neighbor say they saw?" Jerry asked.

"At about 10 AM, they said a white car pulled into Ryan's driveway. Sue got out of the car along with two men in trench coats. They all went immediately to the backyard and may have entered the home through the back door. Later, the two men left in the car and Sue returned to the backyard, where she was observed burning something just before the police arrived.

"Ryan's father was worried Ryan had become involved in a methamphetamine drug cult of some sort that practices black magic."

"Was he worried his son's death might have been some sort of black magic ritual?" Jerry asked.

"He wasn't sure and since Sue refuses to discuss the incident with us, it leaves us with suspicions but no answers."

"I can't think of anything else about this case, Ray. How about you?"

"Not at the moment. I was thinking I'd let it percolate for a while and maybe the team could look it over at this point for a suggested conclusion."

21.

CREED'S QUANDARY

Ross Manzola's trip to Mexico to meet up with Joe Creed began with a 20-minute shuttle flight to the Seattle-Tacoma International Airport, where Ross deplaned and looked for his connecting flight to Los Angeles. Once he arrived at LAX, he boarded Alaska Air flight number 1304 for a 2-hour trip to Loreto, Mexico. He looked forward to seeing Joe again.

Joe Creed's return to La Paz, Mexico, allowed him to renew friendships made several years prior during the search for fugitive narcotics detective Nicolas Cabot. He recalled the dreadful events at the border and the loss of his friend Snake, and the civilians killed from the blast set off by the cartel. He also recalled the death of Nicolas Cabot and the painful loss of his former girlfriend, Lola Flores, aboard the sailboat, 'Just Dandy.'

Joe could not calm his mind about the recent attack against his wife Lydia, and the burning of their home instigated by former Yakima County Prosecutor Karter Truman. His excitement in purchasing the large sailboat 'Hannah" from his friend Kirk was muted by future plans to deal with Karter Truman. Joe kept these deadly intentions to himself, however, except for a few trusted friends. Those who inquired why he was lining the inside of SV Hannah with bullet-proof Kevlar were advised that it was for insulation and noise reduction in preparation for long-distance cruising. A two-day sail northbound, into the wind, allowed Joe to judge how Hannah managed her windward tacks with the extra weight of Kevlar aboard. He remembered the promise to his friend Ross Manzola to discuss his truculent plans with Catholic priest, Padre Papa, pastor of Santa Casa church in Loreto, Mexico. The quaint little pueblo soon came into view off Hannah's port bow. Joe was also looking forward to seeing Ross, who was arriving at the Loreto Airport soon.

There was no safe anchorage from the wind for SV Hannah off Loreto. The tiny marina sheltered by the breakwater was too small for Hannah, so Joe dropped anchor about 150 yards from shore in 30 feet of water and reminded himself to monitor the wind while ashore. Capitán Verónica Sabroso, on leave from the Mexican Navy, and husband Vietnam veteran nicknamed Sniffer, rolled up Hanna's headsails while Joe flaked the mainsail and set the anchor deep into the sandy bottom by running Hanna's diesel motor slowly in reverse. Sniffer released the tender, a 14-foot dinghy powered by a 50 hp Honda outboard motor, from the davits at the stern of the sailboat. Veronica jumped into the inflatable dinghy and started the outboard motor to let it warm up prior to their trip ashore.

"Here's a list of provisions we need and some pesos; see what you can find at the grocery store here while I meet up with Padre Papa," Joe said during their short trip ashore in the dinghy.

"I need to meet Ross Manzola at the airport." Joe said, handing the cash and list to Veronica, while Sniffer tied the inflatable next to a small Mexican fishing boat in the small marina.

"Que es esto?" a Mexican fisherman asked, pointing at a newly installed .50 caliber machine gun mount in the center of the inflatable dinghy.

"Es para cámara de cine," Veronica responded without hesitation.

"Bueno!" the fisherman responded, displaying a smile.

"What was that about?" Sniffer asked as they walked down the dock.

"He wanted to know about the .50 caliber machine gun mount on the inflatable."

"What'd you tell him?"

"I told him it was a for a movie camera," Veronica responded with a smile.

"We can stay in contact with each other using our portable marine radios," Joe suggested as he flagged down a taxicab.

They all got into the taxi and traveled about 10 blocks until it stopped in front of El Pescador grocery store, where Sniffer and Veronica got out; then the taxi continued to the Santa Casa Iglesia with Joe for his meeting with Padre Papa. Joe had much respect for the highly educated Catholic priest who was also a member of the Society of Jesus. Often called the Jesuits and designated by the letters "SJ" after their names, they are the largest Roman Catholic religious order, formed in the year 1540. There are nearly 20,000 members, including over 13,000 priests, 3000 students, nearly 2000 brothers and almost 1000 novices. With headquarters in Rome, Jesuits make a profession of perpetual poverty, chastity, and obedience, serving as soldiers of God.

"Welcome, my friend! All is well, I assume," Padre Papa exclaimed with a handshake and a hug.

"Yes, all is well, for now. However, I'm facing a very difficult quandary in the near future, Padre," Joe responded as he embraced his friend.

"A quandary we can talk about over good food, mi amigo. Let's walk up the street for some lunch," Padre suggested.

"How about Maria's Cocina across from the marina?"

"Maria's it is, Jose."

Maria greeted the two men and spoke in Spanish with Padre Papa, who asked for a quiet table. She seated the men at a table in the corner near a window that looked out onto the Sea of Cortez.

"This is perfect, Padre," Joe said while looking at the wind in the palm trees.

"What are you looking at, Joe?"

"Our sailboat is anchored just offshore, and I need to keep an eye on the wind. That's her out there," Joe explained, while pointing to Hannah.

"My, what a beautiful sailboat, Joe. Tell me about her and where you are going."

"Hannah is a 62-foot Deerfoot cutter sailboat with an aluminum hull. She has three staterooms, with a head and shower in two staterooms and a head and bathtub in the master suite, giving the crew and me plenty of room. She's outfitted with all the latest equipment for long distance cruising, including the best in electronics for navigation and weather reports. She is fast on the water when necessary, flying her mainsail and two headsails. A water maker supplies all our needs for freshwater, a compressor mounted at the stern refills SCUBA tanks for unlimited diving, and a generator plus solar panels keep the batteries charged up. The galley and salon are large enough to seat 10 people if necessary, and we can last for six months at sea when she's fully provisioned. There's no protection from strong winds where she's anchored at the moment, Padre, so I have to keep an eye on her in case the wind picks up."

"She must be a pleasure to sail. I might suggest the gorditos with a banana refresco," Padre said as Maria waited to take their order.

"Sounds delicious, por favor, Maria," Joe responded.

"What is a sailboat head, Joe?"

"It's the toilet in nautical terminology, my friend. I must say, however, we are not preparing for a pleasure sail. We are fortifying Hannah and her crew for an assault against a personal enemy in an effort to eliminate the threat permanently. Tunnel Rat Sniffer is a Vietnam veteran with plenty of warfare experience, and Veronica is a warrior in her own right. Plus, I have more help on the way."

"Is it your goal to take this person into custody and have him face a court or tribunal for his crimes?"

"No, my goal is to eliminate him as a threat, Padre."

"In violation of the 5th commandment?"

"That's my quandary, Padre."

"The 5th commandment says, 'Thou shalt not kill,' doesn't it?"

"It's not as simple as that, Padre."

"Explain it to me. Who do you plan on killing?"

"It's complicated and goes way back to when I was a young downtown foot patrol officer and continues even to this day. The Yakima County Prosecutor, Karter Truman, the most powerful person in the county, misused his authority to avoid justice for his crimes and to further organized crimes for the benefit of himself and others. I was able to initiate an FBI investigation of this corrupt prosecutor, which resulted in criminal warrants for corrupt officials and felony warrants for the prosecutor himself."

"So, why is it not possible to serve the warrant on this corrupt county prosecutor and bring him to justice?"

"He is now in control of a wealthy drug cartel in Colombia and is being protected not only by his cartel gang, but also by the government and armed forces of Colombia. He's basically untouchable since his legal knowledge and his position have allowed him to launch attacks against those he perceives as his enemy—including me and my family. The only way I can see to protect myself and those I love is to launch a covert raid in Colombia and take this guy out, Padre."

"There must be another solution, Joe. The church teaches us that, 'God alone is the Lord of life from its beginning to its end: no one can under any circumstance claim for himself the right directly to destroy an innocent human being.' So, maybe you're saying this man is not innocent. Is that right, Joe?"

"That's right!"

"Therefore, you think you can take his life without moral incriminations?"

"That's just part of it, Padre."

"Take a long, slow drink of your refresco, Joe, and explain," Padre said while biting into the gordito.

"Let me quote a phrase, Padre," Joe said. "*Legitimate defense can be not only a right but a grave duty for someone responsible for another's life. Preserving the common good requires rendering the unjust aggressor unable to inflict harm. To this end, those holding legitimate authority have the right to repel by armed force aggressors against the civil community entrusted to their charge.*"

"Where does this information come from, Joe?"

"From the Catechism of the Catholic Church."

"So, as I understand it, you have the right to repel aggressors by armed force. This man is living in Colombia and is not, at this moment, an aggressor, correct?"

"Padre, there is no doubt in my mind he is planning another attack against me. Besides, the church also teaches, and I quote:

'*Love toward oneself remains a fundamental principle of morality. Therefore, it is legitimate to insist on respect for one's own right to life. Someone who defends his life is not guilty of murder even if he is forced to deal his aggressor a lethal blow.*

'*If a man in self-defense uses more than necessary violence, it will be unlawful: whereas if he repels force with moderation, his defense will be lawful.… Nor is it necessary for salvation that a man omit the act of moderate self-defense to avoid killing the other man, since one is bound to take more care of one's own life than of another's.*"

"So, you're going to kill a man you believe is bent on killing you. I cannot give you absolution for such an act, Joe, even though your action may be just in your mind. I emphasize your actions *may* be just. I think it will be between you and God," Padre Papa asserted as they finished lunch.

"I'm not sure you settled my quandary, Padre, but since the

wind is picking up, I'll need to get back on board soon. Would you give me a blessing before we part?"

"Of course, my friend. Father in heaven, watch over this protector of his community. Help him to act in a just manner in the mission in which he is engaged. Guide him in protecting himself and those he loves and give him compassion for his enemies as he deals with them. Saint Michael, patron of law enforcement, spread your protecting wings around this man and direct your prayers to God the Father on behalf of the mission in which your servant is about to engage. In Jesus' name we pray."

"Thank you, Padre," Joe said as he embraced his friend and slowly walked away.

"Via con Dios," Padre Papa said softly while making the sign of the cross toward his friend.

Joe decided to walk toward the center of the pueblo, down a peaceful tree-lined pedestrian promenade with tiny, quaint shops on both sides, to the central square. People were waiting in line at a nearby bank, while others passed the time sitting at outdoor restaurant tables. The central square, where many festive events took place, was quiet, with just a few people sitting on benches under the palm trees.

Palm trees, Joe thought as he looked up to the fronds swaying in the light breeze.

Approaching a taxi stand, Joe asked a driver, "Quanto a la aeropuerto?"

"Fifty pesos, one hundred round-trip if I don't have to wait too long," the young, smiling driver answered in English.

"Round trip sounds good. I need to meet a friend at the airport," Joe responded as he climbed into the Nissan Sentra taxi.

"I can get you some good Cuban cigars," the taxi driver said during the short drive to the airport.

"Most of the Cuban cigars are too strong for my liking. I'd rather smoke a Mexican cigar like Te Amo or a Rojas Firecracker," Joe responded.

"Copado! I can get those too," the driver responded with a grin.

"I'll come and help with the bags," the taxi driver said as he parked in the taxi zone.

Joe spotted Ross as he descended the stairway from the Alaska Air Boeing 737, thinking he looked tired.

They waited a few minutes while Ross made his way through Mexican Customs and was officially welcomed to Mexico.

The two men shook hands and embraced until Joe said, "Here, let me help you with your bag. I have a room reserved for you at the Posada de las Flores hotel on the central square in Loreto."

"That's not necessary, Joe. I can stay on your sailboat," Ross responded.

"Well, I'm afraid SV Hannah is booked up, Ross. I've got a full crew aboard, but you'll like the Posada de Las Flores. It's a colonial mansion that has been converted into a hotel. It is fully air-conditioned and has a nice swimming pool on the roof," Joe explained as they arrived at the hotel.

"I thought you'd like to relax before supper and get a good night's sleep. I can meet you here for breakfast tomorrow morning and then we can discuss the future," Joe suggested.

"That sounds fine, Joe. It was a long flight. How about let's meet at the restaurant next-door at 9 AM? And I'm buying breakfast."

"It's a deal, Ross," Joe said as he took a portable marine radio from his pocket and called out,

"SV Hannah tender to SV Hannah, come in Hannah."

"Yo tender, are you ready to come home?" the radio responded.

"Yes, I can be at the marina in 10 minutes."

"See ya there, Capitan!" a man's voice responded as Joe got up to leave.

"I'll see you in the morning, Ross," Joe said as they shook hands.

During his 10-minute walk to the marina, Joe could see

Sniffer launching the tender from the stern of Hannah where she was anchored offshore. They met at the marina at about the same time, Joe jumped aboard, and they headed back to Hannah.

"How'd it go, Joe?" Sniffer asked.

"Fine, I need to be back here at 9 AM for breakfast with Ross. Were you able to find the provisions we need?" Joe asked.

"Yes, we found everything we need. I meant how'd it go with Padre Papa?"

"Oh, that. We had a long discussion and I feel better about things, Sniffer."

"The weather forecast is for a light breeze out of the west tonight and all day tomorrow, Joe. We can stay anchored here if you wish."

"Good, I need to spend some time with my attorney friend discussing the legal aspects of the mission tomorrow. Then, I want to show him around and treat him to a good time."

22.
Planned Engagement

At about 8:00 AM the next morning, Joe put a pot of coffee on in Hanna's galley and then took a quick shower while the rest of the crew slept. He poured himself a cup of freshly brewed coffee after his shower and went up on deck. He released the lines holding the inflatable on its davits at the stern of the sailboat and slowly dropped the dinghy into the water. He started the outboard motor, letting it warm up for a few minutes before untying from a cleat and heading for shore, while holding his cup of coffee. Isla Carmen and the beautiful anchorage, Puerto Balandra, visible nine miles east across the sea, were bathed in the sun's early morning warmth. Local fishermen had been leaving the Loreto marina for a day of fishing for the past hour, leaving plenty of spaces for Joe to tie up his dinghy. He then walked several blocks south to Juan Maria Salvatierra Avenue and then west four blocks to the hotel Posada de las Flores and the small restaurant next door. Joe looked inside the restaurant, and not seeing Ross, took a seat at a table outdoors. Before long, Ross showed up with a pleasant smile on his face.

"How'd you sleep, Ross? Was the room comfortable?" Joe asked as Ross took a seat at the table.

"It was excellent. What a beautifully restored old colonial style hacienda, Joe. Thank you for picking that place."

"My pleasure, Ross. I'm honored that you came to visit."

"You've been a friend for a long time, Joe, but my visit is not entirely for social reasons. I'm seriously worried about your plans and hope you'll discuss them with me."

"Ross, I'll answer any questions you may have, and I'll listen and seriously weigh any advice you have for me."

"Good. Did you have time yet to discuss your plans with a spiritual advisor?"

"Yes, I met yesterday with Catholic Priest Padre Papa, and we had a long philosophical discussion. It hasn't changed my mind, though."

"Ok, putting aside metaphysical constraints for the moment, Joe, let's take a look at the legal aspects of your mission. You are a citizen of the United States, making preparations for your mission here in Mexico to take place in Colombia, correct?"

"Yes, that's correct."

"In preparing, I understand you've been acquiring weapons and taking defensive measures. Some weapons are illegal, not only in the United States but also in Mexico and Colombia. Possession of fifty-caliber machine guns can put you in jail for a long time, Joe. I'm sure you know that, so please tell me about the shipping manifest I received at my office in Yakima that said you had 2 fifty-caliber machine guns delivered from overseas to you at Bercovich Boatyard in La Paz, Mexico."

"I took care of that problem, Ross. No worries."

"You took care of a felony crime, Joe? How did that happen?"

"Well, I'm not proud of what I had to do, but it's done."

"What did you do, Joe?"

"As you know, Mexico has very strict gun laws. The country has only one retail gun store, and it's in Mexico City. Strict gun laws in Mexico can be overlooked, however, if you know the right people. I am personal friends with Senor Narciso Agundez, the governor of the state of Baja California Sur, and he has given me permission to possess the firearms."

"How did you manage that, Joe?"

"I donated to his political campaign," Joe answered, looking down.

Ross didn't say anything in response. He had a far off look in his eyes until he looked directly at Joe and said, "What about Donna Ashford?"

"Her? She's agreed to help me."

"So, let me understand. You are being scrutinized by an ATF agent for weapons violations, you've outfitted your sailboat to be an armed battleship, and you've recruited some of the most lethal warriors existing to assist you in your planned assault against an official of the Colombian government. Does that about sum it up?"

"There are a couple other things, but yes, that about sums it up, Ross," Joe responded with a sly smile.

"Where are the machine guns being kept, Joe?"

"Abel Bercovich has them securely stored at his boatyard in La Paz, along with some other weapons I've acquired."

"Other weapons?"

"You don't want to know."

"Ok, then tell me about Donna Ashford, Joe."

"That's a complicated story, Ross. Where shall I begin?"

"Just tell me why you're in league with a wanted international murderer whose name causes extreme fear in the cold hearts of cartel soldiers?"

"She is a construct of the U.S. Central Intelligence Agency and is used to motivate and control opposing drug organizations in some third world countries like Mexico, Guatemala and others," Joe explained.

"She still works for the U.S. Government, even now? What about the Interpol warrants for her arrest?" Ross asked.

"Just a formality in order to keep her cover."

"How can she help you, Joe?"

"The CIA has decided, off the record, it would be good to rid the world of wayward prosecutor and drug kingpin, Karter

Truman, also known as Pedro Escobar," Joe explained.

"Headquarters has assigned Donna Ashford to accompany me on the mission and has also asked an armed rebel faction in Colombia to assist in developing a rendition plan to extricate Truman. Oh, and that ATF agent that was looking for me—he's also part of the team," Joe continued.

"What if you get into trouble, Joe? Who's going to help you?

"The CIA has international lawyers on their payroll who are ready to act if necessary."

"How soon will you execute your plan?"

"That depends on Karter Truman's movements. He's being tracked and we'll go after him when he's in the right position, but it's hard to tell when that will be, Ross."

"We sure could use you back in Yakima now that Ray and Jerry have studied most of the investigations."

"How're they doing on the Sara Bustos murder?"

"That's where they could use your help the most, since it involves the Yakima City Police Department, your former employer."

"What's the problem?"

"The PD has a tight control on the evidence and they're not being very forthcoming. They've absolutely refused to let us examine the victim's diary. Some of the text from the diary is in Spanish has been released, but not all of it," Ross explained.

"Why is that happening?"

"We think it could be because the person who controls the release of information in this matter is the same person who was, and is, a person of interest in the Sara Bustos' homicide."

"Who are you talking about, Ross?"

"Deputy Chief Kensley Twindler of the Yakima City Police Department."

"Does the chief of police know about this conflict of interest?"

"Former Chief Granato says he was unaware of it when he was chief, and former Chief Rizzi later tried to resolve the issue by hiring outside police detectives we believe, to investigate and clear Twindler of any wrongdoing."

"Outside police detectives, investigating a small part of the case is not appropriate. This whole case should have been assigned to some other law enforcement agency to be investigated. There is a major conflict of interest in this investigation with the Yakima Police Department."

"I agree, Joe, but that didn't happen. Sara Bustos' ex-boyfriend and drug supplier, Eliberto Diaz Rivera, was charged with her murder. He was later found not guilty at a jury trial. You see now why we need you back in Yakima?"

"Ross, I promise I'll come home just as soon as my mission is completed. Let's finish breakfast and then go for a walk around this charming little fishing village. I want to show you the very first of the mission churches established on the Baja. Then later we can walk to the marina, take the dinghy out to Hannah, and have lunch on deck and continue our discussion. It's a beautiful day, and I want you to meet my crew before you return to Yakima."

"That sounds great, Joe. I must say, however, I'm looking forward to getting back home and assisting Ray and Jerry."

"I understand, Ross. I'll return to Yakima as soon as I can. I promise."

23.

Bustos Diary

Tired after his frenzied trip to and from Mexico meeting with Joe Creed, Ross decided to take a couple of days off to recuperate before he returned to the office. Arriving at about 10 AM on Tuesday, he noticed Monique was busy making copies of some legal documents while the door to Jerry and Ray's office was standing open.

"Good morning!" Ross said.

"Welcome home, Ross. How was your trip?" Monique asked.

"Good, I had a nice visit with Joe and met some of his crew on the sailboat," Ross responded as Jerry and Ray came out to greet him.

"You didn't get much of a tan, Ross. How's Joe doing?" Ray asked.

"Joe's fine, except he's engaged in some activity that takes precedence over our work here, and I'm not sure when he can return to help us. I explained some of our difficulties, including the reticence of Yakima PD to allow viewing of some of the evidence in the homicide. He said he would return as soon as he was able."

"That's good enough for me. Do you think he could use our help with his project in Mexico, Ross?" Jerry asked.

"He has plenty of help, I believe, and it's not something you'd want to be involved in, I suspect, Jerry."

"He's a brother law enforcement officer and if he needs help, it doesn't matter what it's about. All he has to do is ask."

"He knows that, I'm sure. So, how are things going on the Bustos murder investigation?"

"We just received a copy of a partial translation of the Bustos diary. They still refuse to let us view the water damaged diary in-person, but they have released some of the scanned text in Spanish. I hired a Spanish interpreter to translate the few pages we've been given. This is what we have so far. It's sad, reading the words of this troubled young lady," Jerry explained.

Bustos Diary

Page 307
12-3-98

Today is Thursday, and it's my second day here at Mom's house. Yesterday I spoke with her and asked her if I could be here again, and she let me. And yesterday Raúl brought me here and thank God that I am here. Today I was with Mom all day and I went with Ruby to the mall, and she bought a lot of clothes. But before that my friend the police officer came here, and he was here at the house. He was here talking to me and Ruby. He was here for a while and then he left. And well, he's a good friend. I then helped mom make enchiladas, and I invited Juan and according to him, he was going to come around 4 PM. I called him, and until now he has not called. It's 7:50 PM and he hasn't even called me. I have called his beeper two times, and he hasn't called back. But oh well, it's up to him. I'm alone right now. Mom went out with Raúl to the store, and Chava went with Zito and Nacho. I was left alone. I've been calling him, and he hasn't called back. But hey, he told me that he was going to call me. Let's see what time he decides to call me. I'm going to call him again.

12-04-98

Today is the third day here and my mom told me, "You better be writing good things, otherwise all that will go to waste and I need to see that it is good. So, changing the subject, last night Juan called me supposedly from his friend's. He went to go watch the ball game and bet money. That's why he didn't come, and I called him later and he didn't call me. Today I'm not going to _____ his house and...

Page 308

He told me, "That it was lies and if I believed what Ramón. Juan told me, "Then that's on you. You must not love me anymore." I told him that I did. But that I noticed that he was very different, and he that he prefers his friends and his ball game. Raul is going to go get him right now, and he's going to bring him to my house. Raúl is going to bring the movie and I'm going to watch it with Juan.

12-6-98

It's 4:00 PM, and I got up at 3:00 PM and I started cleaning the bathroom, the kitchen, the living room. I called Juan three times, and he didn't answer me. I then took a bath. I just called my friend, the police officer, and I'm here alone. I'm going to wait to see if Juan calls me. I'm listening to Juan's cassette and I'm thinking of Juan. My mom scolded me and told me to start reading the Bible. She then brought up Juan and said that I'm the dumb one for sitting here thinking about Juan. And he's out there with another female. She said she was not surprised by what Juan does, but by me allowing it. Because I invited him, and he went out and was dancing with another female. And I'm the dumb one. But oh well, let's see if he comes later or calls me. But I doubt that he will come.

Page 309

_____and I feel comfortable with him. Right now, I'm watching the video of her graduation with Ruby and Miguel. Let's see if Juan calls me. If not, I'll call him after a while.

12-8-98

It's now 4:00 PM, and I've already called Juanito. Let's see what time he will call me. Today I bit my tongue, and I got a big bruise. I can't eat because it hurts, but I finally was able to eat something. My dad liked what mom made and said it was good. Well, I've already taken a bath. Let's see when Juanito is coming for me. I hope he comes to see me. I asked the Lord Jesus for his help, because I don't feel good without using drugs. Well, I know that the Lord is going to do something great in my life because I already feel different. I'm going to call him, but the phone is disconnected. I'm going to call my friend, the police officer. I left him a message so he can call me back. Well, I hope he calls me because I want to ask him to see if he can help me go to treatment. Let's see what Juanito tells me. He is my love. I love him very much. That's why I want to live with you, my handsome daddy. He is my love. I want him to love me, and always think about me, just as I think about him every moment that passes. You are in my thoughts.

Page 310
12-8-98, 10:43 am

Ruby, I'm going to call my friend the police officer. Let's see if he will call me. I left him a message telling him that I'm very sick. I'm going to tell him that I've been having seizures since yesterday, and today, too. My mom is taking care of me. She knows that I am no longer using drugs, and that is why they I have the seizures. Because when I use them, they don't happen. When I stop using drugs, I get the seizures. But no one told me, "Go use drugs, Sara." I went all on my own with my friends. I give thanks to my mother that allowed me to be in her house and I'm going to behave. Thank God for all his help. I already ate, it's 11:00 AM, and they already called Ruby to go to work. She is going to take me to the Welfare office, and she's going to drop me off there. I will then come back on the bus. I think that, if I go, I'm going to come on the bus. If not, tomorrow I'll go early.

Well, maybe it's better if I go tomorrow. It's 1:48 PM, and I arrived a while ago from the Welfare office. I met such a lovely little old lady and her son who is of older. They invited me to eat at Salsita's. Right now, I'm looking at them through the window. She is 81 years old. She is the cutest little old lady I have ever seen. They were such good people to me. I introduced them to my mother and told them that I was having seizures and that they had taken ____ away from me. Mom showed them who ___ was and the little old lady said look, he looks like you. I thanked her, and she said, "God bless you, Sarita." I told her the same thing, and they went to wait for the bus. I have seen that little old lady and her son before, but she has always been talkative with all the other people. I thank God because she is still able to breathe. She told me that she has her own house, and she has 14 children, and they are all…

Page 311

…teachers and they have everything. But that when her husband left her, she didn't look for another man and that her children never saw her walk around them, prancing another man in their face. I felt some kind of way to hear that from her. I went with them to Salsitas. I am forgetting something very important when I went to eat at Salsitas. My friend, the police officer, came. He came to talk to me because I left him a message that I had been having seizures for the past three days. And that I had been having them often. It's 2:50 PM, and the little old lady just got on the bus. The bus left with her on it. God be with her and take care of her, help her and don't leave her for a second. She is yours and keep her son in your arms, too. I'm going to call my friend, the police officer, and I'm going to leave him a message. I called him and left a message. I spoke to the pastor's wife, and she told me to go to the doctor, to get more pills for the seizers. It's 2:35 PM, and I'm done throwing out the trash, and I'm done washing dishes again. I'm going to look for a ride to go to the hospital. I'm going to call Yesenia, but her car is not running. My friend, the police officer,

called me, but I was on the phone with Yesenia, and he hung up on me. And I called him again to see if my handsome little friend would call me again, since Juan didn't pay me any attention. I'm dying and he doesn't care to know anything about me. The lovely little old lady is gone. I want to continue seeing her and talking to her. God be with her and take care of her and her son. Also, be in her hands, help her in whatever she does (Amen). God, I also ask you for my Juanito that you be by his side in the good times and the bad. Be with him to help him move forward. Juanito, I want you to remember that I, Sara, love you very much, daddy. And the memories of you and ____ , although you are not with me, but your memories

page 312
12-9-98

Live in my thoughts. God is going to grant me the miracle of having him with me, because nothing is impossible for God. And he's going to help me get him back. Me, his mother, Sara, and his father, Juan Gutiérrez. I thank God because right now I am with my mom. I have done so many things to Mom and I do them over again and she forgives me. I know that ____ will forgive me for leaving him with his aunt for a while. And I ask you, God, to help me. Mom's cousin came over. Well, my aunt. She looked at my tongue and told her that I needed to go to the hospital. Megan called me and said that neither Juan nor I went to court. She said that they spoke with him and for me to call her at 3:16 PM. A friend invited me to go swimming, my friend, the policeman, and he asked me, "If I missed him?" I said, "Yes," and told him, "I'll let you bathe. When you're done, I'll call you." He said yes because he asked my permission, and he said OK. Well, I must look for a ride now, because my tongue hurts. Lourdes called me and told me not to go to Megan and ask her about the pills. And that Juan spoke to —– and told her that he was not going to sign any papers regarding —-. Lourdes said that it would be something ugly to take away the child from — – after they have raised him.

I recognize that they have taken good care of my little cute chubby. And that Enrique's parents can't live without little chubby ——. But I thank God because — – and — – have my baby and they take good care of him, thank God. I called to Nuni, but I didn't find her, and left her a message. Mom's cousin is going to take me to the clinic right now. It's 4:00 PM, and Mom's cousin Teresa is going to take me to the clinic right now. I thought…

Page 313

…we were on the 8th and today is the 9^h. Thank God for this day. It's 4:56 PM. I just got home from the clinic and Mom's cousin brought me. I was prescribed the medicine. And I'm going to go get her, and they told me too that I needed to shape up. So that's what I'm going to do. Well, now I'm going to behave. It's 5:35 PM, and I gave them Raúl Juan's address too, because they say they're going to give him a good lesson and even give him some of my medicine. At 6:30 PM, I'm going to go to church, but first I want to talk to Juan. Let's see what he's doing, and I told Ruby that my friend, the police officer, had come over, and she got angry with him. She doesn't like him. The truth is that this happened to me because I said something. It's 6:15 PM. I spoke to Juan, and he had the music at full volume. And I asked Juan, "What are you doing, dummy?" He told me, "I'm doing chores." I told him. "You know Juan, it's better that you do not call me anymore." And he said, "OK, if that's what you want." Then we hung up. And that's how we left it. That's because in the end I prefer to be alone than know that Juan is reluctantly hanging on me in a bad way. But hey, he didn't want to talk to me. I'd better go to church instead of thinking about things I don't know. Gaby wants me to go to church, she wants to talk to me. And well, I would rather talk to her and not be here at home. And right now, I'm going to talk to my friend, Ernesto. He talks to me in a good way and doesn't leave me on the line or on the phone, like an idiot, as always. Well, at 6 PM, I'm going to church to pray to God for all of us and for me.

Page 314

I make such a fuss. The policeman is going to give me a ride over to visit Juan. I'm going to go. I'm just waiting for the policeman, my ride. Well, I'm going to go see Juanito and see what's going on. It's 9:30 PM, and I just arrived. I went to where Zeterino was and then I called Juan from there. Nacho brought me. It's 10:00 PM, and Juan was supposed to call me, but hasn't called me. He just has me waiting like this. And he asked me if I want to have his thing. Well, I'm here at home and that's what I've been wanting for a while, to come home and thank God I'm here. I'm going to go to bed. It's already 10 PM, and as they say, let's go to sleep. Hopefully tomorrow is another day that God will let me live. I didn't have a very good day today, but I enjoyed it because I know that God won't abandon me. Well, just now I called Juan's beeper, and I called him at home. He answered and told me nice things. He told me that he loves me very much; he sent me a kiss, and I sent one back. And I told him that I love him very much. And I'm going to make my bed and go to sleep, because tomorrow he's going to call me on the phone from work. I hope it's true and my cute sweetie calls me. It's already 10:58 PM, and I've already gone to bed. And well, it's time to go to sleep. What else is there? Today when they gave me those candies, they weren't anything, because I didn't even feel anything, but oh well.

Page 315

I'm writing down scriptures and I'm here having a good time with her. I drew Adam and my mom saw the heart I drew, and I put Raúl in it. She told me that it was supposed to be the heart of God and not to put anyone in it. Well, I must take the application to the welfare office, and I haven't taken it. I must go run my errands. It's 11:00 AM, and my mom gave me $3.00 and told me to go to the welfare office to take the applications. So, I'm going to get ready to go right away. Today I am sending a letter to Alma to find out how my baby — — is doing. I already got dressed. Candy is coming over right now, and my mom is making something to eat. I felt like I was going to have a seizure. Candy prayed for me, and it didn't happen. And I told my mom that they were hiring someone to make tortillas there at Salsita's, and she and Candy were going to go get an application. I want to go but if a seizure happened there, it won't be good. I called Ken; I left him a message to see if my little white boy would call me. I called him a while ago and a friend of his answered. He told me that he had gone on vacation. And let's see if he calls me back. I dialed Juanito's beeper at 12:10 AM. Let's see if my little cutie will call me back. It's 12:00 PM. 15 till 1:00 PM, my little cutie was just leaving to go to work, and he told me that if I could get him a ride he would come, but if not, then he would come early tomorrow but…

Page 316
12-11-98

…I told him no. It's 2:15 PM, and my friend, the police officer, called me and invited me to his house. He gave me his address to go to his house right now. But Candy is here right now and I'm watching a video with her. Gaby is going to come pick up Candy right now and they're going to leave me at the welfare office. I'm going to leave my application that I filled out yesterday. Let's see what they tell me later. It's 3:15 PM, and today I'm with Mom and Candy watching a Christian video on the TV. And he is preaching beautifully, and I like how he preaches. Well, right now I'm going to go to the welfare office with Gaby and Candy to see how it goes. I hope I don't think about anything else or about drugs. I just need to do what I'm going to do and come back without thinking about bad things or thinking about using drugs, because I haven't used them. I feel good and I don't want to use them again. Because that's how it starts, with just one time and then I don't stop. It's 15 until 5:00 PM and I just arrived 15 minutes ago. I went to the welfare office, but I must return tomorrow. I must wait a while for them to give me help. Raul arrived 15 minutes till 5:00 PM and brought some meat for his girlfriend, and the girlfriend was in the room talking to her lover. Raul was angry. My mom is going to go with Raul to church. I'm going to stay and then I'm going to call Juanito. I dialed Juan again at 5:00 PM to see if my little cutie would call me. Well, Juanito, my love, I love you, darling. Nacho went out right now.

Page 317
4-10-99

Today it's the 10th, it's 5:00 PM, and I'm here with mom. Yesterday something very ugly happened to me that God made me witness. The day before yesterday I was giving drugs to a little old man. I had used more than a 16 and God made me see him as my grandfather and then I regretted everything I did. I thank God I ran from there to my mother's house. And my mom opened the door for me and laid down with me on the couch. I asked her for forgiveness and then I talked to Ruby. She didn't pay attention to me and then my mom forgave me and so did God. I thank God for everything he did for me. Well, right now it's 6:00 PM, 5 until 6:00 PM, and I would like to receive Juanito's letter. I want to know how he is. When my little cutie writes to me, I'm going to tell him this. When he gets here, I'm going to kiss him and hug him and tell him many nice things. Well, God, thank you for your help. I want to go to the altar and testify what God has done for me, and how he helped me, and tell what I told my mother, and my mother knows what I said. Well, now I'm going to see which friend wants to go to Jesus's and ask for money, and go buy a 16th, but at the same time, I don't because God is going to help me. And I know that by doing good things, God helps me even more. Thank you, God, I pray for Juanito and —–, that you are with them, and that you make me see some other things so that I won't be the same person. I know that you, God, are the one to…

Page 318 is a duplicate of page 317
Page 319

…make me do everything good. Amen. Well, it's 6:15 PM, and

here I am at the house with mom, Lourdes, and Chava. I'm here and Lourdes is talking about —, my son and mom are talking to Lourdes, and mom is here. Well, I am here with mom and the phone's ringing. I can't answer it. No one calls me. I called my friend, the policeman.

It's 11:00 AM, and today it is April 11th. I talked to Alma, and she told me, "Sara, have you already asked Juan for the address in Mexico?" I told her no. Just in case they send me to Mexico and the truth is, that is what I'm going to do, honestly. Because I know they are going to send me to Mexico. Because yesterday Zito came and threatened to kill me. Lourdes told him that if something happened to me, she would be a witness for the police. Well, the truth is my family already knows what Zito told me. And well, God knows what the truth is. I didn't break into Ofelia's house. But they still blamed me. Anyway, only God knows. God, I hope Juan has received my letter, and he will answer me soon, Lord Jesus. Because I want to ask him for the correct address in Mexico. The best thing to do is to write a letter to Juan and…

"This is what we have up to this point. I'm waiting on YPD for another installment of the diary," Jerry explained.

"Who is Zito?" Ray asked.

"Detectives eliminated him as a suspect. The last part of December 1998, all of January, February, March, and part of April 1999, is missing from the pages of the diary we've received thus far. Remember, Sara Bustos was murdered in September 1999, and her activities with other people prior to her murder are especially important. Let's see what she has to say in the translated portions we've recovered about Yakima Police Officer Kensley Twindler, whom she described as 'my friend, the police officer.' She later identifies him as 'Ken' in her December 11th entry, and since there are no other Yakima police officers named 'Ken,' we believe Sara is referring to Yakima Police Officer Kensley Twindler," Jerry explained.

- December 3rd, 1998, the 'police officer' went to Sara's home and talked to her and Ruby. She described him as a 'good friend.'

- December 6th, 1998, Sara called her boyfriend, Juan, three times and when he didn't respond, she called her 'friend the police officer' while she was alone.

- December 8th, 1998, 10:43 AM, Sara said she called her friend, the police officer, and left a message.

- December 8th, 1998, 4 PM, Sara was having withdrawal symptoms and called her friend, the police officer, and left a message because she wanted to go to treatment and mentioned that she was having seizures. She said he came by and talked to her. Later, she said the police officer called her but hung up because she was on the phone with Yesenia. She then said, "And I called him again to see if my handsome little friend will call me again, since Juan doesn't pay me any attention."

- December 9th, 1998, there was some discussion about her friend, the policeman, inviting her to go swimming and during this conversation, it appears the policeman asked Sara if she missed him. It seems strange that Twindler would ask Sara if she missed him since he'd stopped by to see her the day before. The invitation could be explained by her being invited to the policeman's residence to go swimming. This conversation could add to the evidence Officer Twindler and Sara Bustos were in an intimate relationship. Did he invite her to go swimming at the place where she was later murdered?

- December 9th, 1998, Sara said she told Ruby that her friend, the police officer, had come over and Ruby got angry with the officer because she didn't like him. Sara then said this happens because she (Sara) said something. Sara didn't explain further, but Ruby may know.

- December 9th, 1998, 9:30 PM, Sara said she was waiting for the policeman to give her a ride over to visit her boyfriend, Juan.

- December 10th, 1998, Sara was worried about having seizures from withdrawal when she called 'Ken,' whom she named in the diary and left him a message. She called him a 'little white boy' and said when she called him a while ago, his friend answered and said he was on vacation. She said she waited to see if he would call her back.

- December 11th, 1998, 2:15 PM, Sara said her friend, the police officer, called her back and gave her his home address and invited her to his house.

- April 11th, 1999, Sara said, 'I called my friend the policeman.' This is the last entry we have so far, prior to Sara's murder, on September 17th, 1999.

"When you add up the number of contacts between Sara and Officer Kensley Twindler during the short period of time as noted in the diary, I would say Sara and Officer Twindler were involved in an intimate relationship," Ray commented.

"I agree. We can assume that was the case, especially taking into account the personal notations and sharing of the officer's home address. There's something else that is interesting," Jerry said.

"What's that?"

"It appears Sara attempted contact with Officer Twindler during times when she was dope-sick, and my guess is there's a reason. Is it possible Twindler was giving her money to buy drugs when she was in withdrawal? If so, was there a quid pro quo for sex?" Jerry asked.

"Do you think it's also possible Officer Twindler was using Sara as a confidential informant? Giving her money from a snitch fund for information is not uncommon," Ray explained.

"That's correct, Ray, and there should be records showing any payments to Sara from Officer Twindler. Remember, Twindler was either working in the uniform patrol division or he was assigned to the traffic squad. Working confidential informants was not part of his assignments and would have probably been beyond his authority. I would like to talk to Deputy Chief Twindler myself, to see what he has to say," Jerry responded.

"We've both got the itch to move on this case to see what evidence is available and prepare to press charges, but that's not what Ross Manzola hired us to do, was it?" Ray asked.

"You're right. Our task is to assess each case to see if it can be investigated further and, if possible, which direction to take each investigation. We need to start preparing an in-depth assessment of the cases now, but without Joe Creed's involvement thus far, I'm wondering where we go next. We need to bring Ross up to date on our work," Jerry suggested.

Ray got up and went to the office door and looked around the corner and said, "Hey Monica, is Ross busy at the moment?"

"He's with a client now, but I'll give him a phone call to see if he'll be free soon, if you wish."

"Yes, please, Monica."

"Ray, Ross says he'll be out in a minute. He has someone he wants you to meet," Monica explained as she hung up the office phone.

24.
THE RENDITION

Jerry and Ray were at their desks when Ross walked into the office with someone following him.

"I think you've met Donna Ashford before," Ross said as they approached.

Donna smiled slightly as she looked Ray and Jerry over. She appeared much rougher than before, with a bandage over her left eye, her left arm in a sling, and scratch marks on her face. Her spiked haircut was much longer, and shaggy, with some streaks of gray. She was wearing black cargo pants, a Mariner's baseball team T-shirt, motorcycle boots, and a jean jacket.

"What's up?" she asked as she nodded.

Ross explained, "It's been more than a month since I met with Joe Creed in Mexico. At that time, Joe was preparing for a confidential mission organized by the Central Intelligence Agency. Donna was part of the crew, along with others, in a rendition attempt to capture Karter Truman, also known as Pedro Escobar, the heir to Pablo Escobar's drug empire. She spent the last several months working with Joe Creed and some other folks on a mission to the country of Colombia, where Truman was hiding. She has quite a story to tell about the mission and when she's finished, she's agreed to maybe answer some of your questions."

"Welcome, Donna. Would you like a cup of coffee?" Ray asked.

"No, thanks."

"Are you still wanted by Interpol?" Jerry asked, looking her in the eye.

"We can get into that after she shares her story. Donna, please go ahead," Ross responded.

"Ok, I've known Joe Creed for some time. I worked with him and Casey Abbot from the CIA on the Mexican border, resulting in a big mess when I was a DEA agent. Joe used to be a cop, and later an international insurance investigator with arrest commissions from Mexico and some other third world countries. The agency director decided Karter Truman was becoming too much of a successful narcotics distributor and threat to border security. Plans were made to have him spirited out of Colombia and brought to stand trial in the United States. Joe Creed is personally familiar with Karter Truman, a.k.a. Pedro Escobar, and was therefore asked to join the mission, along with Capitan Veronica Sabroso of the Mexican Navy, her husband and Vietnam veteran, Sniffer, and me, along with others. Our mission was simple: find and capture Karter Truman, serve the Interpol warrant, and bring him back to the United States to stand trial. It was a little tricky because Truman was hiding behind Colombia's armed forces while there was an outstanding Interpol warrant for me, and another was subsequently issued for Joe Creed. This is what happened as I understand it," Donna said as she raised her right hand and ran three fingers through her hair.

"After Joe and his wife were attacked, Joe contacted Casey Abbot about putting a stop to Karter Truman. Truman was a county prosecutor who went rogue. He was in league with drug cartel leaders and mafia bosses while acting as a prosecutor. When they tried to arrest him, he ran to Mexico, and then to Colombia, connecting with the Escobar cartel. He took over the cartel when the leader, Pablo, was killed, and since then, while managing the drug business he has launched attacks against Joe and his family.

Joe, Casey, a guy named Snake, Veronica from the Mexican Navy, numerous others, and me all worked on a previous mission at the Mexican border against the same cartel. A lot of people died on that mission, including Snake, the Vietnam tunnel rat soldier.

"So, Supervising Agent Casey Igor Abbott, the CIA, along with Joe, and other agency assets, put a rendition plan together to capture Karter Truman, and return him to face justice in the U.S. The mission roster included Casey as the field supervising agent, Joe Creed who can positively identify Karter Truman (a.k.a. Pedro Escobar), Captain Veronica Sabroso from the Mexican Navy, her husband and former Vietnam tunnel rat soldier, Sniffer. Don't ask me what Sniffer's real name is because I only knew him as Sniffer. There also was this new guy named Junior, an athletic and smart young man, but very weird. He is the son of Snake, the tunnel rat who was killed during the border mission. And then there were the rebel soldiers in Colombia whose mission was to attack the cartel compound and provide a distraction for us to capture Truman. We traveled to Colombia on Joe Creed's specially outfitted sailboat, Hannah. The boat provided us with a command post to coordinate the attack while it was anchored offshore. The sailboat was outfitted with every kind of electronic equipment imaginable for communications with the rebels, our team, and for monitoring mission activities. We even had live contact with Washington, DC.

"The ranch-compound where Karter Truman lived was about 15 miles east of Buenaventura, Colombia. The property was surrounded by jungle near the river Danubio, and included a large main residence, a smaller home plus several outbuildings, all of which were protected by tall metal fencing which was electrified. The entire property was 80 hectares, or about 200 acres in size. There was a tunnel that led from the main residence to a secret underground bomb shelter structure situated about 100 yards north of the residence. The

Escobar family sought protection in the shelter when there was a conflict or when the compound was attacked. There was a second entrance, or escape hatch, at the north end the underground shelter.

"The plan was for Junior to be dropped off by dinghy on the banks of the Danubio to reconnoiter the compound on foot. It was about a ten-mile hike for him, and he was to report via radio what was taking place at the Escobar compound. He was prepared to watch the place for a month, if necessary. A man fitting Karter Truman's description was spotted by Junior outside the main residence two days later, so a plan was launched for the rebels to attack from the south the next morning, at daylight. Meanwhile, Joe and I made our way to the underground shelter's escape hatch with Junior's help. We opened it and waited inside the shelter for Karter Truman to arrive."

"Where was Veronica and Sniffer during this time?" Ray asked.

"Veronica and Sniffer were backups to Joe and me. They followed us to the shelter entrance and stood by in case we ran into trouble. Casey remained on the sailboat and coordinated the assault by radio and kept everyone updated."

"What happened next?" Jerry asked as Donna took a small, rectangular metal box out of her pocket and began to open it.

"This is Karter Truman," she exclaimed with a smile as she opened the box, revealing a shriveled human finger.

"Oh, my God!" Ross replied.

"I sent a piece to the lab in Washington, DC, for a DNA analysis to verify its owner," Donna explained.

"So, Karter Truman is dead, is that correct?" Ray asked, as Donna stuck the box back in her pocket.

"Do I have the right to remain silent?" Donna asked. "I'll let Joe Creed tell the rest of the story when he returns," she added with a smile.

"One thing I can tell you is that this finger bone will be added to my necklace soon," Donna announced as she sat down.

"Donna will be staying in an upstairs bedroom and her motorcycle is stored in the old garage out back until I can get the Interpol warrants for Joe and her quashed," Ross explained.

"Where's Joe?" Jerry asked.

"He should be returning soon, but I want to keep his whereabouts low key until the warrants are resolved," Ross explained.

"We have more work to do on these cases before we're ready to submit them to you for your appraisal, Ross," Ray explained.

"Good, and when Joe returns, we can include him in the final dispositions of the four cases," Ross added, as he and Donna got up to leave.

"We want to consider some of the following investigative tools that may be used to further resolve the four cases," Jerry explained.

25.
CIVIL ACTIONS

Ray declared, "Wikipedia defines a lawsuit as… *A proceeding by one or more parties (the plaintiff or claimant) against one or more parties (the defendant) in a civil court of law… The term «lawsuit» is used with respect to a civil action brought by a plaintiff (a party who claims to have incurred loss as a result of a defendant›s actions) who requests a legal remedy or equitable remedy from a court. The defendant is required to respond to the plaintiff's complaint or else risk default judgment. If the plaintiff is successful, judgment is entered in favor of the plaintiff, and the Court may impose the legal and/or equitable remedies available against the defendant (respondent). A variety of court orders may be issued in connection with or as part of the judgment to enforce a right, award damages or restitution, or impose a temporary or permanent injunction to prevent an act or compel an act. A declaratory judgment may be issued to prevent future legal disputes…*

"It is likewise important that the plaintiff select the proper venue with the proper jurisdiction to bring the lawsuit. The clerk of a court signs or stamps the court seal upon a summons or citation, which is then served by the plaintiff upon the defendant, together with a copy of the complaint. This service notifies the defendants that they are being sued and that they are limited in the amount of time to reply. The service provides a copy of the complaint in order to notify the defendants of the nature of the claims. Once the defendants are served with the summons and complaint, they are subject to a time limit to file an answer stating their defenses to the plaintiff's claims, which includes any challenges to the court›s jurisdiction, and any counterclaims they wish to assert against the plaintiff…

"A pretrial discovery can be defined as 'the formal process of exchanging information between the parties about the witnesses and evidence they'll present at trial' and allows for the evidence of the trial to be presented to the parties before the initial trial begins. The early stages of the lawsuit may involve initial disclosures of evidence by each party and discovery, which is the structured exchange of evidence and statements between the parties. Discovery is meant to eliminate surprises, clarify what the lawsuit is about, and also to make the parties decide if they should settle or drop frivolous claims or defenses. At this point, the parties may also engage in pretrial motions to exclude or include particular legal or factual issues before trial.

"There is also the ability of one to make an under-oath statement during the pretrial, also known as a deposition. The deposition can be used in the trial or just in the pretrial, but this allows for both parties to be aware of the arguments or claims that are going to be made by the other party in the trial. It is notable that the depositions can be written or oral.

"At the close of discovery, the parties may either pick a jury and then have a jury, or the case may proceed as a bench trial. A bench trial is only heard by the judge if the parties waive a jury trial or if the right to a jury trial is not guaranteed for their particular claim (such as those under equity in the U.S.) or for any lawsuits within their jurisdiction…

"A deposition in the law of the United States, or examination for discovery in the law of Canada, involves the taking of sworn, out-of-court oral testimony of a witness that may be reduced to a written transcript for later use in court or for discovery purposes. Depositions are commonly used in litigation in the United States and Canada. They are almost always conducted outside court by the lawyers themselves, with no judge present to supervise the examination…

"The person to be deposed (questioned) at a deposition, known as the deponent, is usually notified to appear at the appropriate time and place by means of a subpoena. Frequently, the most desired witness (the deponent) is an opposite party to the action. In that instance, legal notice may be given to that person›s attorney, and a subpoena is not required. But if the witness is not a party to the lawsuit (a third party) or is reluctant to testify, then a subpoena must be served on that party. To ensure an accurate record of statements made during a deposition, a court reporter is present and typically transcribes the deposition by digital recording or stenographic means. Depending upon the amount in controversy and the ability of the witness to appear at trial, audio or video recordings of the deposition are sometimes taken as well.

"Conduct of depositions

"Depositions usually take place at the office of the court reporter or in the office of one of the law firms involved in a case. However, depositions are also sometimes taken at a witness's workplace or home, or in a nearby hotel's conference room. Generally, the deposition is attended by the person who is to be deposed, their attorney, court reporter, and other parties in the case who can appear personally or be represented by their counsels. Any party to the action and their attorneys have the right to be present and to ask questions.

"Prior to taking a deposition, the court reporter administers the same oath or affirmation that the deponent would take if the testimony were being given in court in front of a judge and jury. Thereafter, the court reporter makes a verbatim digital or stenographic record of all that is said during the deposition, in the same manner that witness testimony is recorded in court. Some jurisdictions allow steno mask technology in lieu of traditional stenographic equipment, although many jurisdictions still prohibit steno mask because of its disconcerting effect on some lawyers and witnesses.

"Attorneys for the deposing litigant are often present, although this is not required in all jurisdictions. The attorney who has ordered the deposition begins questioning of the deponent (this is referred to as "direct examination" or "direct" for short). Since nods and gestures cannot be recorded, the witness is instructed to answer all questions aloud. After the direct examination, other attorneys in attendance have an opportunity to cross-examine the witness. The first attorney may ask more questions at the end, in re-direct, which may be followed by re-cross.

"During the course of the deposition, one attorney or another may object to questions asked. In most jurisdictions, only two types of objections are allowed: The first is to assert a privilege and the second is to object to the form of the question asked. Objections to form are frequently used to signal the witness to be careful in answering the question. Since the judge is not present, all other objections, in particular those involving the rules of evidence, are generally preserved until trial. They still can be made sometime at the deposition to indicate the serious problem to judge and witness, but the witness must answer the question despite these objections. If the form objection is made, the opposite party still has the right to re-phrase the same question and ask it again. Indeed, in Texas, lawyers were so aggressively using objections to indirectly coach their witnesses on the record that all objections outside four narrow categories are now prohibited and making such prohibited objections waives all objections to the question or answer at issue. California is the major "outlier" on deposition objections; under the California Civil Discovery Act as enacted in 1957 and heavily revised in 1986, most objections must be given on the record at the deposition (and must be specific as to the objectionable nature of the question or response) or they are permanently waived.

"As with oral examination at trial, depositions can become heated at times, with some attorneys asking harassing questions to provoke witnesses into losing their tempers, some witnesses giving evasive answers, and occasional use of profane language. In *extreme situations, one side or the other may ask the reporter to mark the record, then may suspend the deposition, demand a rush transcript, and file an emergency motion to compel a response, for a protective order, or for sanctions. Some courts have magistrates or discovery commissioners who are on call for such contingencies, and the parties are supposed to use them to referee such disputes over the telephone or via email before resorting to filing motions. In extreme circumstances where the relationship between the lawyers, parties, or witnesses has totally broken down, the court may require the use of a discovery referee who will have authority to sit in on depositions and rule immediately on objections as they are presented, may order that all further depositions take place in court in the presence of a judge, or may grant terminating sanctions if the record is already clear as to which party or attorney is responsible for the breakdown in civility.*

"The point in this civil action information is that it can uncover evidence which can later be presented in a criminal trial. The depositions taken under oath from witnesses are transcribed and become part of the official record. Witnesses will have a difficult time if they refuse to respond to a subpoena demanding they be deposed. If a person refuses a subpoena, they can be found in contempt of court and a warrant can be issued for their arrest. It's possible for a person to refuse to answer questions during a deposition by citing the fifth amendment to the Constitution. However, refusing to answer questions because they might incriminate themselves would be a red flag in an investigation. Information received from depositions under oath can be presented later in a criminal trial and can be incriminating enough to garner a guilty verdict. We need to keep this in mind as a possibility for one or more of the cases we've reviewed," Ray explained.

26.

SPECIAL INQUIRY JUDGE

"This is another possible tool that can be used to inquire into criminal activity when traditional methods have been unsuccessful. Here's a copy of the Revised Code of Washington State or RCW," Jerry explained.

RCW 10.29.050 Powers and duties of statewide special inquiry judge. A statewide special inquiry judge shall have the following powers and duties: (1) To hear and receive evidence of crime and corruption. (2) To appoint a reporter to record the proceedings; and to swear the reporter not to disclose any testimony or the name of any witness except as provided in RCW 10.27.090. (3) Whenever necessary, to appoint an interpreter, and to swear him or her not to disclose any testimony or the name of any witness except as provided in RCW 10.27.090. (4) When a person held in official custody is a witness before a statewide special inquiry judge, a public servant, assigned to guard him or her during his or her appearance, may accompany him or her. The statewide special inquiry judge shall swear such public servant not to disclose any testimony or the name of any witness except as provided in RCW 10.27.090. (5) To cause to be called as a witness any person believed by him or her to possess relevant information or knowledge. If the statewide special inquiry judge desires to hear any such witness who was not called by the special prosecutor, it may direct the special prosecutor to issue and serve a subpoena upon such witness and the special prosecutor must comply with such direction. At any time after service of such subpoena and before the return date thereof, however, the special prosecutor may apply to the statewide special inquiry judge for an order vacating or modifying the subpoena on the grounds that such is in the public interest. Upon such application, the statewide special inquiry judge may in its discretion vacate the subpoena, extend its return date, attach reasonable conditions to directions, or make such other qualification thereof as is appropriate. (6) Upon a showing of good cause may make available any or all evidence obtained to any other public attorney, prosecuting attorney, city attorney, or corporation counsel upon proper application and with the concurrence of the special prosecutor. Any witness' testimony, given before a statewide special inquiry judge and relevant to any subsequent proceeding against the witness, shall be made available to the witness upon proper application to the statewide special inquiry judge. The statewide special inquiry judge may also, upon proper application and upon a showing of good cause, make available to a defendant in a subsequent criminal proceeding other testimony or evidence when given or presented before a special inquiry judge, if doing so is in the furtherance of justice. (7) Have authority to perform such other duties as may be required to effectively implement this chapter, in accord with rules adopted by the supreme court relating to these proceedings. (8) Have authority to hold in contempt of court any person who shall disclose the name or testimony of a witness examined before a statewide special inquiry judge except when required by a court to disclose the testimony given before such statewide special inquiry judge in a subsequent criminal proceeding.

"The following is a quote from a document issued by the Washington State Association of Prosecuting Attorneys," Jerry added.

Washington's Special Inquiry Judge Proceeding was established by the legislature in 1971 and has been in statewide use since that time. Akin to Grand Jury Proceedings, which have been in broad national use since this country was established, the Special Inquiry Judge Proceeding, or "SIJ Proceeding" enables a judge to issue subpoenas, order the production of records, or take other action as the court deems justified to allow a prosecutor to investigate suspected crime or corruption. Like the Grand Jury, Special Inquiry Judge Proceedings are confidential and used only during investigations; they cannot be used after criminal charges have been filed. Also, like Grand Jury Proceedings, SIJ proceedings gather evidence based upon a lower standard than probable cause, in this case, "reason to suspect" crime or corruption within the court's jurisdiction. This term is not defined in the statute or case law, but may be interpreted by our courts as roughly equivalent to a Terry stop standard (articulable suspicion). In a Special Inquiry Proceeding, the Special Inquiry Judge may, upon determining that the standard has been met, issue subpoenas for records and testimony to obtain evidence in furtherance of the investigation. While a prosecutor may seek to initiate an SIJ proceeding, the prosecutor must first convince the Special Inquiry Judge of the basis for it. The Special Inquiry Judge then presides over each step of the SIJ proceedings. Both Special Inquiry and Grand Jury proceedings are intended to be confidential proceedings. Confidentiality is necessary, in some criminal investigations, to protect the safety interests of the public, and the integrity and effectiveness of the investigation. Many prospective investigative options would be foreclosed if the information related to and received by the Special Inquiry Judge were to be prematurely made public. Confidentiality is also frequently necessary to protect the safety of witnesses and/or victims, as well as to protect those who are wrongly suspected of crime or corruption and therefore never charged with any criminal activity. Washington's SIJ Proceedings are less expensive and more flexible than Grand Jury Proceedings. The SIJ model created by our legislature has numerous advantages that are not generally found in Grand Jury Proceedings: First, an elected Superior Court Judge(selected by his or her fellow judges) participates in the proceeding. Second, SIJ subpoenas are issued by the elected SIJ Judge, who is familiar with the investigation for which the subpoenas are issued. Third, the SIJ Judge presides over the taking of witness testimony. Fourth, the SIJ proceeding avoids the public costs that would be inherent in convening a Grand Jury. These savings include savings of public taxpayer dollars, as well as savings to business, industry, and individuals, because citizens are not being compelled to miss work to participate as Grand Jurors. In contrast, as a general rule, no judge actively participates in Grand Jury proceedings, reviews Grand Jury subpoenas before they are issued, or presides over the taking of witness testimony. Fifth, a Special Inquiry Judge is trained and experienced in the law as well as in sitting as a neutral and detached magistrate, whereas any citizen can be called to sit as a Grand Juror. While a Special Inquiry Judge assures that the investigation is conducted fairly, the Judge does not issue indictments. A Grand Jury is empowered to call witnesses, issue grand jury reports, and issue indictments. Washington prosecutors have found Special Inquiry Judge Proceedings especially useful when sophisticated criminal activity is suspected, such as offenses involving public corruption (bribery, bid fixing, misappropriation), organized crime (gambling, theft, fencing, arson, vice, prostitution), and fraud (theft from the elderly, securities, real estate, insurance, inventory theft, false billing, embezzlement, identity theft). It is important to recognize that a Special Inquiry Judge Proceeding may not be used as a discovery tool against a defendant as to already charged crimes. The purpose of the SIJ Proceeding is to investigate suspected crime, not charged crime. Use of SIJ Proceedings to investigate charged crimes would not only be a violation of the statutes, but may also constitute interference with a defendant's constitutional right to a fair trial. Remedies for such violations include suppression of evidence and possibly dismissal of the charges. It should also be recognized that certain witnesses may acquire transactional immunity as a result of testifying before a Special Inquiry Judge and that witnesses testifying about public corruption may receive *immunity automatically (self-executing immunity). It is recommended that the prosecutor should request the initiation of SIJ Proceedings only where there is reason to believe that more traditional investigative techniques will not be effective, for example: When investigators lack the probable cause necessary to obtain a warrant for the sought evidence; where law enforcement is confronted with an uncooperative witness and needs to compel the witness to speak; or when investigating corruption or other crimes which require confidentiality while under investigation.*

27.
GRAND JURY INVESTIGATION

"Here's some information from the same source," Ray added.

The function of a grand jury is to accuse persons who may be guilty of a crime, but the institution is also a shield against unfounded and oppressive prosecution. It is a means for lay citizens, representative of the community, to participate in the administration of justice. It can also make presentments on crime and maladministration in its area. Traditionally, a grand jury consists of 23 members.

The mode of accusation is by a written statement of two types:

1. *in solemn form (indictment) describing the offense with proper accompaniments of time and circumstances, and certainty of act and person, or*

2. *by a less formal mode, which is usually the spontaneous act of the grand jury, called presentment.*

No indictment or presentment can be made except by concurrence of at least twelve of the jurors. The grand jury may accuse upon their own knowledge, but it is generally done upon the testimony of witnesses under oath and other evidence heard before them. Grand jury proceedings are, in the first instance, at the instigation of the government or other prosecutors, and ex parte and in secret deliberation. The accused has no knowledge nor right to interfere with their proceedings.

If they find the accusation true, which is usually drawn up in form by the prosecutor or an officer of the court, they write upon the indictment the words "a true bill" which is signed by the foreperson of the grand jury and presented to the court publicly in the presence of all the jurors. If the indictment is not proven to the satisfaction of the grand jury, the word ignoramus or «not a true bill» is written upon it by the grand jury, or by their foreman and then said to be ignored, and the accusation is dismissed as unfounded; the potential defendant is said to have been «no-billed» by the grand jury. If the grand jury returns an indictment as a true bill (billa vera), the indictment is said to be founded and the party to stand indicted and required to be put on trial.

"The following is a copy of the Revised Code of Washington State, or RCW," Ray explained.

RCW 10.27.030 Summoning grand jury. No grand jury shall be summoned to attend at the superior court of any county except upon an order signed by a majority of the judges thereof. A grand jury shall be summoned by the court, where the public interest so demands, whenever in its opinion there is sufficient evidence of criminal activity or corruption within the county or whenever so requested by a public attorney, corporation counsel or city attorney upon showing of good cause.

RCW 10.27.080 Persons authorized to attend—Restrictions on attorneys. No person shall be present at sessions of the grand jury or special inquiry judge except the witness under examination and his or her attorney, public attorneys, the reporter, an interpreter, a public servant guarding a witness who has been held in custody, if any, and, for the purposes provided for in RCW 10.27.170, any corporation counsel or city attorney. The attorney advising the witness shall only advise such witness concerning his or her right to answer or not answer any questions and the form of his or her answer and shall not otherwise engage in the proceedings. No person other than grand jurors shall be present while the grand jurors are deliberating or voting. Any person violating either of the above provisions may be held in contempt of court.

"It would be less expensive for Yakima County if a federal prosecutor initiated a federal grand jury investigation, since the costs would be borne by the federal government. The last time a federal grand jury investigation was launched in Yakima was in 1985, when the Yakima County Prosecutor had the Yakima County Sheriff's Office and elected Sheriff Dick Nesary investigated, resulting in the sheriff's resignation," Ray explained.

"How did he get the feds to open a grand jury investigation?" Jerry asked.

"According to reports back then, the prosecutor received information sheriff's patrol cars and uniform purchases were not being offered in a bidding process required by state law, so he contacted the FBI. That got the ball rolling. Once the grand jury probe was underway, it sought out and uncovered other illegal activities."

"Sort of like a fishing expedition?" Jerry asked.

"I suppose that may be true, since the men were political enemies. The sheriff had been investigating the prosecutor for corruption and it appears the prosecutor was intent on removing the Yakima County Sheriff for a more agreeable replacement. The grand jury investigation was the tool that caused the elected sheriff to tearfully resign."

28.
UNMARKED GRAVE LOCATION, LiDAR

"Here's a of couple articles about locating unmarked gravesites using a new technology called LiDAR," Ray responded.

"The first one is a short newspaper article about how the technology has been tested," Ray continued.

Using LiDAR to find unmarked graves of murder victims

by Bob Yirka, Phys.org
Credit: CC0 Public Domain

A team of researchers affiliated with several institutions in the U.S. reports that LiDAR can be used to find the unmarked graves of murder victims. In their paper published in the journal Forensic Science International, the group describes the technique and how well it worked.

Oftentimes, a murderer will seek to hide the body to avoid being caught and imprisoned. One well-known method of victim hiding is simply to bury the body in a remote location. This approach has proven effective in the long run, as nature will eventually hide evidence of digging—but not all the evidence, it seems. The researchers in this new effort noted that when a body is buried, it takes up a certain amount of room beneath the ground. But as the body decays, it takes up less room, causing the dirt above to settle. This slight bit of settling can look like a depression on the surface of the ground to the observant eye—though less so when covered by debris such as scattered leaves.

The researchers noted that LiDAR has proven to be quite effective at mapping terrain—one example was its use in uncovering hidden Mayan ruins in the Amazon. LiDAR is an acronym of the words "light" and "radar." It is used in the same way as radar—light beams, in the form of laser blasts, are fired at the ground, and a sensor reads how much light is bounced back. Improvements over time have led to LiDAR systems that can detect changes in ground texture to the centimeter.

Because of its accuracy, the researchers wondered whether LiDAR could be used to find unmarked graves. They obtained several corpses that had been donated to science and buried them in several unmarked graves. Some of the graves held just one body, others held more, and of course, one held none to serve as a control. The researchers then flew over the graves in a helicopter periodically for almost two years and monitored the ground using LiDAR. They report that they were able to make out the outlines of all the graves—even those that were covered by leaves and other debris.

"The second article is from the government laboratory at Oak Ridge," Ray explained.

Oak Ridge National Laboratory

Sight unseen: Novel method detects evidence of unmarked human graves

August 13th, 2018

A new approach to find unmarked gravesites could help narrow the scope and potentially speed up the search for clues during crime scene investigations.

Geospatial researchers with the Department of Energy's Oak Ridge National Laboratory, and forensic scientists at the University of Tennessee, used sophisticated laser scanning and 3D modeling techniques, known as LiDAR, to detect telltale signs of recently buried human remains.

The team's method could complement existing technologies and procedures currently used in forensic casework, including pedestrian surveys that rely solely on the naked eye and ground-penetrated radar, or GPR.

"Unmarked graves are difficult to locate once the ground surface no longer shows visible evidence of disturbance, which poses significant challenges in finding missing persons," said Katie Corcoran of ORNL's Geographic Information Science and Technology group, who led a study published in Forensic Science International.

Law enforcement and others surveying an area who rely on their vision alone may not notice unmarked human graves because their surfaces are often camouflaged by grass or weeds, leaf litter or other debris. GPR is useful in detecting subsurface abnormalities but is limited in how much area it can survey.

With near-field approaches such as GPR, investigators must already know the approximate locations of a suspected grave. However, remote sensors like LiDAR can be operated from a standoff distance, allowing investigators to cover more area in their search.

Corcoran partnered with colleagues and students from the Forensic Anthropology Center at UT Knoxville, who prepared a site with three human graves of varying sizes, including one mass grave; one control pit, and surrounding undisturbed ground.

Using a tripod-mounted terrestrial LiDAR sensor, the team scanned the test area four times over a 21-month period, picking up millions of data points that collectively painted a digital picture of what was happening at the ground's surface. The sensor returned a 3D coordinate that is representative of the object encountered in the field.

"We analyzed the sensor data from all four scans and compared changes in the elevation of the ground's surface—changes that were caused by disturbances of the soil as the bodies were decomposing," Corcoran said.

"Our study is the first to quantify the differences in elevation and demonstrates the future potential benefit of incorporating terrestrial LiDAR into existing data-collection approaches to locate unmarked graves," she added.

LiDAR and other remote sensing technologies are also important tools for humanitarian contexts.

"This study helps forensic human rights investigators better understand the geophysical signature of graves, because it reduces the amount of time a team must be on the ground in active conflict situations," said Dawnie Steadman, director of the Forensic Anthropology Center at UT.

The paper's coauthors included Katie Corcoran of ORNL and UT; Amy Mundorff of UT; Devin White of ORNL, UT and Sandia National Laboratories; and Whitney Emch of The National Geospatial-Intelligence Agency. Corcoran is part of ORNL's Computational Sciences and Engineering Division.

Funding for the study was provided by the Army Research Office and the Defense Biometrics and Forensics Office to support the Defense POW/MIA Accounting Agency and supported by a Cooperative Research and Development Agreement with the National Geospatial-Intelligence Agency.

ORNL is managed by UT-Battelle for the DOE Office of Science. The single largest supporter of basic research in the physical sciences in the United States, the Office of Science, is working to address some of the most pressing challenges of our time.

"A drone with LiDAR can be deployed over a property without having to secure a search warrant," Ray explained.

"Anything else?" Joe asked.

"Yes, if the prosecutor wonders if there's enough evidence in this case to file homicide charges without Larry's body, then he should research the most recent no-body prosecutions in other jurisdictions. This is an FBI training bulletin which came out recently about no-body prosecutions," Jerry said as he handed the bulletin copies to Ray and Joe.

29.

NO-BODY HOMICIDE PROSECUTIONS

*FBI **LAW ENFORCEMENT BULLETIN** Provided by FBI Training Division*

November 9th, 2016

No-Body Homicide Cases: A Practical Approach

By Michael L. Yoder, M.A., M.A.

*S*pecial Agent Yoder is assigned to the FBI's National Center for the Analysis of Violent Crime, Behavioral Analysis Unit 4, in Quantico, Virginia.

In 2014, the FBI's National Crime Information Center (NCIC) entered 635,155 missing person records into its database. Records cleared or canceled during the same period totaled 634,367—a clearance rate of 99.87 percent with 788 records remaining. Possible reasons for these removals included 1) a law enforcement agency located the subject; 2) the individual returned home; or 3) the entering agency removed the record after deeming it invalid.

Every day, people file reports on approximately 1,740 missing Americans—both children and adults. This does not account for U.S. citizens who have vanished in other countries, individuals who disappeared but were not reported as missing, or homeless adults and their children. About 70 percent of all reported missing *persons are found or voluntarily return within 48 to 72 hours. Not all individuals indicated as missing are victims of kidnapping, murder, or some other criminal act; however, each account represents the concern of someone reporting a person who disappeared.*

Disappearing Voluntarily

A variety of reasons—mental illness, depression, substance abuse, credit problems, abusive relationships, or marital discord—exist for why people voluntarily disappear. Due to the high number of missing persons' reports assigned to criminal investigators and the vast quantity of cases resolving themselves, investigators tend to 'wait and see' or prioritize a case lower than an identified crime. With enough re-prioritization, an investigation easily loses momentum and becomes part of the load of other missing person cases. Often, no one submits requests for electronic data or captures timely eyewitness interviews and victimology. Consequently, timelines become vague, and memories fade.

Becoming a voluntary missing person does not constitute a crime. Any adult can walk away and decide to ignore family, friends, associates, and employers. Because this type of behavior lacks criminality, law enforcement officers experience limitations regarding how they proceed.

Investigators sometimes receive inadequate information in the beginning of a missing person investigation. If people portray the victim as routinely running away, being reckless, or acting irresponsibly, others may express less concern and possibly not even file a formal report. Investigators could treat the case as a reported event, rather than a potential criminal act. However, when facts and circumstances indicate a strong possibility of foul play or the disappearance occurs due to criminal action, investigators should consider the missing person case as a potential homicide.

People falsely report someone missing for various reasons. Perhaps the person died due to negligent homicide, accidental death, or murder, and the individual responsible for the death wants to create distance (time and space) from the act by establishing an alibi, obstructing justice, or avoiding detection. Offenders sometimes believe that the longer a victim is presumed missing and not found, the easier they remove themselves from culpability. Someone creating the illusion of a person voluntarily missing requires extra effort, which investigators should view as an element of staging.

Preserving Essential Data

A no-body homicide often begins as a missing person case. In such scenarios, an early determination that the matter is more than a routine case often results in successful prosecution. The amount and variety of electronic information—cellular data, social media postings, automated searches, surveillance camera footage, and video or audio recordings—accumulated, stored, purged, and then replaced with new data results in a limited shelf life before becoming lost forever. Investigators must make the effort as soon as possible to preserve, freeze, capture, and gather this information.

The same holds true for forensic details. People sometimes 'wipe' data or compromise the integrity of a crime scene when they do not detect or preserve information, possibly because no one originally acknowledged it as the location of a crime. Correctly assessing where a crime occurred and gathering forensic evidence from the scene proves crucial to the investigation.

Capturing details of actual memories becomes important for the investigator to discern truth over lies. Successful preservation of conversations, observations, and interactions with others directly correlates to when the investigator captured them and how important they are to the beholder. Over time, seemingly routine behavioral clues become nebulous, and once-memorable events become forgotten. A simple communication with another person often blends with memories of other interactions. Topics discussed or specific words spoken turn into less memorable or irrelevant recollections over time. The exact dates and times that activities occurred shift to vague estimates, and the timeline of events diminishes.

Encapsulating Routine Activities

When an investigator suspects foul play, the missing person investigation needs to focus on capturing the victim's routine activities. Individuals impact the world around them through their relationships, electronic footprints, personal and professional obligations, financial decisions, and other routine activities. Investigators should identify the victim's actions prior to the disappearance. Relationally, this may include individuals the victim recently had contact with, the last known sightings of the missing person, latest conversations, topics discussed, and the victim's mind-set. These events also consist of the missing person's future itinerary or plans, such as appointments, goals and expectations, upcoming celebrations, or impending tasks. Electronically, the person's latest texts, messages, postings, photographs, Internet searches, or voicemails indicate both routine and unexpected events.

Leaving family members, close friends, and loved ones without explanation might appear out of character for this person. Emotionally significant items—a cell phone, a favored blanket, a keepsake, special photographs, favorite clothes, house or car keys, and a purse or wallet—left behind often indicate an unplanned departure. Abandoning financial assets (e.g., cash, a savings account, credit or debit cards, or a checkbook) or personal records (e.g., driver's license, birth certificate, military discharge papers, or a social security card) to start a new life makes no sense if the individual left deliberately and voluntarily. By identifying sudden disruptions in the missing person's normal routine that have no plausible explanation, investigators can prove the negative: The victim did not plan the departure, and, consequently, the disappearance may be the result of a criminal act or other endangerment.

Gathering the Clues

Many criminals strive to create an illusion of distance in time and physical proximity from the victim's last-known whereabouts.

Successful disposal of the body is another way offenders detach from the crime. The longer the victim remains missing, the greater the opportunity for important clues to disappear. Memories become vague as they lose their link to precise events, and timelines turn out to be more abstract. Once enough time passes, offenders often claim they were in a different location at the point in time the murder occurred, thereby creating an airtight alibi. When this happens, investigators often shift their focus to other suspects.

In today's society, individuals affect the world around them by leaving heavy electronic footprints. Every person experiences a past and a present and has expectations for the future; interacts with family, friends, neighbors, or associates; and e-mails, texts, phones, or uses other social media to communicate with people. Individuals access their financial accounts through ATM or debit cards, credit cards, checks, or in-person interactions. Through conversations, they often discuss current or future plans and financial or emotional limitations to pursuing their goals and dreams. Most people have responsibilities, goals, relationships, and routine activities that anchor them to the planet.

Persons missing under circumstances where investigators suspect foul play probably were torn from their anchor points. Their abrupt, unexpected disappearance creates an atypical void. It appears that no planning or preparation occurred, and the person's routine activities suddenly were disrupted. When individuals leave behind people they love, valuable items, beloved pets, important electronic devices, secure shelter, favorite clothing, and their money, something is amiss.

Conducting Dual Investigations

When investigators suspect criminal activity, it becomes critical to conduct a dual investigation with hope for a live recovery, but with a perspective that the victim may be deceased. Investigators immediately should collect all electronic devices the victim could have operated, including those containing the individual's social media, all forms of communication, and every type of computer usage, such as Internet searches and financial transactions.

Once investigators decide to conduct a homicide investigation, they must address the fundamentals of the crime of murder. They need to prove that the victim died via homicide (criminal act), on or about a certain date (when), in a particular jurisdiction (where), and by a specific person or persons (who).

While a motive may prove unnecessary, it helps explain the reason for the murder. The motivation for the crime provides important clues, particularly when investigators have no body to confirm death or location where the murder occurred. Investigating circumstances leading up to the disappearance emerge as critical to the case. Sometimes, what appears on the surface as a perfect, harmonious domestic situation in reality equates to an abusive relationship. Understanding the missing person's background often exposes truths known only to the offender and the victim.

A no-body homicide prosecution seems similar to other murder prosecutions, except the prosecutor must demonstrate the likelihood that the victim is no longer alive. This often proves a difficult, but not impossible, prosecutorial challenge. In a homicide case, the corpus delicti—main body or element of the offense—consists of proof that an unlawful death has occurred.

The corpus delicti does not mean that the subject of the crime must be so extant as to fall under the senses, but that the loss sustained is felt and known. For example, in the crime of murder, although the body cannot be located, a particular loss is identified.

The body itself provides the best evidence of an unlawful death. However, other ways exist to determine that a person died. Many homicide prosecutors often base their cases on circumstantial evidence. They must establish 1) that the victim died; 2) that the person was murdered; 3) the approximate time of death; 4) that the likely location of the crime is within the prosecutor's jurisdiction; and 5) the person responsible for the murder. In one particular case, the judge determined that "the fact that a murderer may successfully dispose of a victim's body does not entitle the offender to an acquittal. This illustrates one form of success for which society has no reward."

Discussing Best Practices

In April 2012, the FBI's Behavioral Analysis Unit 4 (BAU 4) hosted a symposium to discuss best practices with 50 law enforcement investigators and prosecutors who successfully litigated no-body homicide cases. This event resulted in a 2014 FBI manual titled *No Body Homicides*. In addition to highlighting historical precedent cases to underscore the validity of prosecuting homicide cases without locating victims' bodies, the manual includes chapters on investigative and prosecutorial issues and associated best practices.

Since the 2012 symposium, BAU 4 has created a database that contains over 660 no-body homicide prosecutions in the United States, including over 477 cases prosecuted since 1995, along with the prosecutors' contact information. BAU 4 often recommends that a prosecuting attorney who never has taken on a no-body homicide case and plans to should contact experienced prosecutors who can help assess the strength of the current case and provide guidance and support. The FBI's database serves as a conduit for individuals to locate fellow prosecutors to discuss best practices for no-body homicide cases and investigative steps to cover before proceeding.

Obtaining Assistance

In addition to helping prosecutors, BAU 4 can assist in all aspects of the investigation, including investigative suggestions; behavioral analysis of suspects; victimology issues; and resources, such as the Violent Criminal Apprehension Program (ViCAP) database and FBI laboratory services. BAU staff members also serve as a sounding board to discuss cases, determine probable events and action plans, evaluate suspects, and provide expertise supporting the likelihood that a victim may be deceased.

As investigators move from a missing person case toward a possible homicide investigation, BAU 4 can help with case analysis, personality assessments of known suspects, interview strategies, media plans, and other investigative tactics. As with many homicides, offenders and victims often know each other, and perpetrators generally have a motive to commit a homicide.

If suspects attempt to distance themselves in time or location, investigators must invalidate any fabricated alibis. A concise timeline, forensic evidence, and behavioral analysis help link offenders to the crime scene and wipe away any false illusions. BAU 4 aids investigators and prosecutors by assessing the strength of the homicide investigation and providing collaborative recommendations for a successful outcome.

Conclusion

Every day, people file missing person reports. The majority are cleared because a law enforcement organization located the subject; the person returned home, or the filing agency determined the entry was invalid. Some missing persons disappear voluntarily, while others fall victim to criminal actions. Law enforcement agencies often must determine whether or not the individual became a homicide victim. The body itself serves as the best evidence of an unlawful death; however, other ways exist to establish that the person died or was murdered. The FBI's Behavioral Analysis Unit 4 created a no-body homicide database and a No Body Homicide monolith. BAU 4 personnel are available to assist law enforcement agencies in several ways with such cases.

"As you can see, there are plenty of resources for the prosecutor who wants to litigate a no-body homicide.

30.
JOE RETURNS TO YAKIMA

"Anybody home?" Joe inquired as he slowly opened the law office door.

"Well, there's a sight for sore eyes. How've you been?" Ray responded as he and Jerry stood up.

"I've been better," Joe answered as he walked into the office, with Donna following.

Joe was sunburned, gaunt, and had a tired-hollow look in his eyes. He was wearing what appeared to be a new T-shirt, crisp Wrangler jeans, and spotless New Balance tennis shoes.

"Can I get you a cup of coffee, or a Pepsi?" Jerry asked.

"A Pepsi would be nice."

"How about you, Donna?"

"Coffee, black please."

"How've you been doing with Ross's four cases?" Joe asked. "I feel bad I've not been able to help."

"We understand Joe. Most of the research is completed, and we're just waiting for a couple PDR responses. We could start looking at conclusions now for each case, since the remaining PDR responses are not critical." Ray advised.

"Donna explained some of your mission activities to us, but I was wondering if you could share with us what you've been doing?" Jerry asked.

"Sure, no problem. I'd appreciate it if you kept what I tell you to yourselves for the time being, since there's currently a warrant out for our arrests. Ross is working now to get the warrants quashed."

"After Lydia and I were assaulted, K-9 Buster was killed, and our Yakima home burned to the ground by soldiers from Truman's cartel a couple of years ago, I realized Truman would never stop trying to eliminate me. I had to do something, so I contacted a friend, Casey Abbott, with the CIA.

"Casey did some checking and found that former Yakima County Prosecutor Karter Truman was living in Colombia and engaged in building up the old cartel again after Pablo Escobar's death. Truman, who has taken the name Pedro Escobar, and Maria Escobar were either married or in a relationship. Truman was managing what was left of the Escobar cartel's drug business.

"I worked with Casey to develop a plan to capture Truman and bring him back to the United States to stand trial in federal court. We recruited Donna Ashford for several reasons. There's a whole mythology of legends about her among the drug cartels because of her work over the years in reducing their numbers; and she was an excellent asset to the mission. She and her Ducati Monster motorcycle are well known by almost everyone involved in moving illegal narcotics in Mexico. They call her La Fantasma, 'The Ghost' in English, and she is rarely seen but greatly feared, collecting the small fingers of the cartel gunmen she kills. Her nickname in Spanish is 'Fannie.'"

"You can call me Donna," she interjected with a smile.

"Then there's Captain Veronica Sabroso of the Mexican Navy, and her retired Vietnam tunnel rat soldier husband, Sniffer. Veronica was raised in a remote fishing village on the east coast of the Mexican Baja Peninsula. Her father and brothers were fishermen, and she later went fishing when one of her brothers was lost in a storm. Fishing the Sea of Cortez for a living is one of the most strenuous and dangerous occupations there is, and that's how Veronica became so lean and athletic. The loss of her brother motivated her to join the Armada de Mexico, the Mexican Navy, and become a rescue boat captain. She's tough as nails and knows the sea like the back of her hand. Veronica and Sniffer were recruited as backups to Donna and me for the Colombia mission.

"I recruited Junior, tunnel rat Snake's son. Snake was lost in our mission at the border. He was an irreplaceable asset to the mission and a very unique individual who loved his country.

"Snake was a true warrior and hero who gave his life for the protection of others," Donna remarked. "But his son was one of the strangest persons I've ever met."

"Junior has a doctoral degree in herpetology and is the director of the serpentarium at the San Diego Zoo, a very accomplished young man, and I'm sure his father would be proud of him," Joe explained.

"Did you see him with his shirt off when we were sailing from Mexico to Colombia?" Donna asked. "He has snake scales over his spine that go from his neck to his butt."

"Junior explained he has a condition called Ichthyosis vulgaris. It's a condition that causes the skin to develop scales and is thought to be genetic. Other than that, Junior is not much different from us," Joe explained.

"What about his tongue and his eyes?" Donna asked.

"Some people think a split tongue is a sign of beauty; and Junior does have a second eyelid, but that seems to be a rare mutation," Joe explained.

"I think Junior may be the result of an early gene-splicing experiment. He is as much snake as he is human. He was able to locate the Escobar shelter and needed no compass or any assistance during his hike inland. That thing he did with the poisonous snake was amazing," Donna exclaimed.

"Yeah, that was something. We were guided to Escobar's shelter by Junior, and we saw a cartel soldier standing guard near the shelter's escape hatch. He had to be taken out, and I was preparing to do so when Junior signaled for me to wait. A moment later, this 3-foot-long green snake, with a large triangular head, came slithering out of the jungle and quietly snuck up behind the guard and bit him on the leg," Joe explained.

"What happened then?" Jerry asked.

"The guard turned around yelling and shot the snake about 20 times," Donna answered. "Then he took about four steps and collapsed, dead."

"Junior said it was an Eyelash Viper, and the highly venomous snake knowingly gave his life at Junior's telepathic request. At least that's how Junior explained it," Joe revealed.

"You can believe that if you want, but I can tell you that Junior is a very different life form," Donna responded.

"What happened then?" Ray asked.

"We were able to enter the underground shelter, and it wasn't long before Mister Karter Truman showed his cowardly face. He was given plenty of warning but chose to reach for a weapon when he was shot," Donna explained.

"After he expired, I took a tissue sample, his right little finger, while Joe went through his pockets for anything he had on him and took some photos of the body."

"You're not saying who shot him," Jerry remarked.

"We'd rather not," Joe responded.

"Then it was time to get outta Dodge with the evidence before we were caught," Donna explained.

"The team made it back to the boat without incident and the sail back to La Paz was exceptional, with fair winds and a following sea," Joe said.

"Now, if Ross can get the warrants for our arrest removed, we'd consider the mission a success," Donna added.

"While Ross is working on that, I can help with putting together conclusions and suggestions for the four cases. It will take me a day or two to read over your reports, then we can discuss concluding suggestions for Ross. How's that sound?" Joe asked.

"Sounds good," Ray responded.

"That's a plan," Jerry agreed.

"Is there anything I can do?" Donna asked.

"Not that I can think of. Just stay out of sight until the warrants are pulled," Joe suggested.

31.
Conclusion

Sharon Louise Burch

"What do you think, Jerry?" Ray asked. "You did a lot of research on this case. What kind of conclusions have you come to?"

"There's evidence it was a homicide perpetrated by her adopted father Highland Burch, and adopted mother, Ella May Norton Burch, with the unknowing assistance of sixteen-year-old brother, Archie. This case is so old the chance of finding new evidence is very remote. The suspects have since passed away due to old age. The case could have been more thoroughly investigated in 1953, but sadly it was assumed it was accidental and no investigation was conducted in Yakima until 1988, when Archie and the birth mother made a formal complaint at the Yakima County Sheriff's Office. In 1988, a prosecution of the adopted parents could have been done, but it was rejected by the Yakima County prosecutor due to numerous expenses that would be borne by Yakima County taxpayers.

"I initially suspected the prosecutor's refusal to prosecute two obvious murder suspects was a malfeasance of office on the prosecutor's part but have since learned about prosecutorial prerogatives in our justice system," Jerry explained. "Here's a copy of an explanation from the Wikipedia encyclopedia."

Prosecutorial discretion

United States

In the United States federal system, the prosecutor has wide latitude in determining when, who, how, and even whether to prosecute for apparent violations of federal criminal law. The prosecutor's broad discretion in such areas as initiating or forgoing prosecutions, selecting or recommending specific charges, and terminating prosecutions by accepting guilty pleas has been recognized on numerous occasions by the courts. Prosecutors may decide not to press the charges even when there is probable cause, if they determine that there is no reasonable likelihood of conviction. Prosecutors may dismiss charges in this situation by seeking a voluntary dismissal or nolle prosequi.

Wayte v. United States 470 U.S. 598 (1985) said:

In our criminal justice system, the Government retains "broad discretion" as to whom to prosecute. [...] This broad discretion rests largely on the recognition that the decision to prosecute is particularly ill-suited to judicial review. Such factors as the strength of the case, the prosecution's general deterrence value, the Government's enforcement priorities, and the case's relationship to the Government's overall enforcement plan are not readily susceptible to the kind of analysis the courts are competent to undertake.

Yick Wo v. Hopkins (1886) was the first case where the United States Supreme Court ruled that a law that is race-neutral on its face, but is administered in a prejudicial manner, is an infringement of the Equal Protection Clause in the Fourteenth Amendment to the U.S. Constitution.

Scholarly study of prosecutorial discretion in the U.S. has reported a wide variance among prosecutors' responses to the same potential scenario. The scholars who conducted the study reported observing prosecutors who appeared to be motivated to do justice but who lacked guidelines and supervision.

Prosecutorial immunity

'Prosecutorial immunity' redirects here. Not to be confused with immunity from prosecution.

In 1976, the Supreme Court ruled in Imbler v. Pachtman that prosecutors cannot be sued for injuries caused by their official actions during trial. For instance, a prosecutor cannot be sued for purposely withholding exculpatory evidence, even if that act results in a wrongful conviction. Absolute prosecutorial immunity also exists for acts closely related to the criminal process's judicial phase.

However, the Supreme Court has held that prosecutors do not enjoy absolute immunity when they act as investigators by engaging in activities associated more closely with police functions. Further, the U.S. Court of Appeals for the First Circuit held that a prosecutor is not entitled to absolute prosecutorial discretion when performing purely administrative functions concerning a criminal prosecution. Additionally, the Seventh Circuit has ruled that a prosecutor is not immune from liability for fabricating evidence during pre-trial investigations and then introducing that evidence at trial.

"After reading this, I understand now why Yakima County Prosecutor Karter Truman was able to commit so many crimes during his tenure as prosecutor. He had almost complete immunity by law," Joe remarked.

"There's not much that can be done in the name of justice for little Sharon Burch, it seems," Ray observed.

"There is one thing," Jerry said.

"What's that?" Joe asked.

"It took me three days, with the help of cemetery staff, Mike Byers, to locate Sharon's gravesite in Tahoma Cemetery. After we found it, I went to Mid-State Monument Company and priced a headstone for Sharon Burch. Richelle at Mid-State Monument was very helpful. Tina Pastor and Mike Byers at Tahoma Cemetery will make sure Sharon's headstone is properly placed over the grave if we decide to purchase one.

Pastor Terry Dinsmore of the Wiley Union Church has agreed to do a gravesite prayer service for little Sharon when it can be arranged. The Wiley Union Church is located just blocks from where Sharon died. The church has active children's programs for the area families, and I think donations to this community church in Sharon's name would be a blessing," Jerry said as his eyes glistened.

"That's kind of you, Jerry. What does the headstone look like?" Joe asked.

"The stone is a natural pink color, and the inscription would be simple with her name, date of birth and date of death inscribed along with the notation, 'everything hurt is healed again'".

"That's perfect, Jerry. Let us share the costs with you," Ray offered.

"I agree and let us know when the gravesite prayer service will take place. We want to be there," Joe said while the others nodded silently in agreement.

"This case made me think of my girls, Mo and Andy," Jerry reflected.

"Michelle and Andrea, two little spitfires, looking for adventures," Ray responded with a smile.

"One time I was working on the farm, and I noticed Mo and Andy watching me from an upstairs window. I don't believe they knew I saw them, but I just went about my business thinking they'd get bored and disappear from the window soon. Do you know what happened? They watched me for two solid hours!"

"They love their daddy, that's for sure."

"I can only imagine what it would be like to lose a loved one, yet it seems there was no one for this little 5-year-old girl, Ray."

"Yakima will be her family, Jerry. How's that sound?"

"To tell the truth, my friend, it breaks my heart."

32.
Conclusion

Lawrence Jay Riegel

"This was your case, Ray, and it was a doozy. What are your thoughts, my friend?" Jerry asked.

"I think poor Larry Riegel died from domestic violence on Christmas Day, 2009. If his girlfriend didn't strike the blow that killed him, she knows what happened, in my opinion, and it just amazes me she has gotten away with it for this long," Ray stated.

"Is there anything that can be done to find Larry's body? It seems Larry's family has resigned themselves to his death. They just want to bury him properly in a consecrated grave, according to their Catholic custom," Jerry asked.

"There are several things that can be done even now," Ray remarked. "For instance, one or both of Larry's adult children could ask an attorney to declare Larry deceased. Once that's done, it may be conducive to discovering what happened if the kids immediately initiated a lawsuit against LaDena for the wrongful death of their father. In my research, I found that several of LaDena's real estate assets are in a trust account, which would be shielded from a civil judgement. However, her sister is the trustee, and she is not personally immune from legal action. The family would need to discuss the possibilities with an excellent attorney because, in a lawsuit, sworn depositions are commonly used. Subpoenas are requested by the attorney for witnesses and suspects to be deposed under oath, with a court reporter taking down every word. People are usually reluctant to commit perjury by lying under oath, and if they refuse to respond to the subpoena, a warrant could be issued for their arrest. Suspects would probably refuse to answer questions, citing the 5th amendment to the constitution, but information garnered from others during the lawsuit could establish probable cause for the arrest and prosecution of the murder. Refusing to answer questions by citing the 5th would be a red flag, wouldn't it?

"Another possibility would be the Special Inquiry Judge or, even better yet, a grand jury investigation. A grand jury would be the strongest tool for the investigations; if led by a very good prosecutor, the crime could probably be solved with a successful prosecution of the murderers. A federal grand jury would probably not be possible, but empaneling a state grand jury would be appropriate if a majority of the county superior court judges agreed. Costs to Yakima County would be a barrier.

"There are some other ideas that may produce results but would need legal reviews before trying them. Like putting electronic tracking devices on the suspect's cars. Investigating current activities could produce other witnesses who may have information about Larry's disappearance. If a newly discovered witness is a friend of the suspect, deposing them under oath may be necessary. This next one is a long shot, but the Riegel family has suffered with the disappearance of their loved one for so long and it has caused them so much emotional harm that they may be willing to try something different," Joe explained.

"What are you talking about, Joe?" Ray asked.

"In 2009, there were over 150 satellites circling the earth. Many were observation satellites, watching and recording the movements of everyone, 24 hours a day. Some of the satellites are owned by the U.S. and other countries, and some are commercially or privately owned. It is possible that one or more satellites were observing Yakima's activities from space on and after Christmas Day, 2009. Obtaining a recording of the movements at Larry's residence and other places is possible, but probably expensive. If the Riegel family wanted to spend their reward funds on satellite surveillance, we might be able to find out where Larry was buried."

"Any other ideas?" Ray asked.

"Did anybody check on wood chipping machine rentals after Christmas 2009?" Jerry asked.

"That's a horrible thought, but I'm not sure. It's probably too late now since most businesses only keep records for seven years and we don't know if police investigators checked that lead back then because they refuse to share their investigative records with us. I don't recall reading anything in the newspaper about wood chipping machines.

33.

CONCLUSION

Ryan Glenn Moore

"This is another domestic violence case officially listed as a suicide," Ray remarked. "It's much different from the Sharon Burch or the Larry Riegel cases, even though all endured domestic violence crimes. Some curious and suspicious things happened prior to, during, and after the stabbing death of Ryan Moore, that caused us to take a closer look at what happened. There's a remote chance the initial thrust of Ryan's knife was done by someone other than Ryan. However, when Ryan answered with a nod to the leading question if he caused the wound himself, it precluded the possibility of a successful prosecution of anyone else, we believe. Ryan's response was almost like a legal dying declaration, and since he is no longer alive, he can't be questioned about his response. The two men in long dark trench coats and the burning in Ryan's backyard by Sue Huntington, witnessed by the neighbor and not noted in the police reports, are activities that could have been investigated further at the time.

"Sue Huntington's activities with the goth community might have turned up some interesting information, but Ryan's declaration that his wound was self-inflicted probably makes a deeper investigation of little value.

"It would be nice to know the name of the doctor that

refused to treat Ryan at the emergency room, but because so much time has passed since the appalling incident, a lawsuit would probably be beyond the statute of limitations, and any reprimand would be too late to initiate even if we knew who the physician was," Jerry remarked. "But that's not much consolation to Ryan's parents. I did hear a sermon once at a funeral of a friend that committed suicide, which made me think. The priest said that we didn't know how much torment was being experienced by the person that took their own life. It may have been so painful that it could be likened to a person in a tall building that was on fire. They had the choice of remaining in the fire or jumping from the 14th floor to their death. Would that be suicide? I think not. I can't think of anything worse than a parent who loses a child. Let's keep them in our prayers."

"I spent a lot of time reading over this next case and am shocked at the way things turned out. Can we discuss this final case, the Sara Luz Bustos homicide?" Jerry asked.

"Sure, Jerry, what's it about?" Ray asked.

34.
Conclusion

Sara Luz Bustos

"Sara was a pretty, 21-year-old girl who had been raised and learned to survive in a dysfunctional environment. She was like any young woman who wanted to be liked and loved and who wanted to live a happy life. However, she got caught up in the snare of drug use and became addicted to cocaine, probably first supplied by a boyfriend. After becoming dependent and seeking to chase away the illness of withdrawal, her life slowly spiraled out of control. She seemed to find that her only asset for acquiring cocaine was her beauty, which faded with each new dependent relationship. It appears that men, attracted to her youthful seductiveness, supplied her cocaine habit in return for intimacy, until the costs became too high. A young, newly divorced police officer became one of her suitors, taking advantage of her addiction in return for her attention, like the other young men. But Sara found herself in a peculiar position with both a police officer and a drug dealer as boyfriends. Both men seemed mostly interested in taking carnal advantage of the winsome, destitute, young lady, but were unspoken enemies of each other. In her naivety, she failed to recognize the danger that approached her when the police officer asked her to provide evidence of drug crimes perpetrated by her drug dealer boyfriend. In her quest to avoid the illness that comes with drug use, and her hope in a closer relationship with her 'policeman friend', she secretly did the police officer's bidding we believe, and provided evidence for the arrest of the drug dealer. Then, just three days after this dope peddler was bailed out of jail, Sara was bashed in the head and left drowned in the Yakima River with a large rock sticking out of her mouth. Then, some strange things happened after Sara was murdered that turned this case upside down."

"This is a difficult case and will take a lot of work. Where should we start?" Jerry asked.

"The body recovery site would be a good place," Ray suggested.

"How did the young, off-duty traffic squad officer find out about the recovery of his girlfriend so quickly that he was able to arrive at the body recovery site just as detectives were beginning the investigation?" Ray asked.

"He wrote reports, demanded by his superior seven months later, that he found out about the body discovery inadvertently. He says he stopped at the police department to pick up reports on his day off and was told by a dispatcher about the incident, so he decided to check it out," Jerry explained.

"Isn't it against police department policy to be taking official reports home?" Ray asked. "And weren't the officers assigned pagers back then?"

"Yes, to both questions, and that was before they were issued cell phones. I see what you're getting at. Did anyone go over the pages to and from the officers on that day to determine if someone at the recovery site may have paged the off-duty traffic officer?" Ray asked.

"I was unable to find that out, since those records were not available to me, but it would be interesting to know," Jerry explained. "It is also incredible that so many people were allowed, unrecorded, into the controlled crime scene area, and strange that none of the numerous detective's reports reflect that the off-duty traffic officer entered the crime scene, apparently without permission, and assisted in the investigation."

"The traffic officer wrote no reports about what he saw or did at the crime scene until he was ordered to do so by his superior officer seven months later. Is that correct? Who is this officer?" Ray asked.

"He is Officer Kensley Twindler, Yakima Police badge number 9999," Jerry responded.

"That's a strange badge number."

"Yes, it appears there was some confusion or mistake discovered at the Washington State Criminal Justice Training Center. When Officer Twindler graduated from the police academy years ago, his records were incomplete, and that fact remained undiscovered until recently. Another background check is being done now and when the records are updated, he will be assigned a permanent badge number. Meanwhile, over the years, he has made rank and is now second in command as the Deputy Chief of the Yakima City Police Department."

"That doesn't make it any easier. What do we know about his relationship with the victim prior to her murder when he was a traffic officer?" Ray asked.

"Enough to know Officer Twindler began a romantic relationship with the victim several months prior to her murder. I suspect other officers were aware of the relationship and believe Twindler was alerted by someone about the discovery of Sara Bustos' body in the river," Jerry answered.

"It's common knowledge that the suspect will often return to the scene of the crime. So, if Twindler did not inadvertently discover the incident at the river like he says, he could be the killer, returning to the scene of the crime," Jerry said.

"At that point, the Yakima Police Department would have been investigating if one of their own officers murdered Sara Bustos, an undeniable conflict of interest," Ray remarked.

"It doesn't look like many detectives knew about Twinder's relationship with the victim when the body was discovered-or weren't saying, and Twindler wasn't saying much until seven months later when the victim's diary was found with his name in it. Even then, he lied about the closeness of his relationship with Sara Bustos if you compare his first report done on April 11th to his second report done on April 12th. He had an obvious responsibility to report it immediately at the body recovery site, that he not only knew the victim, but was in an intimate relationship with her. It appeared Twindler's aim was to keep the details of his relationship with the victim secret," Jerry explained.

"Deliberately misrepresenting the truth is considered lying by omission," Jerry added. "And, as such, the incident should have been investigated to see if Officer Twindler kept obvious and important details from investigators of the homicide. If he did so, his name should have been added to the state's Brady List."

"That could still be done, I suspect. Here's a Post Intelligencer newspaper article that discusses the Brady List. Doug Blair, mentioned in the article, was a former Yakima County Sheriff," Jerry noted.

Cops who lie don't always lose jobs

P-I review finds 2 dozen cases where officers weren't fired

By LEWIS KAMB AND ERIC NALDER, P-I INVESTIGATIVE REPORTERS Jan 28, 2008

Lying by police officers is considered a cardinal sin in law enforcement, a so-called 'death penalty' offense that collective wisdom holds will automatically result in a cop's termination.

But a Seattle P-I review of internal police documents in Seattle and other Washington agencies reveals that's hardly the case.

In the five years ending July 2007, just 13 police officers statewide had been terminated and disqualified to serve again as police officers in Washington state because of lying, including the case of a Seattle officer cheating on an exam.

Yet, the P-I found more than two dozen other cases in which officers were alleged to have misled supervisors, misstated important facts, or fabricated information in fieldwork, internal investigations, and court cases without being fired.

Among them, a Tacoma officer accused of falsifying sick-leave reports in 2004; a Federal Way officer who allegedly tried to cover up improperly throwing away drug evidence in 2002; and a King County sergeant accused of making 'misleading statements' about her alleged pressuring of a subordinate regarding a public sex arrest case.

In a 2004 case, a dishonesty charge against Federal Way Officer James Keller was sustained in a car accident he was involved in, but he was not fired.

In several other cases, officers were not even investigated for potentially career-ending dishonesty charges despite allegations or other evidence those officers lied, a review of disciplinary cases statewide found. Two Tacoma officers claimed a third officer in 2002 provided misinformation in a police report favorable to a prominent architect. That officer was never investigated for dishonesty, records show.

Prosecutors are required to notify defendants and their attorneys whenever a cop involved in their case has a sustained record of knowingly lying in an official capacity. That requirement came about because of a U.S. Supreme Court decision known as *Brady v. Maryland*, and thus officers who lie are known as 'Brady cops.'

But the P-I found that only a few of the state's largest prosecutor's offices keep systems to readily track 'Brady cops' in their jurisdictions. The King County Prosecutor's Office only recently began keeping a so-called 'Brady list' after the P-I raised questions about one such Brady cop in 2005.

Dishonesty cases against police officers can be complex and difficult to prove, law enforcement officials and police union representatives say. Such cases often involve one person's word against another's. It's hard to take away someone's livelihood based on unsubstantiated claims, they say.

"You've got to be very careful with these cases," Seattle police legal counsel Mark McCarty said, "because they're a career-ender.

CONCLUSION

We assume they're going to be appealed somewhere down the line."

Proving lying can be difficult "because you have to prove the element of intent," McCarty added. "And that's very difficult to prove."

If a police officer is found lying, "termination is appropriate," Seattle Police Officers' Guild President Rich O'Neill said. "But I don't think a lot of what (internal investigators) say is lying really meets that level. I believe when you're going to put a label like 'liar' on somebody, you should be able to prove that convincingly."

Even if an officer is caught lying, he or she might not face firing or the revocation of a police license.

"It really depends on who you lie to and what the circumstances are," said Doug Blair, deputy director of the Washington State Criminal Justice Training Commission, which oversees police certification.

Only certain types of lies—such as making false reports to other officers, or 'false swearing' by dishonesty in official reports or hearings—warrant an officer having his or her license revoked in Washington, Blair said.

A quirk in state law also makes an officer's lying to internal investigators a disqualifying offense on its own; but when the same violation against an officer is sustained with other offenses, it's not automatically a disqualifier.

"It's a really weird thing that only complicates matters further," McCarty said.

Yet, records reviewed by the P-I revealed cases that appeared to meet disqualifying standards falling by the wayside for some officers; while other officers with seemingly lesser degrees of untruthfulness lost their jobs and sometimes their licenses.

The Seattle Police Department opened at least 13 internal investigations from 2005 through mid-2007 involving officers accused of dishonesty, among other allegations, according to internal records provided to the P-I. Of those cases, four remained open as of late last year. Four other cases were 'inactivated' when accused officers resigned before the investigations were concluded.

In the remaining five cases, not a single dishonesty charge

was sustained against an officer, records show. In at least three of the five cases, lower commanders or then-Office of Professional Accountability Director Sam Pailca recommended dishonesty-related charges be sustained against accused officers. And in a fourth case, a high-profile case involving two officers accused of roughing up a drug suspect in a wheelchair last year, a civilian review board later said internal investigators should have sustained dishonesty violations against the two accused officers.

But in each case, Police Chief Gil Kerlikowske opted to sustain only other lesser charges, for which he implemented discipline far less severe than termination.

Requests to Kerlikowske for comment about those cases were not returned Monday.

O'Neill, the Seattle guild president, said none of the Seattle examples are clearly dishonesty cases. Conclusions drawn by internal investigators were largely based on subjective beliefs that accused officers weren't telling the truth.

"All of these things are not clear-cut cases of lying," O'Neill said. "When the chief doesn't follow the OPA's recommendations, it's usually because he got other information that tipped the scales the other way."

Not included among these cases is a more recent Seattle case in which Kerlikowske fired Officer David Marley for a tangle of charges, including dishonesty elements. The convoluted firing stems from Marley allegedly crashing his motorcycle while intoxicated last year, then hiding from Snohomish County investigators, as well as subsequent actions. Marley is appealing his firing.

Some departments are tougher than others when handling firing cases. The Bellevue Police Department has fired at least three officers in the past three years for dishonesty-related charges, including an officer who allowed a drunken teenage robbery suspect to leave the scene of a house party. That officer, Angela Rockcastle, later reported she'd asked a King County deputy also on scene to keep an eye on the suspect while she conducted other interviews. After deputies disputed her account, Rockcastle was

Conclusion

investigated and fired. The state later revoked her police license, though she denied wrongdoing at a hearing.

Discipline records indicate police departments might use a dishonesty charge to get rid of officers who aren't liked, while ignoring lies by those who are favored.

A Mountlake Terrace police officer, Jonathan Wender, has accused his department and the Snohomish County prosecutor's office in a federal lawsuit of railroading him with a bogus dishonesty charge because he has favored the decriminalization of some drug use. Wender said in his lawsuit that Snohomish County's procedures for handling 'Brady' officers lack due process protections and standards and, as a result of that, "can and has been utilized to sanction officers for unfair and unlawful reasons."

Wender had been with the department for 15 years when he was terminated Oct. 19th, 2005. His lawsuit says he had had no significant disciplinary issues.

He was accused of failing to follow up on a citizen's tip about a drug-growing operation.

"In Sgt. Wender's case, a substantial reason this sanction was imposed and resulted in his termination was his advocacy of drug policy reform, speech that was disapproved of by the defendants but protected by the First Amendment," the lawsuit said.

In the Snohomish County Sheriff's Office, a lieutenant who headed internal investigations—and who had investigated other officers for lying—was fired himself, after he was accused of tipping off a county bureaucrat to a fellow officer's alleged cheating on disability leave. The lieutenant, Gerald Ross, denied the allegation. The deputy association appealed his termination, but lost, though the evidence against Ross was contradictory. One of the witnesses against Ross was himself being investigated for dishonesty at the time by the department, Ross said.

Dishonesty cases have long been sticky issues in the Seattle department. Seattle has fired officers for dishonesty in the past, including David K. Shelton, fired in 2003 for cheating on a promotional exam and later lying about it. But in several other cases, officers recommended for seemingly supported dishonesty charges have been let go.

In June 2002, an unnamed Seattle officer falsely told a superior his patrol car was significantly damaged because of a hit-and-run driver, when experts said he most likely damaged it backing into a fixed object. Two civilian witnesses were parked near the officer's patrol car and didn't see another vehicle hit it. Five accident review board members didn't believe him and termed it as 'false reporting.'

Yet the 10-year veteran signed a police traffic collision report, declaring 'under penalty of perjury' that his account of the accident was true.

"There is compelling evidence in this case to conclude that the named officer improperly reported damage to his patrol vehicle and submitted a false statement," concluded Capt. Mark Evenson, then with OPA. "The named officer's story of what occurred just doesn't add up."

The department sustained a more generic rules violation against the officer, rather than a dishonesty violation that could have resulted in termination and loss of his police officer's license. The discipline meted out wasn't reported in the documents.

Records show that in December 2002, a Hispanic man claimed an officer punched him in the kidney in the International District, then drove him to Rainier Avenue South and South Dearborn, where he shoved him against the patrol car, injuring his nose. The man called 911 from a store after the officer left.

The officer insisted he didn't drive the man to the second location, but instead said in an official internal investigations interview that he left the man in the International District. However, two other officers were 'under the impression' that their colleague was going to drive the man to the second location, and a report said 'it is unlikely (the complainant) could have walked to the 800 block of Rainier and called 911 when he did.'

Pailca, then OPA director, concluded the officer showed 'dishonesty' and likely 'transported the complainant (to Rainier) in *anger and retaliation.' But the department sustained 'abuse of authority' rather than dishonesty.*

Jan 28, 2008
LEWIS KAMB AND ERIC NALDER

"How many Yakima officers are on this Brady List?" Joe asked.

"I was curious myself and found one Yakima County deputy sheriff and three Yakima City police officers on the list. Deputy Chad Sholtys is listed because of a theft; Officer Brian Dahl and Officer Lori Sheely are listed because of criminal offenses they committed and Officer Matthew Myers for making false statements," Jerry responded.

"That's unfortunate about those officers."

"Why don't we list the rumors about this case and determine what needs to be done to verify or debunk each rumor?" Ray suggested.

"Good idea, rumor number one is Officer Kensley Twindler was somehow involved in the murder of Sara Bustos, was alerted to the discovery of her body by another officer, and refused to share critical information about his relationship immediately at the crime scene.

"Rumor number two is that in order to hide information about his relationship with the victim, Sara Bustos, Twindler may have removed pages and caused water damage to the Bustos diary text which we think was discovered after her murder but not logged into evidence until months later. It's interesting to note that lead investigator Rick Watts signed the property tag for the diary and indicated it was found by Detective Mike Tovar. I could locate no report on finding the diary by Detective Tovar. It must be noted that Deputy Chief Ken Twindler oversees the public disclosure requests now, including Sara Bustos' diary, and he has refused us access to the evidence," Jerry explained.

"Rumor number three is that the bi-lingual city police employee who was translating the victim's diary was injured in an assault or fall and subsequently quit working at the police department. I haven't had any luck in reaching the employee.

"Rumor number four is that the victim, Sara Bustos, was recruited earlier by Officer Twindler to be a confidential drug informant, resulting in the arrest of Eliberto Rivera. If this is the case, then it appears the investigators, including Officer Twindler, decided there was no need to protect their informant, even though she was openly suspected of being the reason for her drug dealer's incarceration. Sadly, she may have been murdered for doing what her policeman friend asked of her.

"Rumor number five is that Officer Twindler killed Sara Bustos in order to protect his reputation and employment as a police officer after engaging in drug use with her. This rumor includes the possibility the murder was either perpetrated by Officer Twindler or he was somehow involved.

"Rumor number six is that there was an in-depth investigation conducted on Officer Twindler's relationship with Sara Bustos, which cleared him of being a suspect. The investigation was requested by the Yakima County Prosecutor and carried out by then Yakima Chief of Police, Dominic Rizzi, who reportedly hired two friends from the Chicago police department to investigate and clear Twindler of any wrongdoing. I sent a PDR requesting copies of the investigation but was again refused by Deputy Chief Twindler himself," Jerry explained.

"Rumor number seven is about an improper collection of DNA from Twindler who reportedly was asked to take a DNA collection kit home, during the initial investigation, and return it with a sample of his DNA, totally against protocol.

"Rumor number eight is the withholding of DNA crime scene evidence for laboratory analysis by police. Some DNA crime scene samples were reportedly not submitted for testing.

"I also sent letters to each investigator who was at the crime scene asking for an interview. Just two investigators responded and shared their information with me. Both said Officer Twindler got a close look at Sara Bustos' body after it was removed from the river, including the 'Sara' tattoo on her left wrist.

Both declined to provide me with a written report, signed or anonymous," Jerry explained.

"Why are the investigators so reluctant to come forward?" Ray asked.

"Two Yakima police officers either quit or were encouraged to do so because of this case, Ray. The others are worried about retaliation, losing their jobs or being assigned difficult duties."

"I can imagine what morale is like in a department with such disturbing rumors that nobody wants to investigate. One short-term chief of police doesn't know about it, and the next short-term chief tries to cover it up when the rumors become rampant. So, what's the remedy?" Ray asked.

"The remedy would be citizens concerned enough about their police department to demand the actions necessary to look into it."

"Officers and detectives are afraid to talk about the murder because of perceived corruption within the police department. What actions are available to clean up this Bustos investigation?"

"First, city leaders should find a long-term candidate for chief of police, someone with roots in the department and community. A chief who cares about the department, its members, and the city as a whole and is not a retiree from another department seeking a second retirement income after serving a short term of just 5 years.

"Next, a grand jury investigation was specifically established just for this type of problem with the government. A grand jury investigation would have the best chance of finding the truth in the death of Sara Bustos. There would need to be some strong political motivations, I suspect, for the prosecutor and the judges to agree to proceed. Otherwise, the stain of this case will remain in our police department indefinitely. Costs would be a limiting factor, but when you think about it, how much is the safety and security of Yakima worth?" Jerry asked.

"Deputy Chief Kensley Twindler is in line to be our next chief of police, Jerry. I sure hope that doesn't happen," Ray remarked.

35.
A Dios

Ross tapped on the office door as he opened it and announced, "I understand you're about finished with the investigations and I'm looking forward to responding to your suggestions as soon as possible. For the moment, however, I have some good news and some bad news."

"What's the good news?" Ray asked.

"The good news is Joe is in the clear. Colombia has pulled their Interpol warrant for him, and I just verified it with the local police."

"How did you manage that?" Joe asked.

"We sent DNA evidence to Colombia and in checking it, they determined that Pedro Escobar had no relation to the Escobar family and was, in fact, an American by the name of Karter Truman. Since Karter Truman was a wanted person himself and was not a Colombian citizen, they quashed their warrant for Joe.

"Donna was a different matter, however. The Colombian warrant was quashed; but Mexico has three murder warrants and there's still the outstanding homicide case where she's a suspect in New York State. More bad news is I received a call from the California Highway Patrol inquiring about Donna. She had my business card in her pocket," Ross explained.

"Was Donna arrested in California?" Joe asked.

"I wish that were so because then I could do something. The California trooper said they tried to pull Donna over, but she ran from them on her Ducati motorcycle. She exited Interstate 5 and headed south on old highway 99 at extremely high speeds, out running even their best motorcycle officers, until she rounded a sweeping curve and ran directly into a train crossing. Orange County Deputy John Carson said he assisted and worked up the accident. He determined her speed at 102 miles per hour when she hit the train," Ross explained with a frown on his face.

"She left this envelope on my desk before she left. Please ask Monique to join us since Donna's letter is addressed to all of us," Ross said somberly.

When Monique walked in, Ross began to read the note audibly.

"Hey guys,

I wanted to pay my respects and say goodbye in person, but I think it's better I left your hospitality quietly, without a line of cop-cars chasing me with their sirens blaring. So, I packed up the Duke, and we calmly headed south at 4 AM. Thank you, Monique, for anticipating my every need. Thank you, Ross, for trying to make a regular law-abiding citizen out of me. It just wasn't in the cards, even though your legal skills were remarkable.

Joe, you and I are a lot alike in some ways and in others, not so much. We love our country and want to protect the innocent from predators. Your work to protect us is honorable, Joe, whereas my desire to eliminate the threats has been lawless. I understand and will accept the consequences with my head held high, hoping not to be judged too harshly. Please see that the National Museum on Crime and Punishment receives my bone necklace and notations for each collection, when the time comes.

Jerry and Ray, you two are examples of the finest in law enforcement; working after your retirements to achieve justice in some old outstanding cases. I wish you both the best. Try to spend more time with your families. Finally, let me say I hope Duke and I make it to the area of Santa Rosalia on the east side of the Mexican Baja Peninsula where my little beach house waits for me. I'd appreciate a visit if you have the time, and if the cartels haven't discovered me. Things are a little different from my point of view when I say I'd rather be carried by six than judged by twelve.

Donna

Epilogue

"While we're all here, I'd like to say a few more things," Ross continued. "First, let us remember our sister in law-enforcement, Donna Elaine Abbott. However flawed she may have been, her heart was dedicated to the safety and well-being of our country. May she rest in peace. Let's also remember all the law enforcement officers in our state and across the nation that lost their lives protecting the peace and dignity of our communities. Thank you, Jerry, Ray and Joe for your work on this assignment and for all your years of caring for our citizens."

Joe stood and responded, "What proper gesture of gratitude would be appropriate for you, Ross, that matches your years of efforts in caring for the rights and responsibilities of these same citizens. You are a humble, unsung hero of our community my friend, and we would like to shout that out to everyone, except we know you'd rather remain modestly unacknowledged."

"Thank you for those kind words, Joe. Are we ready to do a final review on the four cases: Sharon Louise Burch, Lawrence Jay Riegel, Ryan Glenn Moore, and Sara Luz Bustos? They were all members of our community, and we need to think of them as our brothers and sisters. We know more about them now than before, but their stories are still incomplete. We need to share the whole truth about each one of them. We owe it to them and to the peace and dignity of our city to remember what happened to them.

"I think of the statement, 'justice delayed is justice denied' when I think of 5-year-old Sharon Burch and the suffering she endured. There will be no earthly judgement for what was done to Sharon, but that doesn't mean nothing further can be done on her behalf. We need to remember her in grief as a family member. Even though it's been over 50 years since she was murdered, providing her with a headstone and a gravesite prayer service is a beginning. We have become more aware of child abuse since the 1950s, but our society needs to be even more mindful of the signs, and more willing to report abuse if we want to protect the well-being of our youth like Sharon. Supporting children's programs akin to what the Wiley Union Church provides is important.

"When it comes to the Riegel family, I can only imagine what the unending agony of losing and not knowing what happened to their loved one for so many years would be like. It's even more difficult when they suspect Larry's girlfriend knows what really happened to Larry and where his body might be. It appears that our police department could have been more proactive in the initial stages of Larry's disappearance. There was even an official apology given to the Riegel family from the police department for not taking Larry's missing report more seriously in the beginning. I would say that the police department and the City of Yakima owe the Riegel family more than just a verbal apology. The honor of the Yakima Police Department could be restored in this matter if they would put a serious amount of effort into finding Larry's hidden gravesite, while at the same time working to prepare a possible no-body homicide charge, using the latest information and technology available. It might be costly, but it's necessary.

"Regarding Ryan Glenn Moore's loss at such a young and promising age. The scourge of drug abuse stands out in Ryan's case, but it's not the only problem. The amount of drug abuse in our country goes directly against the peace and dignity of our communities. More needs to be done in recovery options and mental health treatment or we'll continue to lose loved ones to the abyss of drugs, homelessness, and crime. The loss of one's child must be almost unbearable, and our hearts go out to the Moore family. A demand by the public for better substance abuse and mental health treatment is necessary.

"Finally, the murder of Sara Luz Bustos stands out as a brutal loss of a beautiful, naïve young woman that became largely overshadowed by a scandal from the same police department which was obligated to protect her. Investigators appeared to have no idea that a suspect, who was one of their own, mysteriously appeared at the crime scene and had the ability to alter or destroy evidence. It must have been a huge embarrassment and concern to the police department and the prosecutor's office to find out, long after the fact, about the officer's intimate relationship with the victim prior to her murder. Information that came not immediately from the officer as it should have, but months later, and only after the discovery of the victim's diary. The embarrassment must have been compounded when the suspect arrested in Sara's murder was found not guilty at trial. It appears also that there was a secret investigation of the officer, his involvement with the victim, and the possibility the officer may have been the killer. We requested a copy of that file, but were denied.

"The challenges in getting the murder suspect convicted were insurmountable it appears in the Bustos case," Ross explained. "Monday morning quarterbacking on our part is not the objective. The eyewitness recanted; explaining the motive to the jury was deemed prejudicial by the judge and was prohibited. The suspect came up with alibies from three friends, and after all that, I would have been surprised at a guilty verdict. Even though there was a second investigation in 2013, the scandals remain because many law enforcement officers and witnesses are afraid to share what they know. This case cries out for complete transparency. The best method to achieve that would be a grand jury investigation by a smart and aggressive prosecutor. Once that's completed, and the ghosts in YPD's closets are exorcised, the city needs a chief of police that comes from the community and possibly from within the police department. Someone who is not just looking to pad their retirement income from another department by vesting a second pension after just 5 years with YPD. It should be noted that the three former short-term chiefs from other departments have all left our community, and it appears they never really intended to make their homes here. So, now we are left dealing with their poor decisions. The Sara Bustos homicide investigation should have been done by another law enforcement agency with no ties to the Yakima Police Department. Since that was not done and because the Yakima Police Department insists on keeping files secret, a full grand jury investigation is demanded in the interest of righteousness. If the Bustos case is allowed to languish away in hidden files within the Yakima Police Records Bureau, the rumors may fade, but they'll not be totally forgotten.

I want us to have the safest city in the northwest, with a police department that is compassionate, honorable, transparent, proactive when necessary, keeping the peace and dignity of our city. A city that attracts businesses and families; a city that is growing and prospering.

Instead, we have the possibility that the next chief of the Yakima Police Department could be a man who got away with murder."

# # #

Acknowledgements

Tahoma Cemetery, Yakima
Staff: Tina Pastor
Michael Byers
https://www.yakimawa.gov/services/cemetery/

Susan Riegel Vaughn & Family
https://www.facebook.com/FindLarryRiegel/

Yakima Valley Regional Libraries
https://www.yvl.org/

Yakima Valley Genealogy Society
https://www.yvgs.net/

Retired Yakima Firefighters Association
https://yakimafire.com/

Russ Mazzola, Attorney

Union Gap Police Department
https://uniongapwa.gov/police/

Vicki Baker, Business Owner
Yakima Valley Conference of Governments
https://www.linkedin.com/in/vicki-baker-28b4639b/

Yakima City Police Department,
The records bureau staff
https://yakimapolice.org/

Rolland "Rod" Shaw, Retired Investigator Yakima County Sheriff's Office

Ron and Peggy Moore

Dominic Rizzi, former Yakima City Police Chief

Sam Granato, former Yakima City Police Chief

Robert Udell, Yakima County Sheriff
https://www.yakimacounty.us/220/Sheriffs-Office

Jan Jorgenson, Researcher

Patricia Byers, Mayor
City of Yakima
https://www.yakimawa.gov/council/patricia-byers/

Schab's Bier Den
22 N. 2nd St. Yakima, WA 98901
https://www.thebierden.com/

Inklings Bookshop, Yakima
https://www.inklingsbookshop.com/

Encore Bookstore, Yakima
https://www.encorebooksyakima.com/

Jerrol's Bookstore, Ellensburg
https://store.jerrols.com/

Sports Center, Yakima
Todd Widner
https://www.facebook.com/people/The-Sports-Center-of-Yakima/100093101379475/?paipv=0&eav=AfYHVUP0IeQwxbWS97faaf12Tp_wWfMlf2i7iztCf5_zX7_kKDhM8HIOssjtS-kPv0c&_rdr

Abel French,
Former Yakama Tribal Police Officer

Rick Watts, retired
Yakima Police Detective

Michael Tovar, Yakima Police Detective
Colleen Tovar, widow

Ed and Adrienne Simon

Wiley Union Church
Pastor Terry E. Dinsmore
2711 S. Wiley Rd.
Yakima, WA 98903
https://wileyunionchurch.com/

The UPS Store
Emily Holt
https://locations.theupsstore.com/wa/yakima/420-s-72nd-ave

Ellen Allmendinger, Yakima Historian
https://www.amazon.com/Hidden-History-Yakima-Ellen-Allmendinger/dp/146713841X

Michelle Hafsos Brantingham
Andrea Hafsos Mott

Deborah Ochs

Mid-State Monuments
1612 S. 16th Ave.
Yakima, WA 98902
Ph (800) 774-7951
Jennifer Bush, Richelle Bush
Randy & Lynn Howe
Ryan Howe
https://www.midstatemonuments.com

Donations for Sharon Burch Headstone:

> Retired Yakima Firefighter's Association
> WA State Council of Firefighters (Roy Orlando)
> Linda Gauci Kusske
> Ten-Eight Publishing LLC

Kristen Schafer
Forensic Lab Supervisor

Fiverr.com
Mark Becker, Text Editor
Mark B@markbecker257

Fiverr.com
Philip O. Cover Design
Philip O@design_w_philip

Fiverr.com
Text Formatting
Patrick L@highdef

"Guilty as Sin"
By Ken Wilson
Murder of an adopted child
https://www.amazon.com/Guilty-As-Sin-Ken-Wilson/dp/B0BV4JDYQ6

National Consortium on Preventing Law Enforcement Suicide IACP
https://www.theiacp.org/

BLUE H.E.L.P.
Honoring the Service of Law Enforcement Officers Who Died by Suicide
https://bluehelp.org/

Ellen Allmendinger, author
https://www.amazon.com/Hidden-History-Yakima-Ellen-Allmendinger/dp/146713841X

H.D. Duman, author
Watch for "Wolfscape"
https://www.amazon.com/Path-Peril-H-D-Duman/dp/1621476340

Officer Down Memorial Page
https://www.odmp.org

Yakima Police Patrolman's Association
https://yakimappa.org

Acknowledgements

Yakima Police Department
https://yakimapolice.org

Yakima Fire Department
https://yakimafire.com/

Yakima Herald-Republic
Tammy Ayer, reporter
https://www.yakimaherald.com

Yakima Paranormal
Shellie Sauve
https://www.facebook.com/p/Yakima-Paranormal

KIMA TV
https://kimatv.com/

KAPP TV
Emily Goodell, Yakima Bureau Chief
https://www.applevalleynewsnow.com/

KNDO TV
https://www.nbcrightnow.com/

Wise Media Group-Podcast
Dan Wise
https://www.facebook.com/groups/wisemediapodcast

Linda Gauci Kusske, grazzi qalbi

Ten-Eight Publishing LLC
www.ten-eightpublishing.net

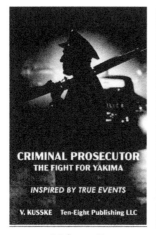 

Volume I   Volume II

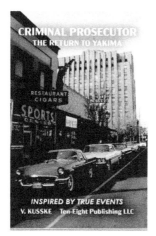 

Volume III   Volume IV

Made in the USA
Middletown, DE
11 August 2024